PATCH SCRATCHING

A Novel by
Steven D. Powell

Illustrations by
Thomas Block

Patch Scratching
by Steven D. Powell

Copyright © 2011 by Steven D. Powell

ISBN 13: 978-1-936447-53-4

cover and book design by
Maine Authors Publishing, Rockland, Maine
www.maineauthorspublishing.com

All works of art provided by
Thomas Block
All rights reserved

Acknowledgements

When I started this novel three years ago, it never occurred to me that actually writing it would be the easiest part, or take the least amount of time. It seems somewhat unjust (at least to me) to thank people by including them on a page or two of the book, of which most readers will never take the time to look at. Still, this is the customary manner so here goes.

What writer is worth their salt without the constant support and encouragement of their spouse? The love and caring support of my wife Linda rests on every page. I have found resolve in the enthusiasm of our two adult children, Amanda and Alex. Thank you to my father Doug, (who at seventy-six years old is still lobstering as a stern man) for being my technical adviser when it came to the ins and outs of lobstering and boats. Thank you Bev Emerson for reading all of the early drafts, over and over.

On the professional side, Thomas Block's visual interpretations of my words brought great joy to me and I hope it does for you as well. My editor, Genie Dailey offered many helpful hints, as did other members of the Maine Authors Publishing team, including Jane Karker, David Allen, and Cheryl McKeary. To Teresa Piccari of The Village Scribe, for her input. Thank you to Hope Creighton for spending an afternoon on the Rockland breakwater looking for a profile photo. Lastly, a special thank you to my English professor (yes he's a real person) Sanford Phippen. Without his guidance, I would not be the writer I am today.

Table of Contents

The Day of the Puffin

It was early, so early the sun was just beginning to make an effort to rise. Jed made his way down the path leading to the raspberry patch. He'd been walking this path to pick raspberries for Deb to use at the bakery for several summers now. There was no need for the path to be lit for him to find his way. Feeling the warmth of the sun on his back would have been nice, though. Ah, but it was the lack of warmth which made the job of picking raspberries this early so much easier and more pleasant. Without the sun, the temperature was just right. He'd have a good hour to work before the sun warmed the air enough to bring the bugs and bees out from their state of dormancy. Which meant that if Jed accidentally touched one of them, they would not be able to sting or bite him, and with the plants thick with dew, he could easily see the spiderwebs. Oh sure, he'd get plenty wet, but that didn't bother him any.

Jed reached the raspberries and looked around. The patch was long, and skirted the edge of the tree line at the entrance to the woods. If he was careful, he could reach most of the berries from one side or the other without having to make his way in too deeply. All the other raspberry patches in the area had been stripped of their harvest already. The tree line and the crest of the hill shaded this patch so it took longer for these berries to mature. Deb had told him that because they developed slowly, the berries had more flavor. All Jed knew was that they were just as dangerous to pick as any others. That was why he always dressed in boots with his jeans tucked in, and a hooded sweatshirt with elastics around his wrists. Only his hands and face were exposed to the threat of the large thorns protecting the raspberries.

Jed picked up a quart basket. He had twelve of them to fill before the sun made the job unpleasant. Deb had shown him how to pick the raspberries so as not to damage them. It had taken him a while to get the hang of it when he was younger, not to mention the difficulty of reaching the berries on the really tall stalks. Now he went at his work not with thought, but with instinct. The growth spurt he'd had last year was showing its value this morning. Jed flew down the outside edge of the patch gently grabbing each berry at the stem and giving it a little tug. If he felt any resistance at all, he knew the berry wasn't ready. He could hear Deb in his head saying, "You can't hurry nature Jed, and if you try, you just cause problems." Jed enjoyed his time in the raspberry patch. It gave him time to think, and he also kind of liked being alone. Life had taught him not to get too attached.

His life had not always been as good as it was now. It took no effort to remember how poor he and his mother had been. Most days it was a treat just having something to eat. Then came that fateful day. It was his fifth birthday. His mother had taken him to Deb's Bakery for a bear claw as a birthday cake. While he was eating, his mom asked Deb if she could keep an eye on him. When he asked his mother where she was going, she said, "It's a surprise." That was nearly seven years ago, but he'd pretty much figured out what the surprise was by the end of that first day. Any image he'd had of his mother had left him long ago. And people had stopped talking about that day—the day his mother ran off with that good-for-nothing Carl Batch. Some said his mother had done Jed a favor, leaving him behind like she did. She weren't much good, and Carl liked to beat up on things, especially kids, or so Jed had heard some of the townspeople say. Seven years! His mother had been gone from his life longer than she'd been a part of it. Jed had gotten used to the idea of Deb being his mom. She was really good at it, too. Even though the bakery kept the two of them busy, especially during the summer when all the rich people came. All and all, Jed saw his life as pretty good.

New Ireland is a coastal town. In the summer, it went from a few hundred locals to a few thousand with the people from away. To the naked eye, it didn't look like much, but Jed thought it looked a lot like what he'd seen in old black-and-white western movies. A single narrow street with just a few buildings lined up on either side. The only difference was that behind one set of buildings was the harbor. On the off-water side, there was the one church at the end, then the hardware/grocery store and the post office. Then on the water side was the marine supply store, an old building that had been empty as long as Jed could remember, the town office, and Deb's Bakery.

In the summer, a small take-out opened at the church to help raise money, but the only place to get a pie, or any home-cooked breads and pastry, was at Deb's. Most of the buildings looked like they'd seen better days. All except for Deb's that is. She was always doing something to spruce up the place, especially the outside. Deb would say, "If they don't like the wrapping, they won't care what's inside." Deb was full of these little sayings. Sometimes Jed had to think about them for a while before he understood their full meaning.

Jed had never asked Deb why she had no husband; as busy as they both were all the time, he had a sense that most of the men were afraid they couldn't keep up with her, and didn't want to look bad standing in her shadow. But Jed didn't mind. He'd been on the move a lot with his mom, never having anything to do, or anyone to do it with. He'd grown to like his life with Deb at the bakery. Sure, he had to get up early, and it was a lot of hard work, but he'd woken up in the same bed every morning since he'd been with Deb. Even still, after all this time, he'd wake up every morning and listen for the sound of Deb working, the pots and pans in the kitchen banging. He was always afraid that one morning he'd wake up to silence and run downstairs only to find Deb gone. Leaving him alone. The feeling was just as strong now as it had been that first morning. He just couldn't shake it. If he could only figure out what it was about himself that had made his mom leave, he could keep watch for it, or maybe even make it go away.

He'd never really opened up to Deb, or gotten close to her because of this feeling. Sometimes Deb would go to Augusta for supplies, and she would always invite Jed to go. He wanted to, but his fear that they'd somehow get separated and he'd be left behind wouldn't let him. Staying home wasn't much better. He'd spend the whole day telling himself that if she didn't come back, it was no big deal. He'd be fine. Then when she returned home and drove into the garage, he felt a sigh of relief, but he'd never show any emotion. When he'd been with his mom, Jed would tell her he loved her all the time and always want her to hold him. Now he believed that as long as people thought you didn't care one way or the other, you were safe, and being safe was better than being loved. That much he knew for sure.

Suddenly a raspberry bush came loose from its entanglement, hit his face, and brought him out of his thoughts. The sun had made its way over the crest of the hill to the apron of the raspberry patch. He could feel the trickle of blood run down his face and settle by his earlobe. Time was running out. All but one of his baskets was full of berries now; just a few more minutes and it would be time to go.

He pulled his sweatshirt off and wiped the blood from the scratch on his face. It was just then that he heard something. He listened for it again, more intently. He could hear cars and people, but couldn't tell where they were. It was still plenty early for so much commotion; clearly something was going on. He quickly finished, gathered up his things, secured the berries in the two boxes he'd brought, and started up the hill. The path was well lit now and filled with color. He had to walk through old man Crockett's blueberry field to get to the raspberry patch. This end of the blueberry field was not so well tended as the rest. Old man Crockett had said, "It weren't worth the effort, being so close to the woods. Just be raising them berries for the forest animals." Because of the lack of care, yellow pigweed and Queen Anne's lace grew proud as a picket fence along each side of the path. Here and there, though, you could see the berries growing close to the ground. They were still mostly green, with a few purple ones around the ledge that looked like it was growing out of the ground as much as any living plant. There were also some spots where straw had taken to seed. Jed managed to grab a nice long piece of the straw and flick it into his mouth as he scurried up the path. Experience had taught him it would be at least another week before he'd need to tell Deb the blueberries were ready for picking. Old man Crockett had told everyone, if they wanted them blueberries, they was welcome to them. No one but Jed had touched them for years. The townspeople all knew Deb depended on them. Besides, no one could do more with blueberries than Deb. In turn, Deb kept the price of her blueberry pies and muffins low because she got the berries for free.

At the crest of the hill, Jed could look straight down onto the harbor. Everything was still quiet there. He turned to his right and looked down across Horseshoe Point. He'd always liked how this point had come by its name so honestly. The fella who named it must have been standing in this very spot, because from here, it looked like a horseshoe. The cove was a safe place to berth a boat from storms. The opening faced southwest, which meant that boats had to come in toward shore to get into the cove. This gave the best protection against any weather coming out of the east or, even worse, the northeast. This was because the land was on the back side, toward the ocean, instead of open to it. If there were a bad wind blowing in the fall or early spring, it would be out of the northeast. Plus, the way the trees had grown in little round groves, they looked like nails in a horseshoe.

Yep, everything looked the same. There wasn't anything going on down there. Then he heard the noises again, and he turned to the left toward Drift End Beach. He could see this was where all the commotion was coming from.

Caught up with the curiosity of not knowing, and wanting to find out, Jed started walking toward Drift End Beach instead of the bakery, forgetting all about the raspberries he was carrying. It was a fair piece to walk, but nothing Jed wasn't used to. Had he not been so accustomed to his surroundings, he could have easily walked right through the blueberries, but his unconscious mind took him down the winding path with nary a misstep from the trail cultivated by time and travel, and with the same care and passion as the blueberries themselves had received over the years.

Upon arriving at the beach, Jed realized he still had the raspberries in his hands. Finding shade under a big spruce tree, he covered the berries with his sweatshirt and placed them at the cool protective base of the tree. No one noticed him, as they were all looking at whatever was on the beach. Once he'd secured the safety of the raspberries, he turned his focus back toward the mystery on the beach. Jed made his way through the crowd thinking it must be something big. But then he realized, if it were big, he would have seen it from the hilltop. What he saw once he'd made it to the front of the crowd was completely unexpected.

A puffin! A baby puffin! Jed knew it was still too young to fly because it didn't have its color yet.

"Must've blown off of Ledge Cliff Island," he heard someone say.

"Yup. Too bad it didn't drown, it's just going to die anyway," said another from the crowd.

As Jed stood there, he was taken back to that day, his fifth birthday at Deb's Bakery. Suddenly, he knew how the puffin felt. It was all alone in a strange place, surrounded by people and things it didn't know. Wondering where its mother was and why she'd left him alone. All the fear and emotions of that day filled Jed's mind. It was no fun not knowing, wondering what was happening; even more scary was the feeling of not knowing what was *going to* happen. Jed felt a sharp pain in his chest. His throat tightened like a collapsed balloon, and he felt his eyes well up with tears. *Am I going to cry over a bird?* he thought. He had not cried since the day his mother left. This hardly seemed like something worth crying over.

Jed was lost within himself as his thoughts raced. The crowd started to break up. They'd seen what there was to see, and taken their pictures. To them, the plight of the bird was of no concern. Jed couldn't help wondering why no one tried to help. How could they not care? This was a living, breathing animal, and they were all willing to let it suffer until it died, or got eaten.

"Well, *there's* a thing ya don't see every day. Last time I seen something like that was a few years back, at the bakery," said a voice from behind Jed.

Jed looked up to find old man Crockett standing there.

"I seen ya tearing down through my blueberry field and thought for sure you'd tromped on my berries. I was fixed on giving you a whooping, but there weren't no damage, so I guess you're safe. For now, anyways. You been picking raspberries for Deb, I imagine."

RASPBERRIES! Jed had forgotten all about the raspberries. Deb would be looking for them. He'd turned and started toward the berries when old man Crockett spoke again.

"What about your puffin, boy?"

"My puffin? What makes you say that?" Jed asked.

"'Cause you two are cut from the same cloth. This bird's abandoned just like you was. Don't you see that, boy?"

"I guess, but what can I do?" Jed answered.

"Why, you can return the favor Deb done for you, and help this bird."

"How? I'm just a kid."

"Well, Deb weren't but a baker when she took to mothering you. On top a that, she should've been the last one to take you in. Besides, I didn't mean just you. I'll help if you really want to do something about it."

Jed knew old man Crockett was right. His feelings toward the bird were strong, and he did want to help. But he also remembered what Deb had said.

"Deb says I should leave nature alone," Jed replied.

"This ain't what she's talking about, boy. I guess I got to learn you something this morning after all."

Old man Crockett told one of the other kids who'd been hanging around to take the berries to Deb and tell her that Jed was with him making things right. Meanwhile, Jed picked up the bird and wrapped it in his sweatshirt so he could carry it without either of them getting hurt.

"Well, boy, what's your plan?" asked old man Crockett.

Plan? He didn't have a plan. But he did know what needed to be done.

"Take it back home, to Ledge Cliff Island," he said.

"By Christ, you ain't as dumb as your mother, is ya? Must've gotten your brains from your father. Come on, boy, my boat's tied up at the wharf, let's take this little fella home."

They walked to the wharf and launched the boat without a word. Jed had never been much for conversation, and old man Crockett had said more to him today than he had since Jed had come to town. Soon they were almost out of the harbor, and a glimpse of Ledge Cliff Island could be seen off the starboard bow about a mile outside of Horseshoe Point. Jed came to that old man Crockett had said something about his dad.

"Mr. Crockett, did you know my dad?" he asked.

The old man had thought maybe he'd gotten away with his slip of the tongue. It wasn't his place to tell the boy his past. He'd often thought someone should have spilled the beans by now, or fessed up to knowing the what-all of it. But it was him that was in it now. He knew that telling the boy would be like running a seining net over a line of lobster traps. It'd be easier to throw the whole damned thing back overboard than to try and sort the mess out to save anything from it. Well, he'd let this mess sit on the bottom long enough; it was time to see what was left to save.

"Yeah, I know your father," said Crockett, "he's my son."

Jed could not believe his ears.

"It's time someone told ya," the old man said. "Guess there ain't no reason why it hadn't ought to be me anymore than anyone else. Before that good-for-nothing mother of yours came along, my Zach was spending his time with Deb. Your mother come to town, flirting and carrying on with near all the menfolk in town. But that was afore she got an eyeful of my Zach. She'd told him some story about needing a boat ride, and Zach the kinda fella that would help anyone and everyone with nary a question agreed to give her a ride. Once she got him outside the harbor, she turned on her charm, and Zach had a weak moment. Him and Deb was working on doing things proper, and getting married before starting a family. But your mother, she could charm the rosary beads off from around the Pope's neck if'n she had a mind to. My Zach never had a chance with that woman."

"She got to Deb before your father did and told her a whale of a tale, but Deb knew better. Zach couldn't face Deb after that, though, so he left town. Went merchant marining. Ain't seen hide nor hair of him since. Your mother came to me, claiming she was carrying Zach's baby, but who the hell knew? You could a been anyone's kid at the time. Though it's clear enough now you're Zach's. It's scarier than a fog at low tide in Horseshoe Cove how much you look like your father."

"Anyways, I took her to the bus station and bought her a ticket. I told the clerk, Chester, not to refund her the money if he knew what was good for him. Thought that was the last of it, but then she showed up a few years later with you tagging behind.

Went straight to Deb's, she did, dropped you off and got back on the same bus she come in on with that lazy bum Carl Batch."

"Now you hear me, boy, 'cause I don't chew my cabbage twice when it comes to the truth. Trading the two a them for the one a you—never was there a better trade made in this town. Anyone who tells you different is a lying sack a shit! May God cut my trap lines and steal the ballast outta them if I don't mean every word of it."

Jed was in a trance. He'd always noticed that old man Crockett treated him better than most. Now he knew why. And Deb, she'd done nothing but good by him the whole time. He guessed maybe having him was better than not having his father at all.

A new and strange feeling came over Jed. For the first time ever, he felt connected to the town and the people there. *This must be what it's like to be part of a family, to belong*, he thought. He looked down at the puffin cradled in his hands and peeking out from under the sweatshirt.

"You might give that bird a herring or two from the bait tub over there, so as to settle it down. Won't be so rambunctious with a full belly," said Crockett. "We're nearly there, but we'll have to drop anchor and take the dinghy from here."

Crockett and Jed climbed into the dinghy and headed for the base of one of the lower cliffs. They had decided that Jed would take the bird up the cliffs as far as he could safely go, with the hope that one of the adult puffins would claim it. Puffins only have one chick at a time, so there was a good chance the bird's parents would be looking for it. They were halfway back to the boat when Jed noticed that two of the larger puffins had made their way to the baby, so they stayed and watched for a moment as the two adult puffins helped the baby make its way back up to where the others were.

Jed and the old man rowed back to the boat, secured the dinghy, and headed out. Jed started thinking about what Crockett had told him. He figured the old man had said all he wanted to about his father, so there wasn't any point in asking questions. He decided to stay quiet and keep thinking about everything that had taken place in the day, and just enjoy the boat ride back to shore. Jed had not had many boat rides, so he wanted to enjoy this one as much as he could.

It seemed like only a few minutes had passed when he heard the engine slow down, which meant they were close to the wharf. Jed looked up at the sky. The sun was high, meaning it was nearly noon. The bakery would be busy now. He wondered how he'd act when he saw Deb, now that he was armed with this new information.

The boat made its way to the dock, Jed jumped out and grabbed the stern line, tied it off, then went to the bow and did the same. Then he turned to old man Crockett.

"Well, guess I better be getting back to the bakery. Thanks for the help and the…the talk."

Jed turned and ran up the street before Crockett had a chance to answer.

As he came through the door, Deb was bringing coffee out from behind the counter. Jed ran straight to her, wrapped his arms around her as if it were the first time, and in fact it was. He hugged her so hard, she nearly dropped the pot of coffee. Without looking up, he began to speak.

"Thanks for taking me in, and for feeding and clothing me, and all the other stuff you've done."

Before he went on, and without letting go, he looked up at her and said, "I love you…Mom."

Deb was still in shock over the hug. Jed's words were so soft and pure, she didn't know what to think. She heard the door open and looked up. It was old man Crockett. She looked back down at Jed, then back at Crockett. Crockett nodded. Deb managed a smile while her eyes filled with tears.

Finally, everyone knew.

CHAPTER 1
Truth or Fiction?

Black ink stained the pale white paper as Jed's fingers danced across the keyboard of his manual typewriter. Each key clacked with the anger harbored within him. His teacher, Miss Polly Wright, had singled him out when assigning this paper for her creative writing class. A class Jed had once looked forward to. Things were different now, however. Now he wished he'd never heard of Miss Polly Wright.

Downstairs, Deb was busy in the bakery getting ready for the day. Hearing the sound of Jed's typewriter always brought a smile to her face and a song to her heart. She would have bought him one sooner had his interest in writing been known to her. Over the two years since making the purchase, Jed had made good use of it. He had not, however, much to Deb's disappointment, shared many of his writings with her. If she'd learned anything since Jed's arrival, it was that sharing didn't come easy for him. As with many things in her life, Deb made the best of what she got. Unbeknownst to Jed, his presence connected her past to the present in both a good and a painful way.

Feeling the pain of her memories brought a new level of awareness to the sound of Jed's typing. She could hear a rawness in it. Like a piece of classical music with its rhythm and beat changing as a way to affect emotions in those who listened. Deb couldn't help wondering whether it was her memory which brought forth this new sound—or had the sound called up the memory?

The clacking continued as letters formed words making structured sentences, thereby developing paragraphs, which filled pages. All the while, Miss Polly Wright's words rang in Jed's head.

"Jed, you're a good writer in that you understand how to write. What's missing is *you*. By that I mean you're not investing any emotion in your words. You must give yourself up to the craft in order to get the best out of it."

Pulling the last page off the spindle, Jed said to himself, *You asked for it, lady.* With the story safe in his backpack, and a quick visit with Deb, Jed was off.

During his walk to school, the past came back to Jed just as it had to Deb. Along with Deb, he now had Gramps for family. How many times had Jed wondered whether or not he'd have known about Gramps if not for a lost puffin? It was that day of the puffin, which Jed had written about for Miss Wright. Then there was Winnie, his one and only real friend.

Jed, however, was adept at getting by on little or nothing. He didn't know it yet, but this was an aspect of his character Miss Polly Wright wanted to change. She wanted him to want more from life, to expect more.

* * * *

With the past filling his mind, Jed wished Gramps wasn't out lobstering so he could stop in and visit for a minute. This time of year, the chance of getting out on the water was fifty-fifty because of the wind. There were no days off unless the wind was blowing. Jed turned toward the harbor. The water looked just like glass this morning, not a ripple could be seen. Every boat was out. Even the ones owned by the men Gramps called "fair-weather fishermen." Gramps would be in from lobstering and back home by the time Jed's English class started.

It was a class Jed had signed up for with great anticipation. The fact that it was at the end of the day was a plus, as it gave him something to look forward to. Just before school had started for the fall, an unexpected event had happened. The teacher Jed was expecting to teach the class unexpectedly retired. The new teacher, Miss Wright, thought she knew kids like Jed just because she'd spent a few weeks in New Ireland every summer as a child. Jed couldn't seem to remember her ever coming into the bakery.

At first, Jed had not been happy about the idea of a new teacher. Then he convinced himself it was a good thing, and got excited about having a teacher from "away." It turned out she was impossible for him to please. No matter how hard he worked, it wasn't good enough. At this point, he was barely passing in a subject he was used to getting A's in. Instead of having something to look forward to at the end of each school day, Jed dreaded his last class. Because of this, most school days dragged. Today, however, Jed was anxious to turn in his story.

The assignment was to be given to Miss Polly Wright at the end of class. As Jed handed her his paper, she asked, "Tell me, Jed, am I going to like this?"

Jed heard himself answer, "Probably not."

Before anything more could pass between them, Jed was gone.

* * * *

Experience had taught Polly to read Jed's paper last. A cup of green tea and a couple of Milano cookies later, she was ready, except that this paper was not for desk reading. Oh no, this story called for an overstuffed chair, a soft light, and the sound of the wind coming out of the east. Last but not least, she wrapped herself in an old quilt her grandmother had bought at a fair years before. It was one of the personal items which had come with the house. "Some things just belong together," her mother had said. Buying the house, contents and all, had provided both comfort and pain for her.

Polly couldn't help becoming emotional whenever she read Jed's writing. This story would be no different. If anything, it would test the very limits of her balance between woman and teacher.

As Polly read the story, she particularly noticed Jed's attention to detail when describing a landscape or a scene. By the time she'd read just a few pages, it was easy for her to transcend her surroundings and put herself in the story and become one with it. Jed's words brought forth the senses of sound, smell, taste, and touch. But most of all, it made one feel emotion. She began to understand why Jed acted the way he did. If these words were true, it was no wonder Jed kept to himself. Polly herself was alone here in New Ireland. But it was by choice, not because she'd been abandoned. Jed's words made her think of her own mother. She set the papers down, picked up the cup of tea, and took a sip as she looked out the window to the water. What must it have been like for him? As the warmth of the tea filtered through her, Polly picked up the story and continued.

She remembered picking blueberries from the spot Jed described, and she knew it well. Of course, that was before Jed's time. She felt a little guilty thinking back on it now. She remembered seeing two men there one day. She'd thought for sure they would scold her for picking the blueberries, but they didn't say a word. Polly wondered now if one of them had been Mr. Crockett.

She finished reading, then set the papers down, removed her glasses, grabbed a tissue, wiped her eyes, and blew her nose. Her feelings were torn between the impact of the story and a sense of disgust. She'd given her senior English class an assignment to write a short story from a past memory. This paper was typical of Jed's writing. She imagined him as a child, painting outside the lines when he colored, telling colorful elaborate lies to cover up his indiscretions. Still, even though this was not what she was looking for from the lesson, the writing skills could not be denied.

Clearly Jedediah had taken a memory and embellished it. She'd been tolerant with him in the past, but this behavior failed to show any improvement. Grabbing her red pen, she started toward the paper with the intent of marking it with an F, but once the pen touched the paper, it wouldn't move. Finally, she wrote, *Jedediah, see me after class* on a separate piece of notepaper.

Polly had moved to New Ireland from Hartford, Connecticut, after graduating from UConn. Her family had owned this summer home in New Ireland for three generations. Granted, it wasn't much, a two-hundred-year-old four-room cape with an unfinished upstairs. Everything about it was out of date. The windows were single-paned, there was no insulation, and it didn't have any heat, other than a wood stove, until Polly had the local fuel company install a furnace. Heat hadn't been a problem before that, as no one in her family had lived in the home year 'round until her. The best part of the whole house was the farmer's porch her grandfather had added fifty years ago. That, and the view of the harbor. Polly had enjoyed the porch all of last summer. But it was fall now, and the cold was beginning to tighten its grip on New Ireland. Her view now included the porch, as opposed to being from it. When she'd decided to move here, it had been with high expectations.

Living here during summers had been a big influence in Polly's becoming an English teacher. The one thing that had bothered her was the local accent. Somehow, the people here had come to omit the letter *g* from their vocal language; words like *doing* and *raining* were pronounced *doin'* and *rainin'*. After moving here full time, it hadn't taken long for her to realize that most people here knew this, and talked with the accent anyway. In fact, she'd met a number of people who, like her, had moved here and then fallen into the habit of speaking the same way. Something she was determined not to do.

To the locals, it didn't matter, though. No matter how she or any of the rest of them talked, or how long they lived here, they'd always be known as *those people from away*. If they stayed and had children, the kids were known as implants. Polly's idealism about bringing the town's language into the twenty-first century died before it ever got started.

On a visit to the Redman Village town library to look for teaching aids, she'd borrowed a film. It was one in a series made by the Maine Public Broadcasting System. Polly got a kick out of a TV series called *A Good Read* at first, but that was before she realized it was about Maine authors. The format was a host interviewing writers from Maine. The first one she watched had been on Stephen King. She'd been so intrigued by it, she'd watched all the rest of them. They were hosted by an English teacher, hence her attraction to them. But this teacher was also a writer, and he was from Maine. His name was Sanford (Sandy) Phippen. It was something Sandy had said that made her realize how silly her idea about the local dialect was.

Sandy had talked about how the identity of Maine's people was being lost because they were all trying to talk like Walter Cronkite, and how he remembered when you could tell what part of Maine a person was from just by the way they talked. But now this identifying aspect of Maine's people was slowly disappearing, and that seemed sad to him. Polly had been fascinated by this, as it was the opposite view from hers. Then she found one of Sandy's books at the library. It was a story about a boy working at an inn to earn money for college. She couldn't help but wonder if the boy was Sandy, and if so, how true it was. After reading the book, Polly decided that Sandy was right. It was then she decided that the idea of trying to change the character of the local people was not only foolish but also wrong. It would be like killing a part of their heritage.

However, surely it wouldn't hurt to convert just one. And Jedediah was the one she'd chosen. He stood out to her. His potential had barely scratched the surface of what he was obviously capable of, and she felt compelled to do whatever it took to bring out his talents. But hard as she had tried, Jed resisted. Nowhere was it more evident than in his writing. He loved using patches of the local slang rather than proper English, but Polly wasn't giving up. This one was going to college. With the comfort of this thought, Polly got up and headed off to bed.

CHAPTER 2
Jed's Story

Jed walked into the classroom and dropped into the chair. He'd been up since 4 A.M. November meant it was time to get gear ready for winter lobstering. His eyes instantly closed. They hurt in that burning way eyes do when the body wants to send a message to the brain telling it *I'm tired*. Jed opened them just in time to catch the disappointment in Miss Wright's eyes as she set the story on his desk. He read the note and shrugged. Was this one so bad that she couldn't even give him a grade? Shop math was looking better and better. At least that was something he could make use of down the road. Writing used to be fun, but with Miss Wright as his teacher, doing the dishes for Deb's Bakery had moved ahead of it. English was now officially his least favorite subject, and his longest class of the day.

Finally, the bell rang announcing the end of school for the day…for everyone but him. Jed sat at his desk as the rest of the kids filed out of the room. Winnie stopped and took the seat next to Jed, as he knew she would. They'd been best friends for as long as anyone could remember.

"You okay, Jed?" she asked.

"Nope," was all he got out before Miss Wright interrupted. Not that Jed ever said much anyway. Winnie had spent more time with him than anyone else over the years, and she was still waiting for their first real conversation. But then Winnie didn't need him to talk in order to know what was going on with him. She just wanted to be next to him, with him.

"Jed has an appointment with me, Winifred. Now run along and he'll be out shortly," said Miss Wright.

"Yes ma'am," answered Winnie as she got up to leave. She hated that name and wished adults would stop using it.

Polly looked at Jedediah. He sat with his head down. If he could look more disinterested, she didn't know how. This was not going to be easy, but it needed doing.

"Jed, I want to talk to you about your story. It's very well written, but I think you misunderstood the assignment."

Jed looked up just long enough to say what was on his mind. "Not good enough for a grade."

"No, that's not it, Jed," she said with her best teacher voice. "This is a good story, it's just not what I asked you to write about. I think I need to have a talk with your parents. So that we can all work on this together."

"Do you mean Deb or Grampy Crockett?" he asked.

"No, I mean your parents, Jed, not the people in your story."

"If you read my story, you know I don't have any parents," said Jed just loud enough for her to hear.

Polly's voice became strained. "Do you expect me to believe this story you've conjured up is real?" she asked.

Jed slowly raised his head, stood up, and looked Miss Wright in the eyes with a distant anger of his own and said, "I don't expect jack from anybody." With that he walked out.

Polly was both angered and relieved when Jed left. This was the first time she'd seen him angry, and it had an immediate effect on how she viewed him. The idea of the story being true still found no home in her mind. All at once, many of the things about Jed which had frustrated her in the past came to light. She needed to confirm this now. Jed had left the story on his desk. Polly picked it up with a new sense of reverence and respect. If the words on these papers were true, Jed had opened up to her and she'd done some serious damage just now. She suddenly felt sick and like not so great a teacher. Placing the story into a folder, she headed to the principal's office to see what Mrs. Welsh knew.

Mrs. Welsh was as "native" as one from New Ireland could get. Her roots could be traced back to the founding town fathers. There was also no question about her being of Irish descent. Some of the fire-red hair still remained, and she was built thick and solid with a low center of gravity. When she walked into a room, the mood changed, and she commanded respect with just a look. Polly was reminded of the day she'd signed her teaching contract with Mrs. Welsh. The money was not what she'd wanted, but when she brought this up with Mrs. Welsh, the look she got put an end to the negotiations on the spot. Without a word, Mrs. Welsh had made clear that teaching at this school was not, nor would it ever be, about money.

Mrs. Welsh had told Polly when she was first hired to feel free to enter her office at anytime the door was always open. Being new however, and wanting to prove herself by making it on her own, Polly had not taken advantage of the offer before this moment.

Mrs. Welsh looked up. "Well, look what the tide brought in. What can I do for you, Miss Wright?" she said with a tone that established her as the person in charge.

"I wanted to talk to you about one of my students, if you had a few minutes," replied Polly.

"Yes, I've been waiting for you to do this very thing. You and Jed have been having a time of it," said Mrs. Welsh with a wink.

"How did you know?" asked Polly, somewhat amazed.

"It's my school. I know everything that's going on, Polly. I know everyone here, their parents, brothers, sisters, aunts, uncles, and grandparents, including yours. In fact, I knew them before you did."

Polly had no argument for her, so she pushed forward. "Yes, well, I asked Jed about setting a conference with his parents but he...well, he walked out on me."

"Did he? That doesn't sound like Jed," said Mrs. Welsh.

"Well, he said that a Deb and Mr. Crockett were his parents, but they're characters from this story he wrote," said Polly as she handed the folder to Mrs. Welsh.

Polly sat quietly as Mrs. Welsh read over the story. She looked for some hint as to what Mrs. Welsh was thinking as she read, but there was nothing. Once she finished, Mrs. Welsh passed the folder back to Polly.

"What was the assignment?" she asked.

"To write a story about a memory," Polly said.

"And...?" said Mrs. Welsh.

"And I meant for it to be a *true* story."

"So if you don't believe it, it's not true. Is that it?"

Polly was surprised by this answer. "Are you telling me that this *is* a true story? My God, what have I done?"

"I'm going to give you some advice and leave it at that," said Mrs. Welsh. "As a teacher—or anything else, as far as that goes—it's not the mistakes we make that matter, but what we do to correct them. Jed saw you as an outsider, yes, but also as a fresh start. Someone from the outside who might see him as something more. Now you're no better than the rest of us. Welcome to the bait bag, dearie."

A smile came across Polly's face. "I guess I'm the one learning today. Thank you, Mrs. Welsh."

"You're welcome, just doing my job, dear."

Jed left school and headed straight for the bakery. Winnie caught up with him as he crossed the street. He slowed down when he saw her, but no words passed between them. Winnie had seen Jed like this before and knew it was best to wait for him to speak first. He'd never been angry with her, but if she tried to get him to talk, he would have been just that much more determined not to. Besides, she could tell by the pace they were walking that whatever he had to say, he was saving for Deb. Winnie was just pleased he wanted her around at times like these, even if he didn't tell her so.

Jed had let her read the story he'd written, and Winnie was sure it had something to do with him being upset now. She had tried to tell him that Miss Wright might not like the story when she'd read it. But despite what Miss Wright believed, Jed wrote from the heart. That was his gift, and his curse. He might have trouble talking about his feelings, but he had no problem writing them down. It was this little detail that made her realize how different he was from the rest of the boys. "The Day of the Puffin" (as Jed had named the story), had brought him out of his shell a little. But it was mostly with Deb that he confided and found comfort. She was the one person Jed opened up to.

Sometimes Winnie thought Jed still saw her as the same little girl he'd first met. She also knew this was, at least in part, her fault. She didn't do or wear anything to show she was a girl. With strawberry blond, shoulder-length hair, no makeup, and always dressed in loose, baggy clothing, Winnie didn't get any attention from the boys like the other girls did, which was fine with her. She was comfortable and felt good about who she was, and didn't need to have boys chasing after her. The boy she was interested in was already spending his time with her. Though she did wish he'd notice that the scenery had changed since they'd first met.

They'd met at the breakwater. A mile-long wall of granite blocks with a lighthouse at the end. It had been built years before as a way to protect the harbor from storms. Winnie had been sitting out in front of the lighthouse with her legs hanging over the edge, waiting for the tide to come in enough for her to dip her toes in. It was early on a Sunday morning in late August. Winnie felt sure she was alone, sitting there on a towel in her birthday suit. Granted, she was only eight years old, but doing this made her feel like one of those rebel hippies she'd seen in a scrapbook her mother kept hidden in the attic of their house.

When Jed came around the corner of the lighthouse, she felt more like the way she imagined Eve must have felt the first time Adam saw her. She hadn't really done anything wrong, but for some reason it felt that way. It wouldn't have been so bad if her clothes had been nearby. But she'd left them up by the base of the lighthouse, out of the wind.

Even though Jed only looked her way for a second before turning away, it seemed a lot longer. Winnie wrapped the towel around herself, knowing she couldn't move without further exposing herself. Then Jed did two things, which surprised her. First, he picked up her clothes and brought them to her. Then he walked to the other side of the wall, took his clothes off, turned around, and faced her. He smiled as if to say, *Now we're even.* Then he turned and sat down with his feet hanging over.

Winnie was pleasantly surprised by his actions. She knew he was the boy from the bakery, but she didn't really know much about him. Before she realized what she was doing, Winnie got up, walked over, laid her towel down, and sat down next to Jed. They sat there for a good half hour with not a word between them. When they heard the voices of people walking toward them, they instinctively got up and dressed. Still without speaking, they started to walk back to the shore together. After a few more minutes, Winnie introduced herself and he told her his name was Jed. Ever since that day ten years ago, they'd been best friends. Even so, Jed had never really let Winnie inside.

Winnie had often wondered if he felt the way she did. When he'd let her read the story, it gave her an inkling that maybe, just maybe, he did. Having read the story, she understood him a lot better. Sure, she'd heard the stories of

Jed's past, but being able to see things from his perspective really helped. Winnie wished it had been her who had brought this out of him. Instead, it had been Miss Wright and her high standards. Even if Jed didn't realize it, Miss Wright was a good teacher for him. Now, however, was not the time to bring this up.

They reached the bakery still traveling at a good pace. Jed's arm was straight out and met the door with the power and muscle that working as a baker and lobsterman had given him. Without breaking stride, he was through the door, across the bakery, and out into the kitchen. Winnie and Deb made eye contact. Deb slipped off her apron and handed it to Winnie as they passed. Jed began running water for the dishes, not noticing that Deb had done most of them already. Since Jed had never been one for small talk, Deb got right to it.

"So I take it Miss Wright didn't like the story," she said, then waited for the silence to pass.

Surprisingly, Jed answered back quickly. "She liked it all right."

"But..." said Deb.

Jed turned the water off and spun around, not looking at Deb. "But she thinks it's not true. She wants a meeting with my parents."

"I'd be happy to meet with her Jed, you know that," offered Deb.

"Yeah, I know. I even said that." It was now that Jed chose to look at her. "She thinks I made up my story, including you and Grampy Crockett. Why would anyone lie about not having parents? Isn't it bad enough not to have any? Do I have to be reminded of it all the time?"

With that, Jed headed up the stairs to his room. Deb had heard this from him before, but it still hurt. She wanted to scream *What about me?* but never did. She'd known his father and wished he'd return every day. And every day he kind of did:

Jed looked more like him with the turn of each tide. It gave Deb an itchy patch she couldn't reach to scratch.

CHAPTER 3
Old Man Crockett

Jed woke at 4 A.M., same as usual. The idea that this was early never occurred to him, as he'd been doing it for so long now. After the way he'd treated Deb the day before, Jed wanted to get out the door without being seen, but he knew it would be difficult. Deb would be up soon, if she wasn't already. Jed knew he had a hard day's work ahead of him, and that taking a shower now would be pointless. Might as well just climb into his favorite jeans, and pull his well-used sweatshirt with an old Patriots logo on it, over his head. As he reached for his sneakers, he remembered that this was a work day with Grampy, so he put them back and grabbed his steel-toed work boots.

Years of repetition made Jed look at the toes of his boots to check the shine without thinking; yep, he could see himself. Grampy Crockett had provided the discipline he'd been missing in his early years. Grampy lived by a few simple rules. "Take care of your equipment, and it'll take care of you," was one of them. A quick look around his room reminded Jed of another rule: "There be a place for everything, and everything in its place." Jed now lived by these rules himself. Deb had mentioned on several occasions how pleased she was that he took care of his things so well. Not that there was so much to take care of. After living on the road and having nothing of his own for years, Jed appreciated everything given to him.

Once he'd started making a little money, Jed quickly realized its value. When other kids would be at the store for ice cream on a hot day, spending their money freely, Jed would go without. Oh sure, he wanted that ice cream all right, but not enough to pay for it just because it was hot. Except when Winnie wanted one, that is. Then he'd agree to buying one, but only if they shared it. Even then, it was a single scoop in a dish with two spoons. Each time, Jed waited for Winnie to complain, but she never had. When Winnie offered to pay, he always refused. Despite his rough exterior appearance, old man Crockett was a gentleman, and he was teaching Jed to be the same. Hence two more rules: "Actions be louder than words," and "Treat all women like ladies, until they prove themselves different." These two rules were the easiest ones for Jed to follow. He'd never been much of a talker anyway, and doing things for others came naturally to him. Working at the bakery was to help Deb. Working on the farm and lobstering with his Grampy just seemed like the right thing to do. The only reason Jed took the money was to make Grampy happy. He'd never once thought of what was in it for himself. And while most people thought that being a lady meant being lazy, Jed knew better. Deb was more ladylike than anyone else he knew. A lady is determined by how she treats others, not by how others treat her.

Jed's mood improved some with these thoughts. Making his way down the stairs, he moved slowly, walking near the wall so that the wood wouldn't pull against the nails in the steps and make them squeak. He reached the bottom pleased with not having made a sound. Halfway out the door, he heard Deb's voice.

"You forgot your lunch," she said.

Jed turned to see her holding out an old metal lunch pail. It was black where there was still some paint, with glimmers of metal visible in the dents and creases that gave it character. Without losing eye contact, Jed reached for the handle. A high-pitched squeak broke the silence as Deb let go and the metal handle and the hinges rubbed against each other.

Deb had told him the first time he used the lunch pail that it had belonged to his dad. With this simple gesture from Deb, the remaining anger from yesterday left him. His mind calmed, and the feeling of not having parents was gone once again. This pail was proof of his father's existence, while Jed's memory held his mother's.

"Thanks, Deb. I'm sorry about yesterday. I didn't mean nothin' by it."

A smile spread across Deb's face. She'd noticed Jed had been dropping his *g*'s now and again, since hanging around his grandfather. But one had to take the bad with the good, and Deb was willing to let this go. Jed needed a male influence in his life, and who better than his own grandfather? If that meant Jed sounded more like a Mainer, so be it. No more words passed between them as Jed walked out the door. None needed to. They'd come to know each other well enough so that words were often unnecessary. Just like old man Crockett had said, their actions spoke louder.

Jed looked out over the harbor as he made his way around front to the street. The water looked like amber ashes in a fireplace as the hint of the sun danced on the waves moving with the force of the tide, while the sea smoke made its way up into the morning light. The reflection in the lit windows of the buildings made the waves look like they were on fire. Boats moored in the harbor took on the look of gray ash within the flames with their white color contrasting with the darkness of the water and flickers of reflective light.

As he stood there looking over the harbor with this image in his mind, Jed began to consider the idea of there being a story here. He reached into his back pocket and pulled out a tattered notebook he always kept with him to make notes at times like these, and made an entry:

Just as water consumes fire, it can also consume man with a burning passion that draws him into it. Never giving anything but pain and disappointment in return. As badly as a man may want to stay ashore, the ocean calls him, like the bottom of a bottle, or the lust of a woman. He goes forth willingly, knowing there will be a price to pay. For with each life lived, another goes unlived. God's beauty, tainted by the devil's desires.

Jed looked at his watch: 4:20, he was going to be late. Turning on his toes, he took off in a sprint. If he didn't get to Grampy's by 4:30, he'd be called a lazy-ass sleepyhead all day.

Each home seemed to light up as Jed passed by, as if he were the flow of electricity they needed. Up ahead he could see a dim light coming from Crockett's kitchen. Even after all these years, Jed knew very little about the past. Most of the time when he'd ask about it, Grampy would say, "Ain't no good in worrying about the past ya can't do nothing about, when there be a tomorrow a-coming to beat ya down."

There hadn't been much snow so far this winter, so the path through the blueberry field was still usable. But no snow meant the odds of a bad crop of blueberries increased. The snow helped to insulate the plants from being damaged by ice and cold, or being eaten by deer. A fact that had been drilled into Jed's head this winter almost daily. But then, his grandfather seemed happiest when he had something to complain about.

Jed went through the door still in stride. His head was pounding from the cold air, and his chest heaved up and down as he tried to catch his breath. The clock above the stove was stained from all the years of wood burning, and the inside had yellowed, but Jed could see it read 4:29. He'd made it. Turning, he saw his Grampy sitting at the table eating his usual. Four eggs fried in the leftover bacon grease from the half pound of bacon on his plate. Grampy continued to bail the food into himself as he started talking.

"What in hell ails ya boy? You can't be all tuckered out just from running up that little ol' hill. Why, when I was your age, I had to get up at three o'clock, do my chores, then work until midday on the boat. Then I had to come here and work till the sun went down. After that, I'd be out chasing the girls around half the night. Caught my fair share of 'em, too. Yessir, them was the days," said Crockett, with a toothless smile.

Jed let him spout off, knowing it was Grampy's way of saying good morning, glad to see you.

"Hey, Gramps. Did you ever catch anyone I might know?" he asked. Jed liked the fact that he was the only person who could call old man Crockett Gramps.

"Heh-heh, a gentlemen don't kiss and tell, boy, you 'member that."

Jed already knew this of course, but he still liked to hear these things from Grampy.

"What's on the agenda today, Gramps?" he asked.

"Well, seeing as you're all tuckered out and probably ain't worth much anyway, I thought we'd take a boat ride outside the harbor and check the traps out there. Then make a run into Redman Village for some supplies. That be all right with you?"

"Heck yeah. I love going to Redman Village," answered Jed.

Crockett grinned and said, "I left some eggs and bacon in the skillet for ya, if you got strength enough to eat."

Jed smiled back and said, "Thanks, Grampy."

They ate in silence.

Deb was pleased she'd had the chance to see Jed before he left. Grampy Crockett had told her he was planning a trip to Redman Village, and she didn't want Jed to go off for the day feeling bad about things and fretting about it all day. Jed still had a tendency to keep things to himself. It was a habit from the past that Deb had not been able to make any headway in changing. She knew Jed trusted her and had feelings for her, but he still had trouble letting people in, including Winnie, including her.

This lack of trust had both a good and bad aspect to it. As Jed continued to grow into a man, the fact that he continued to look more and more like his father made things increasingly difficult for Deb. The lack of trust had created a distance, and provided a buffer for her, not unlike the one she'd had with Zach way back then. But then Zach was not living under her roof, bringing joy and love into her life. Although she'd give anything for this to be the case. It was because of Zach that Deb had remained single.

Oh, there'd been plenty of suitors, but none who could live up to her memory of Zach. Despite her lack of interest in men, Deb qualified as a looker in this small fishing town, or anywhere else, for that matter. The work at the bakery kept her in shape. Being on her feet all day helped her legs stay slim and firm, and she had a tendency to wear skirts that were even shorter than her apron. All the bending and lifting also kept her waist slim and her butt firm. Then there was all that kneading of the dough. This had given her thick arms, but she didn't have those flabby triceps a lot of women developed in their forties. Hers were firm, as were her breasts. Gravity had yet to take its toll—in part due to the hard work, and in part because she'd never had children.

Many a woman had stopped into the bakery with kids in tow; occasionally, one of them would comment on the impact nursing had had on her breasts, causing them to lose shape and head south. Deb would always think to herself, *Sounds like a fair trade to me.* But she'd never said it out loud. She knew they were just venting. There was no way any woman would trade her children for firm breasts. It was just a reaction to the changes in their bodies, that, and the lack of interest from their husbands. Here again, Deb wished she had a husband to be ignored by. A husband named Zach, that is. Still, at five feet four inches and one hundred ten pounds, Deb was a pleasure to look at even though she'd celebrated her thirty-ninth birthday more than once. Her hair had always been short due to her work, and she'd worn the same red Patriots hat for so long, there was now a permanent crease in her hair. It was a hat Zach had given her as a joke. Zach loved the Boston Patriots, and Deb was quick to remind him that he was a sucker for a loser. The franchise seemed destined to always get in their own way when it came to succeeding on the football field. They were called the New England Patriots now. Deb didn't really understand the game, but she'd kept track of them over the years by watching the games when she could, hoping in vain to see Zach's face in the crowd on the TV screen.

Deb heard the motor of Crockett's boat kick over. After all these years of early mornings in the bakery, she'd learned to identify the slight differences in sound from each of the boats in the harbor. Without realizing it, she had subconsciously come to keep track of who left and when. Deb looked forward to the day when she would hear Jed's boat for the first time. Not because she didn't wish or believe that Jed could or would leave someday, but because she couldn't bear the thought of losing Zach a second time. That's how she knew it would feel, if Jed ever left. Losing Zach nearly did her in. The idea of going through that again was unbearable.

Deb stepped away from her work and watched the boat carrying Crockett and Jed make its way out of the harbor before picking up speed once it was into open water, a tradition that was lost with some of the younger lobstermen. A show of respect, which had lost its place in a world of competitiveness and jealousy. This was a conversation Deb had heard taking place in her bakery on many occasions. Who made the most money, whose boat was the fastest, and a collection of other things that had nothing to do with lobstering.

One of the old-timers would make a comment about how one of the younger men had left the harbor at full steam that morning; setting his boat to rocking, causing a problem, or breaking something because of it. The young fellas would then make some comment about the old-timer getting his ass out of bed in the morning and leaving before them, if he didn't like it.

Deb had made a point of staying out of the politics of lobstering. After all, she wanted all the men as customers, and the confrontations seemed to create a unique kind of atmosphere in the shop. She hoped that Crockett's influence would provide Jed with a respect for the traditions.

As the sound of their boat was lost in the density of the fog, Deb turned her attention back to the work at hand. Her thoughts returned to the past, and how Jed was the patch covering a permanent scratch on her heart.

CHAPTER 4
Redman Village

J ed grabbed a bait bag and hung it in the trap, dropped the trap overboard, and watched the line to be sure it didn't snag on anything.

"Was that the last one, Gramps?" he asked.

"Yep, that'll do it."

"Okay, I'll get things cleaned up and secured," said Jed.

"I got a better idea. Why don't you come up here and take the wheel?" offered Crockett.

Jed dropped the mop he was holding. The boat was small, so it only took a few steps for him to make it from the stern to the wheelhouse. Even though he'd been going out to haul with Gramps for a few years now, there'd been few opportunities to get his hands on the wheel.

Crockett waited for Jed to get a firm grip on the wheel before letting go. When he finally did, it was only his hands that moved. The rest of him stood fast; standing by, ready to take the wheel back if the need arose. But Jed was a natural. He understood the balance between a boat and the ocean. How the weight of the boat pushed against the water, and the pressure of the water pushed back. Each telling the other what it wanted to do, striking a balance between the two. But there was more for him to understand, and it was time he did.

"You were born with the sea in your blood boy, ain't no doubt in that," began Crockett. "The ocean's a dangerous place.

Most people know it, but they don't know why."

Jed started to get excited. This was going to be one of those times when Gramps was going to share some of his wisdom. Jed had come to relish these moments, as they were rare, and the information was worth more to Jed than anything he'd ever learned in school. He repeated his grandfather's words in his head to be sure he'd heard them right. *You were born with the sea in your blood boy, ain't no doubt in that. The ocean's a dangerous place. Most people know that, but they don't know why.* Jed knew he needed to be ready to receive Gramps' words the first time. Gramps had told him long ago that you don't get any second chances out on the water. Plus, there was a saying people used to describe Crockett, and Jed had heard the old man say it himself many times: "Old man Crockett don't chew his cabbage twice." Jed wasn't sure exactly what it meant, but he had a pretty good idea.

Throughout this thought process, Jed had not taken his eyes off the water, but the wind changed quickly causing a spray to come over the bow. Had it not been for the plywood enclosure around the wheelhouse, they'd have been drenched.

"Sorry, Gramps, missed that one," he said with a voice full of dejection.

"Ain't nothin' to be sorry 'bout, wasn't nothin' but a kiss."

Jed was confused. "What do you mean, a kiss, Gramps?"

"That's what I be talking about, boy. We got two women fighting over us men. For as long as anyone can remember, the ocean's been called *she*, and we done the same with our boats. Like my boat here, I call *Miss Ellen*."

"After Grammy," said Jed.

"Yup, that be right, boy. Fishermen always have at least two women who love them, three if they have a sweetheart or wife. The ocean has a way of drawing a man out into it."

Jed was reminded of the words he'd written in his journal earlier that morning. Now he knew where they'd come from.

Grampy's lesson continued. "A man will go out fishing even when he knows he shouldn't. The sky and air will be filled with signs a-tellin' him there be a storm a-brewing. But he'll go out just the same. Not 'cause he has to, but 'cause he wants to. Now the ocean's the kinda woman who wants a man all to herself. She wants to take him into her grasp and hold him in it forever, at the bottom for all time. She's not willing to share him with anyone else. But she don't want just one man, she be after them all."

"The fisherman's other woman, his boat, knows this. Oh, but she be true to her man, do anything to protect him from the ocean. When you hear the waves slapping up against the boat, that be the two of them arguing. Miss Boat will take all the beating the ocean can give out, then turn right around and come back tomorrow for more. Why, she'll even give her life, if it means her man will make it back to shore safe. Never once giving thought to her own safety."

"That's why the ocean's so dangerous for a man. He be caught in the middle of two women fighting over him. While he loves and respects both, he'll never choose between them. He loves them each for who they be; different, yet the same. So they fight. Sometimes the boat wins and after years together, she delivers her man home, safe. Never to return out onto the ocean again, free of her hold. Sometimes, the ocean wins. Then she keeps the man for herself, which means he's never to be seen again."

"What about the sweetheart or wife?" asked Jed.

"She be worst off of 'em all, my boy. She must plead with the ocean not to take her man and beg the boat to keep him safe. Oh, she'd fight for her man if she could, but that's not her lot in life. She's doomed to love a man who belongs not just to her, but to others. So she waits. Waits for the day he gives them up and comes home to her. Scorning her life and loving her man. Caught in her own battle."

Just like that, the lesson was over. Jed especially liked

that. There was no big discussion where you talked it to death. By the time all the talking was done, a person had so many thoughts bouncing around in their head, it was impossible to formulate your own opinion. No sir, Gramps said his piece then left you to think and do what you wanted with it. Many a night Jed lay in bed thinking over one or more pieces of advice he'd gotten from Gramps. It was this, more than anything else, that made him feel connected to his own version of a so-called family.

Granted, his family was made up of a woman he'd been left with and a crotchety old man who now spent every free moment with him like the father he'd never met. Still, it was a lot better than being dragged here and there by a mother who couldn't stay put and a man who would hit you every chance he got.

Over the years since his mother had abandoned him, Jed had often wondered why. What would make a mother do something like that? Jed had come to realize it must have been the beatings. Carl must have told her to choose between him or Jed or he'd make the choice for her. So she left him where he'd be safe, cared for. After all, she was his mother. That meant she had to do what was best for him, right? If she had chosen him instead of Carl, he might not be here today.

Jed kept staring straight ahead as the harbor to Redman Village opened up before them. The fog had moved out with the morning tide. It was now possible to see all the way to the horizon. There was a question he'd been wanting to ask Gramps for a while now. The timing seemed right. There was no place for Gramps to go, and they'd be docking in a few minutes. Maybe he could get a quick answer.

"Gramps, what happened to your wife?" he asked. Jed didn't feel right saying *Grammy Crockett*, since he'd never met her.

"She died," came the short answer.

"Yeah, I know, Gramps, but how? Why?"

There was a long silence, to the point where Jed thought he was being ignored. Then, just before he was ready to maneuver the boat, Gramps reached over, pulled the throttle back and popped the clutch out of gear. There was another silence. Jed kept looking at Gramps, and Gramps kept looking straight ahead. There was pain in Gramps' face. Jed was sorry he'd asked the question now. He wanted to say something. But what? Gramps didn't like people saying sorry to him. When Jed had said sorry to him in the past, Gramps would always say, "If you're sorry, ya shouldn't a done it in the first place."

Then Jed recognized the feeling that made the look in Gramps' face. It was the same one he'd felt that first day in Deb's. Gramps was scared and alone because the one person in his life that mattered the most was gone.

Jed reached for the lever that put the clutch into gear. As he put his hand on it, Gramps put his hand on top of Jed's. Jed froze. Gramps had never touched him before. Even though the hand was rough and worn from all the years of hard labor, at this moment, there was a warmth to it. A tenderness Jed felt for the first time. He turned and looked at Gramps. Gramps was looking at him, his eyes full of tears.

"My wife died of a broken heart. She hurt bad when our boy run off. That near killed her. Then that wench of a mother of yours run off with you. It was like losing both of ya to the ocean. She just couldn't bear it. She got sick, and the will to live left her. I got the doc and offered him everything I had to help her. But he said there was nothing he could do for her. It was up to her to live or die."

"I blamed you for a long time. Right up till the day that puffin showed up. You were willing to help that puffin when no one else cared. It was then I saw my Ellen in you for the first time. But it wasn't till later that night I come to believe it was Ellen who sent the puffin to bring us together."

Having said his piece, Crockett popped the clutch into

gear and pushed the throttle forward. Jed stepped aside so that Gramps could take control. Bringing the boat up to the dock was a skill he'd yet to try, let alone master. It would be his job to put the three old tires over the side to protect the boat from running into the dock, and to tie the boat to the dock both forward and aft. Jed was always amazed at how easily Gramps accomplished the task of bringing the boat up against the dock. "Like a hot knife through soft butter," is how Gramps put it. Once the boat was secured, Gramps said Jed had two hours on his own, then to meet him at the marine store to get the supplies.

Now, Redman Village was not a city. Heck, it wasn't even that big a town. But for Jed, it did have one thing to offer which New Ireland didn't: it had a library. Jed could spend two hours just walking around looking at all the books. However, he knew that wasn't going to happen. There was a section he would subconsciously end up in no matter where he started. Even though the trip to Redman Village was about the same in a car or a boat, Jed had only been able to make the trip to the library a few times. When he looked at the books, it wasn't the thought of "so many books, so little time" that crossed his mind. No, his dream was to see his own books on the shelf someday. A dream he'd shared with no one. Not Winnie, not Gramps, not even Deb.

Jed followed this train of thought and ended up once again in the biography section. Reading books about the lives of others helped to give his own life a center. He learned that many of them had lived lives which had started out difficult, to say the least, and yet they still ended up fulfilling their dreams. He especially liked reading books about authors.

Irene Black was the head librarian and nothing got by her. After all, this was her library, and it had been her mother's before that. Her mother had taught Irene that a good librarian should know what her public wanted when they came in.

She was here to serve the public and protect the books. Irene noticed Jed coming in but she waited until he was settled before approaching him. Reaching under the counter for the book she'd been saving for him, Irene made her way toward Jed.

Jed was reading about E.B. White and didn't see or hear Miss Black approach. Whenever Jed came across a writer with connections to Maine, it caught his attention. He nearly jumped when the librarian whispered, "E.B. White, he wrote a book on writing. It's called *The Elements of Style*. We have a copy of it here if you're interested."

Jed looked up. He'd never noticed how young she was. Right away, he could tell she was different from the other women he knew. Even Winnie. He wasn't sure how to answer her. But he finally managed to say, "Thanks, but I'm just looking. I don't have a library card."

"Yes, I know. That can be easily rectified," said Miss Black.

Jed gave her a strange look and she launched into teaching mode.

"Rectify means—"

"I know what it means," he interrupted, a little put out. Then he felt bad and continued, "I've just never heard anyone use it before. And the reason I don't have a library card is that I live in New Ireland. I noticed you only lend the books out for two weeks at a time, and the sign over there says it's a penny a day for every day a book is overdue. I never know when I'll be back, so I can't really promise to have a book back on time even if I did take one out."

"Oh, I see. Well, I have a book here that you could borrow, and bring it back whenever you can."

She handed the book to Jed, and he looked at the inside, the back cover, and then read the cover. *Kitchen Boy*, by Sanford Phippen.

"This isn't a library book," he said.

"No," she replied. "It belongs to me. Mr. Phippen is from Maine, he went to UMO. The book's fiction, but it's based on his teen years. I noticed you like reading about authors and I thought you might like to read it."

Jed took a closer look at the book. The cover had a picture of a man riding a lobster over a boiling kettle. For some reason, Jed connected with the picture. He smiled without realizing he was doing it.

Irene was pleased by this. A smile like Jed's was why she put in all the hard work and long hours. Nothing pleased her more than to see a book in someone's hands, and a smile on their face.

"Why don't you take a look at it while I find that E.B. White book I mentioned? Then we'll *rectify* that library card problem."

As Jed got up, the chair made a scratching sound on a bare patch of the floor. Jed didn't know it yet, but he and Irene were going to become good friends. Friends who did things for each other without asking or telling, friends where when one had an itchy patch the other was there to scratch it.

CHAPTER 5
It's the Not Knowing that Bothers

Jed looked at the two books sitting on top of his bureau, right where he'd put them on Friday when he got back from Redman Village. He wanted to read them, but something inside made him hesitate, as if somehow doing so would have a negative impact on his dream of becoming a writer. In some ways, the dream meant more to Jed than actually accomplishing the goal. What if he tried to become a writer and failed? What then? Then he'd have nothing to look forward to. Not that the life he had was a bad one. He didn't mind going lobstering, or working in the blueberry fields, or even the haying. Spending the rest of his life doing that kind of work would be okay.

Still, there was a lot more to the world than New Ireland, Maine. Jed's memories from childhood were full of things he'd seen, places he'd been. The names of these places had long since been lost, if indeed he'd ever known them, but the vision of a city remained. Jed assumed it was Boston, but he'd never talked with anyone about it. No one except Winnie, that is. Since Winnie had never been out of the county, she wasn't much help. She was a great listener, though. That's the one thing Jed liked most about Winnie. She was a really good listener. Winnie didn't ask him a thousand questions, or give an opinion about everything. She just listened.

Being deep in thought, Jed didn't hear the creak of the steps as Winnie headed for his room. Nor did he hear the soft knock on the door. Not until he heard her voice was he aware of her presence.

"Knock, knock. You decent?" she asked playfully. "Not that I haven't seen you otherwise."

"Hey, Winnie, come on in," he answered.

Winnie liked Jed's room. Though it wasn't very big, it had an interesting shape. One outside wall followed the roofline, slanting in as it rose, while another was nothing more than a small dormer framing a window, and the third wall was the roofline from the opposite side. This design shaped the room like a triangle, a tepee, or (and this was Winnie's favorite) a tower where you'd keep a damsel in distress. That's how Winnie saw Jed at times, as a damsel in distress, and she was the hero whose job it was to save him. The wall which held the door was the only flat one in the room, and it ran up to the peak of the roof, twelve feet up. The remaining part of the room was not a wall at all, but a small triangular opening. It was only three feet high and narrowed down to a point from three sides. Like the lead weights you'd put on a fishing line.

The two of them had spent many hours within this small area playing imaginary games, talking about the future and the past, the comings and goings of their lives. Everything save one. A couple of years ago, they had stopped the games. It was then that Winnie had snuck up and made the marks on the rafter in the very back, at the small end. It was nothing grand, just a simple heart with the initials of herself and Jed within. Giving a home to the one thing they never talked about in this space or anywhere else. The only dream Winnie had never shared with anyone. The only real dream she'd ever wanted to come true. Without realizing it, Winnie was staring at this tiny room and got caught.

"What are you looking at?" asked Jed.

"Oh, nothing," she replied, looking for something to say. "I was just remembering the times we spent in that little room.

It seems like so long ago now."

"Yeah, I know what you mean."

The slightest smile emerged on Winnie's face. Her eyes caught sight of the two books on his bureau. One of them took her by surprise. She stood up and walked to the bureau and picked them both up.

"Did Miss Wright give you these books?" she asked.

Jed cast a confused look at Winnie before answering. "Miss Wright! Why would you bring her up?"

"Well, ordinarily I wouldn't, but I've seen this book called *Kitchen Boy* in her bag at school. I like the cover. A boy riding a lobster. When I saw it, I was reminded of you."

Jed took the book from her, and gave it a good look. The boy on the cover didn't look like him at all. In fact, it wasn't even a boy, but a man. Jed had, however, wondered from time to time what it would be like to ride a lobster. He'd also seen the ocean look like a boiling pot. Although Jed liked the cover himself, he could not see the resemblance Winnie was talking about.

"No, I got this from the Redman Village Library. The author is from Maine," he said.

"The library?" said Winnie with a sly smile. "I didn't know you'd ever been *in* a library, let alone had a library card."

Knowing he was caught, Jed fessed up. "I've only been a few times. Gramps and I went to Redman Village the other day in the boat. I like to read books about writers. Anyway, there I was minding my own business when the librarian offered me a library card. The E.B. White book is from the library, but this book is hers."

Winnie thought she knew everything about Jed, but this was something new. If Jed was interested in writers, it would stand to reason that he was more serious about his writing than she'd thought. Jed had never given her anything he'd written except for school work. She always figured he wrote because he had to, not because he wanted to. Surely he would have shared this interest with her, if anyone. She needed to learn more.

"I didn't know you were that interested in writing," she said in a way that left the door open.

"It doesn't matter," he replied. "I'm no good at it anyway."

"What makes you say that?" she asked.

"Miss Wright," he answered.

"Miss Wright? What did she say?"

"You know that story we had to write last week?"

"Yes…"

"Well, what did you get for a grade?" asked Jed.

"I got an A. What about you?"

"Don't know. She hasn't told me."

Winnie looked at him in disbelief. She liked Miss Wright and was having trouble believing Jed, despite their history together.

"What do you mean she hasn't told you yet? Just look at the paper."

"That's the thing," he responded. "She hasn't given it back to me yet. All I got was a note telling me to meet with her after class."

"So that's why you were so mad last week, because she didn't like your paper?"

Jed took a deep breath. He knew he should talk about it with Winnie. "No, she didn't really say that. She said it wasn't what the assignment was."

"But it was. Didn't you explain it to her?"

"I tried, but she didn't believe it was true."

A look of understanding came over Winnie's face.

She said, "I have an idea. Why don't you show it to the librarian in Redman Village? I bet she'd be able to be objective."

For some reason, Jed liked this idea. "Yeah, maybe I will.

Thanks, Winnie."

"You're welcome," she said with a smile. "You want to do something?"

"Maybe later. I think I'm going to read some of this book now, if you don't mind."

"Not at all. How about I go downstairs and help Deb for a bit, and you can come down when you're ready. It's a beautiful day and I was hoping to walk the breakwater."

"Sure. I'll be down in an hour or so."

Winnie got up to leave and gave Jed a hug on the way by. To herself she was thinking, *You're worth the wait*, but she'd never dream of saying it out loud. Even though she wanted more than what they had, Winnie didn't want to risk losing him over her desires.

Just as she was leaving, Jed spoke.

"Winnie, you're the best. Thanks again."

When she looked back, he was already reading the book, or at least pretending to. His words scratched an itch she'd been trying to reach for as long as she could remember. As she made her way down the stairs, her steps, like her heart, were so light they barely touched the wood.

CHAPTER 6
On the Move

At this time of year, Gramps didn't go out to pull his lobster traps every day, and things were slower at the bakery, so Jed had more free time, time he used to read the books he'd gotten at the library.

Deb had reminded him there was a reason to make another trip to Redman Village sooner than he'd realized. He'd been studying for his driver's license, and Redman Village was the closest place to take the test.

Even though Miss Black had said there was no hurry in returning the books, Jed was anxious to do so. Reading *Kitchen Boy* had stirred something within him. The book had made a connection with him through the things he wanted to write about. It was as if he was holding the proof that his dream could come true, right there in his hands. The other thing reading the book had done was give him the courage to want Miss Black to read his story, just as Winnie had suggested.

Getting a driver's license was a big deal to a lot of the kids his age, but not for Jed. The lack of freedom other kids expressed wasn't present within him. His exposure to the library, however, had changed his desire a bit, but not so much that he lost sight of reality. Even if he had a driver's license, he didn't have anything to drive; nor was he willing to part with any of his hard-earned money to buy a truck just because he suddenly had a driver's license. Still, it seemed important to the people around him. Both Deb and Gramps had taken him out driving and parallel parking. Jed even got a kick out of the fact that Gramps didn't hesitate to let him drive the truck around town, while the idea of steering the lobster boat made Gramps cringe. Jed knew it was because of what the old man had told him about the boat and women. Even so, he still thought it was funny.

Most people kept their distance from Crockett because they thought he was mean. Jed figured they just didn't understand him, at least not like he had come to. He knew Gramps was lonely, and carried around a lot of pain. Some would say Jed was a constant reminder of that pain, and they'd be right. When he'd first realized this, Jed had wondered why the old man kept him around. As they spent more time together, it became clear to Jed that his presence also reminded Gramps of the things he'd lost when Zach left, and that in some way, he eased as much pain as he caused. Jed found great comfort in this belief. Over time, he hoped to learn more about Gramps even though the topic had never come up until that day on the boat. Even then, what was revealed was very little. Sometimes Jed felt like he spent most of his time waiting. Waiting for his mother to come back, waiting for Gramps or Deb to talk about his father. Good thing he was a patient person.

That was one thing Jed remembered about his mother. She liked him to sit still, be quiet, and wait. If he didn't, he paid the price. Carl was not the first one to hit him. However, unlike Carl, his mom didn't enjoy hitting him. After years of thinking about it, he'd come to the conclusion that part of the reason his mother got together with Carl was so that *she* could stop hitting him—she'd found someone else who was happy to do so. Then she left. That was something he was still trying to figure out. But then he was only seventeen, or was it eighteen? He didn't really know. Maybe this was something he wasn't meant to know yet. At least that's what Jed told himself.

For now, he was looking forward to the trip to Redman the

next day. Even though it would mean missing Miss Wright's English class at the end of the school day, a class he'd come to enjoy of late. Miss Wright had been different toward him, and Jed had come to realize that the things she was teaching were starting to make sense to him. His grades had begun to show improvement as well. Miss Wright had even spent time helping him with the story that had started this whole thing.

She explained to him the do's and don'ts of dialect, how it's fine when writing a play or movie script, but when using it in writing literature, one has to be careful or the reader will lose interest in the story if they have to stop and figure out what's being said. She was also teaching him the difference between showing and telling when writing. For example, instead of saying, *The wave was big, making the boat look small*, a writer would say, *The sea rose above the boat, casting a shadow over the expectations of its occupants as they looked up at this mass of impending doom*. With these private lessons, Jed's writing began to improve in ways he could never previously have imagined.

The topics and hints in E.B. White's book had proven to be a big help as well. It wasn't so much the information provided in the book's lessons as it was the fact that a person from Maine was a leading authority in the literary world— which gave him a lot of confidence. Miss Wright also told him something which hit home with him. She told him that grammar had a place in writing books, but more important were the writers who invented new words and changed the world by breaking the rules instead of following them. Reading *Kitchen Boy* helped Jed understand the importance of having a personal style, or "unique voice," as Miss Wright said it was called in the writing world. It was a world Jed was becoming more and more immersed in each day. The more Jed learned about writing, the more he saw to write about and the better he learned to live life.

Deb flipped the sign on the shop's front door from Open to Closed. It was one o'clock and she needed to get moving if she was going to pick up Jed and get to Redman Village in time for his driver's test. Turning around, she stopped to stare at the booth Jed had been sitting at that first day. A day which took place years ago, and yet seemed like just yesterday. Jed might not be her child, but as far as she was concerned, he was her son.

To Deb, today was one of those special days, one of those experiences a parent remembers more than the child does. For Jed, it would be a chance to gain some freedom, a rite of passage. For Deb, it was his first step toward manhood and a chance for her to see if the things she was trying to teach him were really taking hold. Nothing big, mind you, but the little things. The right and wrong of the world, and how one chooses to live in it. Not so much the things that get noticed for being there, but the ones that don't get noticed. These were the things Deb had decided to focus on, just as any mother would— manners, taking responsibility, doing without telling—so that Jed would become the man his father hadn't been.

A single tear made its way down Deb's cheek, into the corner of her mouth. She instinctively licked it, tasting the saltiness. She wondered who the tear was for. Was it for Jed, or for his father? Or was it for herself? Maybe, she concluded, it was for all three of them. This thought made her smile and caused more tears to fall. She thought of what might have been, of how much more this day could be if only his father were here.

A rattling of the door startled her. "Sorry, closed," she called before turning to see who it was. When she did turn, Winnie was looking back at her.

"Winnie, right on time," she said with a soft smile.

"Hi, Deb. You ready to go?"

"Almost. I just need to grab a sweater," Deb said while making her way to the back.

Deb was glad to have Winnie's company for the trip. Jed might not need a friend today, but it seemed *she* did. As she pulled her favorite blue sweater from the coat rack, she noticed the other one hanging there. It was gray with an overlay of white cable and a hood; the sweater Zach had given her. She thought how funny it was to see it today. It had been hanging there all these years, unnoticed. Why today had it chosen to come into view? Deb took it as a sign, placed the blue sweater back on a hook, and put Zach's sweater on. It sat on her shoulders as if tailor-made. Although she'd never worn the sweater before, its effect was calming.

When she came back out, Winnie noticed the sweater immediately. "Nice sweater," she said. "Is it new?"

"Kinda," was all that Deb would say.

They walked out arm and arm, knowing the truth of things without speaking, as girls sometimes do.

Jed was waiting outside the school when Deb pulled up. He was both pleased and surprised to see Winnie in the car. Her presence made him realize the importance of this event, and feel a little nervous about it for the first time. The idea of failing in the presence of Winnie was not something he wanted to have on his mind today. Deb shut the car off and got out. She put her arm around Jed while Winnie gave him a hug.

"You ready to go?" asked Deb as she handed him the keys.

Jed felt the keys drop into his hand. Of the people he knew, these were the two who meant the most to him. Although Gramps was, as of late, making a strong case to join them. He looked at Deb and asked the question that needed asking.

"You sure you want me to drive?"

Deb's answer came with a simple reassuring smile as she slipped into the back seat so Winnie could have the front.

Jed took the hint and climbed in behind the wheel. Before starting the car, Jed looked Winnie's way. His stare was met with her soft voice saying, "I trust ya."

With that, Jed turned the key, checked his mirrors, released the brake, and put the car into drive. With a long patch of road in front of him, Jed felt the transmission scratch itself into gear as the car began rolling toward Redman Village.

CHAPTER 7
Know Your Own Way

Deb and Winnie sat quietly in the waiting area for Jed to return. Winnie found herself looking for something to say. The trip up had been more quiet than a library. It wasn't too often she had a chance to get time alone with Deb. Most of their time together was at the bakery. Winnie could tell Deb knew and understood what she felt for Jed. They'd really never had a chance to talk about it girl to girl, though.

"This must be what it's like for expectant fathers waiting for their wives to deliver," she said. As soon as the words left her mouth, she knew they were wrong.

"I couldn't tell you, dear," was Deb's answer.

"Yeah...sorry Deb, I didn't mean to—"

Deb cut her short. "It's okay, Winnie. To tell you the truth, I think we're more nervous about this than Jed is."

"Yeah, this and th—" *Dang!* thought Winnie. *I've done it again.*

"The what?" asked Deb.

"If you don't mind, I'd rather not say," Winnie answered, hoping to get out of her predicament.

Deb understood that Winnie had nearly shared a secret with her that was between Winnie and Jed. Knowing how close the two of them were, she didn't want to cause any problems.

"I understand, dear," was all she said.

They'd both been watching the parking lot, and when Deb's car turned in, they looked at each other with the unspoken question in their eyes: Had Jed passed the test?

They watched as the tester spoke with Jed. He held up a clipboard, and it was obvious they were going over something. Finally, Jed and the tester got out of the car. Jed waited for him to go ahead before walking in. His head down, Jed looked at the ground the whole way in. Deb and Winnie were still holding their breath when he entered the building.

He spoke without looking up. "I need to go into the inspector's office for a few minutes," he said as softly as either of the women had ever heard him speak.

Deb felt her heart sink. "So does this mean you have to schedule a time to come back?"

"No," said Jed. "His pen ran out of ink in the car. He's getting a new one to sign my license."

Jed then looked up with a grin that made the two women happy, but mad enough to hit him for playing such a mean joke.

In an effort to avoid their teasing, Jed made his way down the hall and returned a few minutes later with his new license.

As they walked back to the car, Jed asked if he could stop somewhere before heading home. Deb looked at Winnie, sensing that this was the same item of business which had nearly transpired between them earlier.

"You're the driver, Jed, I go where you go." Then she winked at Winnie and smiled.

Jed got behind the wheel and made his way out of the Department of Transportation's parking lot. Deb assumed Jed's destination would be further away, and was surprised when he turned toward home.

"Would you like to know where we're headed?" Jed asked, apparently aware of her confusion.

Deb thought for a second. "Nope, surprise me," she answered.

"Okay, if you say so."

Deb was more than a little surprised when Jed turned into the library parking lot. "What are we doing here?" she heard herself say.

Jed parked the car and turned the motor off before answering. "Deb, could you hand me my backpack, please?" he asked.

Deb reached down onto the floor, picked up the backpack, and handed it to him.

"Thanks."

"You're welcome," answered Deb, feeling a little mystified.

Much to her astonishment, Jed unzipped the backpack and pulled out two books and a folder. Deb had seen the books in his room, and had made the assumption they were part of his school work.

"Jed, I never knew you'd been to the library. When? How…?"

A smile crossed Jed's face. "Whenever Gramps and I come over for supplies, I stop in, but I never had a library card until the last trip a couple of weeks ago. This could take a few minutes. Do you want to come in or come back and get us?"

Before Deb could answer, Winnie spoke up and said, "You should come in, it gets better." Winnie broke out into a silly giggle. She jumped out of the car in a single move, opened Deb's door, and extended her hand. Jed was standing on the other side of the car, waiting.

Deb reached for Winnie's hand and the two of them joined Jed. As they walked, Deb thought about how grown up Jed seemed all of a sudden. Here he was, driving, going to a library, and goodness knows what else. She glanced at Winnie and wondered if the two of them were even closer than she had thought.

Winnie felt a swelling of pride for Jed. He was becoming a man. Now, if he would only notice her. For some time, she'd wanted to tell Deb how she really felt about Jed, and ask for her help. The one thing holding her back was the fact that, as far as she knew, Deb had never had a man. If this were the case, Winnie didn't want to remind Deb of it by bringing it up, while part of her did wonder what Deb could possibly know about men. A woman as old as Deb, who'd never had a man, couldn't possibly know or understand how she felt. A simple question might show her she was wrong, but Winnie was confident in her opinion. She didn't think Deb could provide the help she so desperately needed at this moment.

Jed opened the door to the library. The creak of the metal hinges on the big wooden doors caused an echo throughout the building, disturbing the silence. Jed liked this noise. It reminded him of leaving the harbor with Gramps in the early morning fog. He also imagined this would be how people would feel reading one of his stories. As if something that had been hidden away from them was suddenly entering their world.

Irene Black heard the door open and instinctively turned to look. Just as her mother had taught her, Irene could see without being noticed. The library had been empty for the last few hours, but then it was Friday. Not a good afternoon for the library business. Her first thought was that it was a bunch of kids stopping by, acting up, causing a commotion. She was pleased to see that it was Jed, and he'd brought friends.

Jed approached the front desk with Deb and Winnie in tow. "Hi, Miss Black. I finished the two books," he said, handing them to her.

She smiled at him. "Hi, Jed, it's nice to see you again, and so soon. You've really read both of these already? That's very good, Jed."

"Thank you," he answered. "I'd like you to meet Deb. Deb's my..." Jed had never had an occasion to introduce Deb before. He knew what she meant to him, but he didn't have a word for it.

"I'm his unofficial guardian," offered Deb.

Guardian, thought Jed. *She's more than that, but what?* She wasn't his mother, though she did everything he thought a mother should.

"Well, she's more like my mother, except she's not," added Jed.

"I see," said Irene. "And who is this lovely young lady?" she asked, looking at Winnie.

Jed turned toward Winnie. This time he wanted to get his words right.

"This...is my best friend, Winnie."

The soft, upward turn of Winnie's lips, which revealed her dimples, showed proof he had chosen the right words.

Jed failed to notice Deb's reaction to his words about her, and she was just as glad. How long had she waited to hear him say something like that? Once again, the taste of salt was upon her lips, but not from new tears. No, this taste was from all the tears of the past. Tears she'd cried for Jed, and his father. Because a woman's love, real love, is forever. When a woman loves, it's not for sex or looks, but for something much deeper, stronger. A woman loves for the person, the soul. When she's wrong, it's not because she was tricked, but because she can see the man for who he *could* be, even if he isn't. That's what she falls in love with.

Deb looked down at the sweater she'd worn for the first time in years. The very same sweater Jed's dad had given her so long ago. Her heart took her back to that day.

* * * *

September was the month, she and Zach had made plans to meet at the breakwater for a walk. It was their special place. She'd gotten there early but Zach was late. So much so that she'd just about given up on him. The sun was nearly gone and it was getting cold. Deb hadn't planned on it being so cool. As she turned to head back, she saw Zach coming, hurrying. He was sweating and his breath could be seen. Then she noticed he was carrying something.

"Sorry I'm late," he said, passing her the box he was carrying. "I was waiting for Mom to finish this for you. Happy birthday, Deb."

Deb took the box, forgiving him at once. She opened it and grabbed the sweater by the shoulders, letting the box fall. There it was. A gray and white sweater. Her name was knitted into the upper right corner in front. On the back was the very breakwater which lay behind her. It was the best gift she'd ever received in her eighteen years. She loved it instantly. There were no words to express how she felt. Slipping the sweater on, Deb put her arms around Zach and kissed him over and over.

The day Zach left, she stopped wearing the sweater. The day Zach's mom died, she stopped thinking about wearing it. Deb had been sure Zach would come home for the funeral, but he didn't. If his mother's funeral wasn't a strong enough reason to bring him back, Deb knew she didn't have a chance.

And yet she loved him still.

* * * *

"Deb," whispered Winnie. "You okay?"

Deb wiped the tears from her eyes and shook her head yes, knowing if she spoke, her voice would crack and give her away.

"Good, he's about to ask her, and you don't want to miss this," said Winnie with a smile.

Her giddiness had reached a new level as she cuddled up to Deb, smiling big as a jack-o-lantern, her shoulders bouncing up and down.

Deb looked toward Jed and saw that he was holding the

folder he'd brought, in both hands, as he began to speak.

"Miss Black, I was wondering...if you'd read this and tell me what you think?"

Jed hung his head a little. This was a big step for him, and he felt more than a little insecure about it. Sharing this very piece of writing with Miss Wright had not gone well. Now he was doing something he'd never done before. Not only was he asking Miss Black to *read* his writing, but he was also asking for her opinion on it. Jed figured she knew more about books than anyone else he could think to ask. If she liked it, or thought it was good, then maybe, just maybe, he had a chance to be a writer someday.

Irene took the folder from Jed's hand and opened it. Her face lit up when she saw that it contained a story written by Jed. She beamed at him, obviously aware of the effort it had taken for Jed to show it to her. She ran her hand softly down the top page as she scanned the words before speaking.

"How many others have read this?" she asked.

"Just my English teacher, Miss Wright. I wrote it for an assignment she gave. Oh, and Winnie," he answered.

"And why are you asking me to read it?"

Jed thought for a minute. Why *was* he asking her? It had been Winnie's idea, not his. Still, he had liked it. "I guess it's because you're a librarian."

Irene looked at him. "No, that's why you *chose* me. My question is why do you want me to *read* it?"

Jed lifted his head, met her eyes, but didn't speak. Not that he needed to. Within his eyes was her answer. She could see the passion and desire to be acknowledged as a writer. The wanting, the wondering, the insecurity. This was all she needed to know.

"I'd be honored to read it," she said. "Is this your only copy?"

Jed seemed surprised by her question, but his answer was simple, as usual. "Yeah."

Irene stood up and walked to the copier. She ran off two copies, then handed the original to Jed and a copy to Deb.

"I'm guessing you'd like to read this as well, and if I'm going to, you should," she said. Then she turned to Jed.

"If Deb means as much to you as you say, it's important to share your writing with her. I can tell you whether it's technically correct and the grammar is proper. But you need someone who knows you to tell you if it's true. By that I mean true to yourself. Do you know the first rule of a good writer?"

Jed shook his head, but the eagerness to know was all over his face.

"The first rule of a good writer is to only write what you know. Writing fiction is about being creative, not making things up," Irene said. "Do you understand what I mean?"

"I'm not sure, but I think so. You're saying that I shouldn't write about Boston if I've never been there, right?"

"Right. That's exactly what I mean. Now, once I've read it, how do I get in touch with you?"

"You can reach him at this number," said Deb as she stepped forward and handed Irene a business card.

"Oh, Deb's Bakery. I've heard of your pies." Irene turned to Jed again. "Thank you for this opportunity. I'll be in touch."

Jed smiled and said a simple, "Thank you, Miss Black."

Deb put her arm through Jed's on one side, while Winnie took the other. As they got back to the car, Deb had an idea.

"Hey, Jed, you know who's waiting to hear how you did? Gramps. How about we stop in on the way home?"

Jed liked this idea. "Okay. How about you, Winnie? Can you go?"

Winnie smiled her best smile. "I'd love to."

With that they were back on the road to New Ireland,

each of them pleased by the developments of the afternoon, but none more than Jed. He felt the events had given him a new patch from which to harvest fruit; to scratch out a life for himself. He settled back into the seat and for the first time in a long time, he felt comfortable, like he was home.

CHAPTER 8
A Patch of Road

Crockett was sitting in his usual chair. He didn't own a TV, and the only radio in the house was on a shelf over the small old Philco refrigerator in the kitchen. He'd built that shelf for her, for Ellen. He'd also bought the radio for her. He never did figure out which of the two she liked better. That was over fifty years ago now. Of their thirty-nine years together, it seemed like thirty-eight of them had been spent in this kitchen. Why, he couldn't conjure up a single memory of Ellen that didn't start, finish, or just plain happen, in this kitchen. Even Zach had been conceived here. They'd been married for some time and both wanted children, but nothing they tried worked. Crockett surmised that perhaps they were just trying too hard and that they should just let it happen.

He'd gotten up at his usual time to go lobstering one morning, only to find it blowing hard. Ellen was awake, but still in bed. One thing Crockett had learned from his father was that it was important for women to know where their husbands were. The memory was alive and in full color in his mind now. It was as if he could see himself standing at the end of their bed. The scent of Ivory soap and lavender rising up from her body and filling his nose. He stood watching her breasts gently move up and down with her deep breaths, before speaking. It was in moments like these that Crockett found his belief in God, and felt love in its fullest measure.

* * * *

"Ellie, it's blowing too hard to go out. I'm just going to check the boat, make sure the mooring is holding, then I'm going to work on gear in my shop. Give a holler if you need something."

"Okay, dear. Why don't you come back after you've checked the boat and I'll make breakfast."

Crockett liked that idea. He gave Ellen a big hug and kiss and said, "See you in an hour. Love you."

By the time he'd gotten back to the house, the wind had given him that extra feeling of being alive. It was early spring, but the wind was still coming out of the east, carrying with it the dampness of the water. Even after all these years, he could feel the cool sting of its presence on his face as he walked back into the house through the kitchen door. A feeling he quickly lost when he caught sight of Ellen.

She had a fire going in the wood stove to keep the chill off, but she'd forgotten to close the door. He could see the flames dancing on the wall behind her, almost in sync with the song on the radio. She was still in her cotton nightgown, and the flames of the fire were providing glances of the treasures covered only by the pale green cotton.

Crockett couldn't help himself, he had to have her right there on the kitchen counter. This moment of spontaneity and passion had done the trick. After years of trying, Zach was born nine months later.

* * * *

Since Ellen's passing, this memory was the one that haunted Crockett the most. If it hadn't been for Jed's unexpected arrival, Crockett might well have joined Ellen before now. Not that he minded being alone, it was the feeling-lonely part that

Jed had taken away. Jed had given him a purpose, a vision for the future.

Yet here he was, living in the past. Listening to Ellen's radio, staring at the counter. Doing the one thing he hated the most—thinking about the woulda, coulda, shoulda's of life. It was deep within this pull of the past where Crockett found himself nearing a point of no return, when he heard a car driving up his gravel road. Wiping the tears from his sun-dried, sea-salted face, he poured himself a new cup of coffee while he waited.

Winnie looked at the house all dark and empty. "I think he's gone to bed," she said.

"No," said Deb. "It always looks like this; he's up and waiting for us."

Jed had also expected the house to be dark, which is why a ray of light coming from an unusual place caught his attention. Jed had been coming here long enough to know when something looked wrong. At the far end of the old barn was a newer section. On the front of the add-on were double doors hinged to swing outward. In all the time Jed had been coming here, there had been a chain going through the door handles and secured by a big padlock. Tonight, not only were the lock and chain missing, but the door was ajar and a light was on inside. Seeing this gave him a feeling of concern.

Leaving Winnie and Deb well behind him, Jed could hear the radio getting louder as he got closer to the kitchen door. Having learned long ago that knocking was not required, Jed bolted through the door praying to see Gramps in his rocker.

If Crockett hadn't heard them arrive, he might well have been startled by the force with which Jed entered.

"Where's the fire, boy?" he asked.

"Gramps," Jed panted, while trying to think of a way to save face. Then it came to him. He reached for his wallet and pulled out his license. "Look, I passed the test."

Crockett squinted his eyes and snorted. "'Course you did, I taught ya everything you needed to know." He smiled at Jed, taking the edge off what he'd just said.

Before they could take the conversation any further, Deb and Winnie entered.

"Well, I see you brought your support group," said Crockett. "Nice to see you, ladies. If I'd-a known you was coming, I'd-a baked a cake," he said with a chuckle.

"Oh, that's okay," said Deb. "We just thought you might be waiting to hear how Jed did."

"Nah, I knew he'd get by all right. You and I taught him, after all," said Crockett with a wink.

"Now wait a minute," began Jed. "Before they came in, you—"

"Oh, you just hush up and never mind, boy. Besides, I got something to show you.."

Crockett got out of his rocker. "Make yourself useful and pick up that bag there on the table and follow me. You two can come along if you like."

Jed looked toward the table and saw a plain paper bag sitting there. Shaking his head, he picked up the bag. *Same old Gramps,* he thought to himself.

The women met Jed outside and each took an arm again. Jed was so caught up in the moment, he didn't notice where they were going until they were there. Gramps was opening the doors to the building Jed had seen the light coming from.

As Crockett moved inside, he offered a playful, "You coming?"

Inside, there was something covered by an old canvas.

"Is this what you wanted us to see?" asked Jed.

"Not quite," answered Gramps. "Hand that bag to one of the girls and give this here canvas a pull."

Winnie reached for the bag saying, "Here, I'll hold it for you."

As Jed pulled the canvas off, a white 1965 Corvette

convertible in mint condition revealed itself. Jed couldn't believe his eyes. He walked around the car slowly, admiring every detail. He'd seen pictures in some of the old photo albums Gramps had showing this car, but had never seen the real thing. Jed looked at Deb and Winnie. Winnie made a downward motion with her eyes. Jed made his way to the front and looked down. There on the front was a brand-new license plate. A vanity plate which read simply JED.

This left Jed completely perplexed. He looked at Gramps. The expression on his face was priceless. There was a look of complete satisfaction, and yet underneath was a hint of sadness.

"Gramps, where did you get this, and why?" he asked.

The look of satisfaction gave way to the sadness.

"In all our years together, this was the only thing my Ellie ever asked for. I bought it, brand new, right off the showroom floor in Boston. She didn't drive it all that often. When Zach left, she stopped driving it altogether. When she passed, I built this building and put it in here. I figure it's about time it was put to use."

"Now, where's that bag?" asked Gramps.

"Here it is," said Winnie, handing it over.

Crockett took the bag and opened it. "Come here, boy."

As Jed stood in front of him, Gramps emptied the bag.

"Here's the manual, the other plate for the back, the keys, and last but not least, the title. She's all yours, Jed. See here? I've signed the title over into your name."

Jed could hardly believe this was happening. Gramps had called him by his name instead of "boy." He looked at his grandfather. "I don't understand, Gramps."

"It's simple, Jed. You got your license now, so you be needing a car. I got a car I don't need, so I'm giving it to you. You going to stand here and just look at her, or take her for a drive?"

Jed reflected back on the events of the day. This would be

a day he'd remember for a long time. Winnie couldn't contain herself anymore.

"I'll take a ride home," she said, moving next to Jed and encircling him with her arms.

Jed turned to Winnie and smiled. "Sure, Winnie, I'd be honored to give you a ride home."

He opened the passenger door and Winnie climbed in. He was just about to get in himself when he stopped and asked, "Gramps, would it be all right to keep the car here? I don't really have a place for it."

"Well, I hadn't thought about it, but sure, that'd be all right by me."

As Jed and Winnie pulled out, Deb put her arms around Crockett, giving him a bear hug. To her surprise, she felt the air leave his body as if the boom had swung and left the sail empty. She'd never known Crockett to be sick or show pain before. Pulling back, Deb saw the tears in his eyes.

"Don't say anything to the boy," said Crockett with a look that begged for compassion.

This was something new for Deb. She'd never seen this side of the old man. He'd always been a thin man, but Deb could see he'd lost weight. The years of hard work had found their way into the lines and character of his face. Still, there was something else there. Or perhaps not there. She could see what was missing now, even in this poor light. Deb slid her hands into his. The feel of his leathery skin and bone had a softness to it. It occurred to her that some time must have passed since he'd felt a woman's touch. Deb knew she'd never held his hands before. Although Deb closed her hands around his, Crockett kept his open. As if showing any affection toward another woman would be a sin against Ellen.

"I won't say anything to Jed," said Deb softly.

"You promise?"

Deb smiled. "I promise. Have you been to the doctor?"

Crockett's eyes cleared and he found his composure. "Yeah, I seen him."

Deb waited a bit, hoping for more.

"He said it's cancer," Crockett finally offered.

"How bad is it?"

"He said there are patches of it everywhere."

"Did they say if anything could be done?" she asked.

"It's too advanced. All they could offer was a lot more pain for a little more time. I don't need no more of neither."

Crockett was struggling with the words, and Deb sensed that he'd already made some decisions about the future.

The old man took a breath and went on. "Since we're on the topic, I've named you as the executrix of my estate. It won't be much trouble; I've left most everything to Jed."

Deb was touched by the honor of being chosen, and saddened by its reason. Crockett had always been in her life. She and Zach had been friends as kids, long before they'd fallen in love. Now she was being told that another part of that connection was coming to an end. But when?

"Have they told you…how long?" she asked.

"Without treatment, less than a year."

Deb was shocked by the time frame. To think that by this time next year, Crockett could be gone. His reason for not telling Jed became a little more understandable. This was Jed's last year of school, and such an important time for a teenager. It was the end of one era and the beginning of another. Jed's life would be more difficult if he knew that the only male influence in his life would soon be gone.

"I see," was all she could think to say.

"Jed knows all that needs knowing to run this farm and lobstering. But I'm going to have him pull the traps for the winter. After I'm gone and he takes over, he won't have any free time no more. The break will do him good. Best if he spends less time with me, anyway. Who knows? Maybe he'll notice the woman Winnie's become."

This last comment made Deb smile. "Yeah, I've been waiting for him to notice her, too."

She thought back to the time she'd gotten Zach to see her as a woman. Tired of waiting, she'd bought a new bathing suit. She knew he was going to the quarry for a swim, and she wanted to surprise him. She put the suit on under her jeans and t-shirt. As she approached the swimming hole, she saw Zach, but he wasn't alone....

"I just hope he don't wait too long in noticing her. Like my Zach did with you," said Crockett.

Deb was fighting her own tears now. She hadn't known it that day, but it was Jed's mother who'd been with him. Instead of the beginning she was looking for on that day, it was the end. The end of any relationship she'd hoped to have with Zach. Many a time, she'd played out a different scenario in her head. One where she had not turned around and left, one where she had interrupted the two of them and fought for Zach. But she hadn't, she did turn around and leave that day. Put the swimsuit and her dream of becoming Mrs. Zach Crockett back in the chest of drawers. Forever, as it turned out.

"Well, I'm going to head back to the house," said Crockett. "The sun's near gone, time for bed."

Arm in arm, they walked back to the house in silence.

Deb got Crockett settled inside and promised once again not to say anything to Jed.

She made it home before breaking down completely. She was glad Jed wasn't there. Keeping Crockett's promise wasn't going to be easy. But Deb knew this had been a big important day for Jed, and that was how she convinced herself that doing so was necessary.

Winnie hardly took her eyes off of Jed the whole way home. He was becoming the man she hoped he would be, right in front of her eyes. She cursed the bucket seats. *If the car had a bench seat,* she thought, *I'd be able to make my way next to him. With the bucket seats, it would be too obvious.* It took all the self-control she could muster to suppress every ounce of her being, which ached to put her arm around him and profess her love. Her heartbeat was making time stand still. The ride home seemed to take forever. Until they pulled into her driveway, that is. The sound of the gravel giving way to the pressure of the tires brought her back to the present. Before Jed could get out and open her door, she had to say something.

"So, this has been a big day for you."

"Yeah, I guess," he answered.

"What do you mean, you guess? You got your license, shared your story with someone, got a car. If this isn't a big day, I don't know what is!"

Jed smiled and chuckled. "You're right, Winnie, you're always right."

"Well, thanks for finally admitting it," she said with a tilt of her head and a wink. "So what do you think Deb will say about your story?"

This thought gave Jed a tingly shock throughout his body. With all that had gone on today, he'd forgotten about Deb having a copy of his story.

"You forgot about that part, I see," Winnie continued. "Well, I for one think it's about time."

"Don't forget, I made a lot of that up."

"Yeah, so?"

"So what if I got some of it right? The last thing I want is to cause her more pain about my father."

"Oh, she's a big girl, Jed."

"I know that, Winnie. It's just that I owe her everything. I mean, where would I be today if she hadn't taken me in? I think about that sometimes. Would I be in some foster home? Jail? Living on the street? Or worst of all, DEAD!"

"Oh, Jed, that's just your literary creativity getting carried away. You're with Deb because you're meant to be. Just like you're meant to be a writer."

This comment really hit home. "How do you know I'm meant to be a writer from just one story?"

"Because I can tell it's what you want to be, and I know you can be anything you want."

Jed smiled at Winnie and took her hand in his. "You're a good friend, Winnie."

She watched from the living room window as Jed drove away with a patch called her heart. A patch instead of the whole quilt. A heart that was just itching to be scratched—by Jed.

Another promising night gone to hell, is all Winnie could think. *Maybe I should talk to Deb.*

CHAPTER 9
What You Don't Know

Irene Black felt a warmth from within. She'd read many books in her time, but knew no authors personally. Granted, Jed was no author, but someday he might be. At five o'clock promptly, she locked the library doors and then went through her routine of closing up—checked to make sure no one was left in the building, collected all the stray books and put them back in their proper places, picked up the trash and personal items left behind, and lastly, turned all the equipment and lights off. With the single exception of the light at her desk.

She then made a cup of tea, sat at the desk, and read Jed's story. Normally, she was a quick reader, but with this story, she wanted to take her time. This turned out to be a good thing, because the story did have a few grammar issues. Nothing unexpected. Given the fact that Jed was a high school student in a small town. Chances were good that time was not given to the full study of the English language and its rules of grammar at this level of education. Most of the time, it was enough for the kids to grasp the basics. Since most of them would never consider or even attempt to speak without the local accent, time in English class was better spent on other things.

As Irene made her way from page to page, the truth of the story's origin revealed itself. There was more fact than fiction here. Clearly, this was something written from Jed's life, something which came from his heart and soul. Because of this, the story touched her heart and soul as well. Although she was able to keep her composure while reading, emotion after emotion moved through her mind and body. The ending, however, required a tissue.

After collecting herself, she read it again at her normal rhythm and speed. The story was well organized, with a good plot, had strong characters who were well developed, and an appropriate ending. On top of that, there was the hint of a moral to it. What surprised her was the maturity of its subject, not so much in the parts, which appeared to be true, but in the ones she assumed he'd made up.

It was at this moment that Irene understood her purpose, what was being asked of her. Knowing that the post office was on her way home, Irene stood up, walked to the copier, and made another copy of the story. She then wrote a one-page letter and attached it to the story, along with one of her business cards. Next, she addressed an envelope, weighed and attached the appropriate postage to it, placed the letter and story inside, and sealed it. Although she had second thoughts on the way, she chose to deposit the envelope in the freestanding mailbox just outside the post office door, believing this was what she was meant to do.

Unaware of the impact this single simple action would have on future events, Irene drove home.

Deb walked into the bakery with a heavy heart, in part because of what she now knew, and partly because she could not share it with anyone. Not that she wasn't good at keeping a secret. Many a customer had chosen to share their secrets with her. Sometimes she felt more like a bartender than a baker. But none of the others had anything to do with her personally, nor had she been asked to keep these secrets from anyone special to her. No, keeping this new secret was not going to be easy.

It was getting late for an early riser, and she needed to

find a way to clear her mind before anything close to sleep would come to her. Then it hit her: Jed's story. She reached into her bag and pulled it out. Realizing it was going to take more than a few minutes to read the whole thing, she decided to get ready for bed and read it there.

Deb climbed into bed, propped up a couple of pillows, and settled in. With a sip of hot chocolate, she began the story. Before the first page was turned, the cup of hot chocolate in her hand was replaced by a tissue. The day of the puffin was something she'd thought about a lot over the years. She'd heard many versions of the story, but never Jed's. As she read his story, she wondered how much was based on truth and how much was fiction. There were, however, some details she knew were fiction. Not because they were unbelievable, but because she knew the truth of them herself.

Reading the story reminded Deb of how alone Jed must feel, and why he kept his distance. Having been abandoned by his mother had left him with trust issues. Abandoned by his mother, never knowing his father. A father that she'd been in love with for as long as anyone in New Ireland could remember. Deb began to wonder if Jed had written anything else that would give her some insight into how he'd felt all these years.

Before going to sleep, Deb made up her mind to talk with Jed about it in the morning. She was just too tired to wait up for him. With any luck, he'd be late. At least she hoped so for Winnie's sake. Deb had seen herself in Winnie on more than one occasion, and thought about sharing what she knew with her, but that wasn't in her nature. As much as she desperately wanted to help, Deb was the type who waited to be asked.

Jed got up at the usual time even though he hadn't slept much. The events of the previous day were slowly beginning to sink in and reveal their importance to him. Having a driver's license hadn't been that big a deal to him. He felt differently about it now. Having a car *and* a license made a huge difference. The car and license together meant that he would never be stranded again. Not that he wanted to go anywhere. New Ireland had become his home, or what he thought a home should be. Granted, he didn't have a mother or a father, but he did have Deb, and Gramps—oh, and Winnie. How different would his life have been without Winnie all of these years? A lot more lonely than it was, that was for sure.

Suddenly, the smell of coffee filled Jed's nose, which meant Deb was up. He quickly got dressed and made his way down to the bakery's kitchen.

"Morning, Deb. Is that coffee I smell?" he asked.

"Morning, Jed, and it is. Would you like some?"

"Sure, I'll have a quick cup with you."

Deb poured two mugs of coffee and set them on the table. Then she walked over to the counter, and Jed watched as she picked up her copy of his story. She came over to the table and sat down with him. He had known when Miss Black had given a copy to Deb that this conversation was coming. Jed decided to face it now, rather than make an excuse to leave.

"Is that my story?" he asked, knowing the answer.

"Yes, Jed, it is. I was hoping we could talk about it."

"Sure," he answered.

Deb took a deep breath and a drink of coffee, than began, "First of all, I like the story very much. I'm no writer, so I wouldn't even pretend to offer ways to make changes. The thing I want to talk about is more about keeping your fiction separate from the truth."

This statement confused Jed, but he chose to remain quiet and just listen.

"Your father and I were never together. We were more like you and Winnie are. Having said that, I would never deny my feelings for your father."

This surprised Jed, he had always figured they were a couple. "Okay, thanks, Deb."

"There's another thing that's important enough for us to

talk about right now."

Deb paused and took another big drink of coffee. Jed had the impression she was trying to push her emotions aside and stay focused.

Deb finally spoke again. "The part about your mother going to Gramps for money, that's true. But she never went to your father."

Deb paused again, letting these words sit in the air for a few seconds so they could sink in. Jed thought about what Deb had just said. He took a couple of sips from his mug before responding.

"I'm not sure of what you're trying to say, Deb."

Deb sighed. "What I'm trying to say, Jed, is that your father left because of what happened between him and your mother. He didn't leave because of you. As far as anyone knows, he knows nothing about you."

Upon receiving this new information, Jed's expression changed dramatically. His head dropped and his shoulders rounded, as if to enclose his entire body. Even the coffee mug was barely visible in his tightly clenched hands. Deb could see that he was withdrawing, going to his safe place. She had seen Jed do this before. She needed to say something that would keep him talking.

"Jed, it's not my place to tell you about your mother or your father. Everyone in town has their own opinion of each of them and what happened."

Deb had more to say, but she wanted to see if Jed was listening. As she watched, his hands opened, revealing the coffee mug, and his elbows moved back toward his body, forcing his shoulders up. Lastly, his chin slowly began to rise. But not so much that Deb could see his eyes. Still, it was enough for Deb to know he was on his way back to her. She continued.

"You're old enough to know that, given the right opportunity, people will show you who they really are. We just have to be open-minded enough to see it. People also move in and out of our lives. Sometimes it's a good thing, sometimes it seems like the worst thing that could ever happen. The important thing is to stay true to yourself. If you can do that, you'll get through life just fine."

Jed didn't show it, but he heard and understood Deb. Truth was, Gramps had been telling him the same thing for some time now. Hearing it again from Deb, the words took on a different kind of meaning. As he sat there thinking about it, it dawned on him how much Deb's life was like Gramps. Both of them alone except for him, their lives seeming to revolve around work and nothing else.

"Is that how you do it every day?" he said.

"Yes, Jed, that's exactly how I do it," she said with a smile.

Deb glanced at the clock as the first sign of the sun lit its face.

"It's nearly five-thirty. Gramps will be wondering where you are."

Jed turned and looked at the clock. He knew that the time showing on it should be causing a panic in him, and yesterday it might well have done so. But it wasn't yesterday. It was today. He was reminded of a quote, though he couldn't remember from where: "Today is the first day of the rest of your life." The meaning of these words was somehow clearer now.

"Yeah, I expect he is," Jed said as he got up to leave. Before doing so, he finally looked Deb in the eye. "Thanks, Deb. I'm glad to know it wasn't me who drove my father away."

He gave her a soft smile, and Deb stood up to give him a hug. It was the first hug she'd given him in quite some time. The way she hugged him told Jed she needed it as much as he did. He waited for her to let go, then turned and left without looking back. He had seen the tears in her eyes. If he'd looked at her, he probably would have teared up himself, and there was no way he was walking into Gramps' place looking like he'd been crying.

What he couldn't help feeling was that a hole in his life had been repaired with a patch of knowledge. What he didn't know was that it was only a temporary fix. Soon it would be scratched open. Wide open.

CHAPTER 10
Change Moves with the Tide and the Wind

Jed walked into Gramps' house thinking that he'd be ready with some remark about how late it was, and that the whole day was ruined because of it. But something was different; Gramps didn't say anything when he came in. Jed noticed there was no lunch box on the floor next to the rocker, and Gramps had work boots on instead of hip boots. It was clear Gramps wasn't ready to go lobstering.

"Morning, Gramps, sorry I'm late. Deb and I had coffee together, and we lost track of time."

"That's all right, boy. I been sitting here looking out the window thinking about things."

Jed's suspicions were now confirmed. As he took a closer look at Gramps, it became obvious that instead of sitting up in the rocker, he was resting into it, taking on the shape of the rocker. His hands were in his lap, rather than firmly gripping the arms of the chair. Jed's thoughts returned to the previous night. He'd felt something then. The open shed door, Gramps sitting in the kitchen rocker at night rather than in the living room, not to mention the actual events of the evening. Even when he'd returned the car and saw the kitchen light still on, something was funny, but he let it go. These subtle changes viewed independently could, and did, go unnoticed, but together they had meaning. A meaning Jed was not sure of, but the feeling was a pit-of-the-stomach kind of thing he couldn't ignore.

"Thinking about what, Gramps?" he asked, not sure he wanted an answer.

"I got a feeling this is gonna be a long, bad winter. I've seen this kinda weather before. The wind will be coming off the water from the northeast all winter. What few days we'd have to go out lobstering will need to be spent cleaning up after the snowstorms. It ain't worth fighting. I think we should bring the traps in and put the boat up for the winter."

Although this sounded a little strange coming from Gramps, Jed had learned to trust Gramps' gut feelings as much as Gramps did himself. Still, it meant not working, and that was the strangest part.

"So, what are we going to do for the winter once everything is ashore?" he asked, trying not to sound too inquisitive.

"Oh, there'll be plenty to do. We have to go over the traps one by one and fix anything needing fixing. Then there's the boat. It's been a while since I give it a good going over. This'll be a good chance to show you a thing or two about boat and engine repair. Things you'll need to know when you have your own boat."

My own boat, thought Jed. He didn't know how to feel about that, nor had he given any real thought to *having* his own boat. But then he hadn't thought about having his own car, either, and now he owned a Corvette. *Maybe that's the bigger message here,* Jed thought to himself. Maybe he needed to start thinking about the future, rather than just living day to day aimlessly. After all, this was his last year of high school. Jed's thoughts were interrupted by Gramps' voice.

"So we need to get the barn ready for the boat and make a place to store the traps out of the weather. Once winter sets in, we'll need to be ready and settled 'cause there won't be no letting up."

"Okay, Gramps, whatever you say. When do you want to

get started?" he asked, expecting the answer to be today.

"Oh, I can get by on my own today. Why don't you take the day for yourself, have some fun for a change."

Jed watched as Gramps reached for his wallet and pulled out a fifty-dollar bill.

"Here," said Gramps. "Take this and go spend the day with Winnie. Show her your fun side."

Jed hesitated, then reached for the money. Gramps didn't part with his money foolishly, and Jed knew it was his place to respect the offer and accept.

"Okay, Gramps, if you say so. Thanks!"

As Jed was leaving, Gramps called out, "Hey boy, tell Deb I'll be down for lunch later. I'm in the mood for her soup."

Jed smiled to himself. That sounded more like the Gramps he knew. "You got it, Gramps."

Deb knew Crockett would be in early, before the dinner crowd. At 10:50 A.M., the bells on the door jingled, announcing his arrival. Without turning, Deb filled a bowl with beef stew, dropped in not two but three dumplings, and poured a fresh cup of coffee. The sound the old man made moving to his favorite booth was slower than Deb was accustomed to hearing. Deb knew today must be a bad one, since Gramps had given Jed the day off. Making her way to his table, Deb set the food in front of him and sat down across from him.

"So, a day off. That's a rarity for you," she said.

Crockett gave a smile. "Yeah, I told Jed we're not going lobstering this winter. We need to go over the boat and traps to make sure everything's in good shape for the spring. Besides, it's going to be a bad winter and I don't want him out there in it."

Deb heard what Crockett said, but more importantly, what he didn't say. He must be sicker than he'd let on last night. What other reason could there be for him to decide not to go lobstering through the winter for the first time in some twenty years? Since before Zach left, Deb realized.

"It was good to see Winnie last night," said Crockett.

"Yes, it was. Aside from you and me, she's all Jed's got. At least as far as I know," said Deb.

"So are they friends, or something more?"

"That's a good question, but as for the answer, I'd say for Winnie it's more, but Jed doesn't have a clue," she answered.

Crockett gave her a look straight on. "Sounds like someone else I know."

Deb's lips twitched, giving credence to Crockett's words.

He shook his head. "Well, let's hope he wises up faster than his father. Not that he *ever* did. That's the only mistake my boy ever made that I regret. He should have made an honest woman out of you, Deb. I never told you that, did I?"

Before she could answer, the bells on the door rang again, announcing the arrival of more customers. As Deb got up, Crockett fell into the game they'd come to play over the last several years.

"These dumplings are raw, and there's too much salt in the soup!" he exclaimed, loudly enough for the new arrivals to hear.

"You're the one who's got too much salt in ya," she hollered back. "Eat it or leave it, you're paying for it either way."

She walked over to the table of new customers, greeting them with a wink and a joyful, "What can I get ya?" *Business as usual*, she thought to herself.

Crockett smiled into his soup. He'd been a little worried about Deb's ability to keep his secret. He knew now how silly that was. After all, she'd kept a bigger one than this. As he well knew. He also knew life wasn't about the patch of cloth, but the way you used it to cover up the scratches life made in your soul. Deb was made from the best kind of cloth, and she had the hidden scars to prove it.

CHAPTER 11
Making Patches

As fall moved toward winter, Jed and Crockett gradually removed the lobster traps from the water, twelve at a time, the most *Miss Ellen* could safely hold. More and more, Jed was doing the bulk of the work, while Crockett did less. This change took place without Jed even noticing at first, much to the old man's surprise. Perhaps it was because Jed had gotten caught up in the excitement of all the new responsibility—everything from driving the boat, to pulling the traps and baiting them, to taking care of the lobster catch. Crockett knew Jed would be okay; he was more than capable of running a lobster boat on his own.

When they'd started, the number of traps in the water was an even one thousand, each with a lobster buoy attached to it with Crockett's colors. His colors had been in the water longer than any of the lobstermen in New Ireland. Each lobsterman is assigned colors for his buoys when his license is issued. It's the way everyone knows whose traps are whose. Crockett's were red and yellow, both colors are easy to see on the water because they contrasted with the blue-green of the ocean. Today, the last of them would be hauled out. Crockett's traps had not been completely out of the water since the day he'd started lobstering over fifty years ago.

In the past, he would add more rope to the traps and move them out into deeper water for the winter. This was something a lobsterman needed to do if he wanted to lobster year round. The water on the coastline froze, so the lobsters moved out into deeper water. When Crockett did this, he'd bring in the traps that needed to be repaired or patched. This gave him something to do on the days he couldn't go lobstering. This winter was going to be different though, with no traps out there waiting for him. He'd spent the last eighteen years trying to get used to not having anyone ashore waiting for him. It was just as hard today as it had been the first day. And tomorrow would be just as hard again.

Jed heaved the last trap out of the water, up onto the deck. He pulled the crabs out and threw them back. Next he checked the lobsters to be sure the size was right. Every lobsterman kept a measuring gauge on board. A gauge is flat and made of copper. On each edge there's a recessed area, with one longer than the other. The way to measure a lobster with the gauge is from the tip of the head to the end of the back. If a lobster was too small, or too big, the law requires them to be thrown back into their watery home. The other important thing to look for is females. When you catch a lobster, you have to turn it upside down to check the lobster's sex. Males have what looks like horns at the top of the tail and females have fins. When you find a female, then you have to check for eggs in the tail. Also, any female carrying eggs has to be released. Everyone knew this was the right thing to do. After all, these eggs represented the future of lobstering.

The last lobster Jed picked up was a female with a tail full of eggs. He stared at all the eggs for a few minutes, thinking about how the last lobster he'd caught until they put the traps out in the spring, had to be released. As he gently lowered the lobster back into the water, he said under his breath, "See you in the spring."

He turned toward Gramps and said, "That's the last one. I'm going to head in. Can you check to make sure the traps are tied tight?"

Crockett didn't speak, just a nod of his head indicated he'd heard Jed. But then Jed hadn't expected a response. When they were out on the boat, Crockett didn't talk much—not that he did any other time, either. Jed knew it was because on the water, you had to pay attention all the time. Out here was no place for idle chit-chat.

Jed looked out over the water. Turning a boat was nothing like a car. You needed to check the water to see which way the tide was moving, was there a current nearby? What direction was the wind coming from, and at what speed? If he turned too quickly or in the wrong direction, the water would not hesitate to claim them. The days that were the most treacherous were the ones when the water was flat calm, ones where the ocean looked like a mirror, a reflection of the sky. You could easily be lured into a false sense of safety, only to be caught broadside to a wind out of nowhere, but not Jed. Over the years lobstering with Gramps, he'd been taught all of these things. Before they happened, Gramps would call for his attention and show him how the shape of the waves would change, to be mindful of which way the buoy was lying, if the leaves of the trees were turning over; even the birds' actions changed with the weather. Right now, most of them were sitting on the water with not a care in the world. There were no signs of trouble anywhere.

Other lobstermen watched Crockett as much as they did any danger signs they might be aware of. When Crockett headed in early, he did so with a convoy of boats following him. Even if they didn't know why, no one stayed out when Crockett headed in. Jed loved seeing this show of respect for his grandfather. Even the ones who clearly didn't care much for his Gramps didn't question his reasoning. Jed wondered if each time, some of them were hoping Crockett would be wrong so they could hold it over him forever. He never had been, and Jed was sure he never would be.

Everything looked right, so Jed slowly turned the boat, mindful of the traps on the stern. He watched as the harbor moved across the bow from port to starboard. The harbor, however, wasn't what he was looking for. The tide was coming in, and if he could find the current, they could ride it all the way in to the harbor. This was something most of the other lobstermen didn't bother with. There were no ledges or other hazards to be concerned with in the waters off New Ireland, so they'd just motor straight for the harbor. By using the current, though, a boat could almost bring itself in. So much so that Jed could take the boat out of gear to save wear and tear on the engine and transmission. "Watch the pennies and the dollars will take care of themselves," was another of Gramps' favorite sayings.

The other advantage of this tactic was that it provided time to do chores on the way in. By the time Jed and Gramps tied up to the dock, the lobsters were ready to be unloaded and the boat was clean and ready for the next day's work. Because of this, they were always the first in line to sell their lobsters to the dealer, the first one to tie up to the mooring, and the first ones in the truck and down the road toward home.

Until they started bringing in the traps, that is. Now they had to unload the traps from the boat, then load and secure them onto the truck before anything else. This was the eighty-second time they'd done this. Over the last several weeks, they'd found and retrieved nine hundred and eighty-two of the one thousand traps. Jed figured it must have been more than Gramps had expected to find, because he didn't complain about the eighteen that were missing. In fact, Jed noticed Gramps wasn't doing much complaining at all lately. Even when he'd slip up now and again, Gramps hadn't said a word. Part of Jed wanted to say something, but most of him was happy not to hear about it. Even though Gramps hadn't said anything during recent days, Jed heard the words echo in his head. Jed thought maybe that was why Gramps wasn't saying anything, because he could see there was no need to anymore.

As they slowly made their way back to the farm, Jed grew uneasy with the fact that Gramps had not said more than a few words all day. Crockett was keeping an eye on the traps in the back and didn't notice Jed staring at him. As he looked at Gramps, Jed noticed there was something different about him, and wondered what he was thinking about, but he didn't ask. It just didn't feel right doing so. It wasn't his place, or nature, to ask questions. Especially of his elders. So they sat in silence flying down the road at a top speed of twenty-five miles an hour.

Not that Crockett would have noticed either way. He may have been looking at the traps, but he didn't see them. He was a thousand miles away, or at least a hundred years. His mind was on Ellen, as it was most of the time these days. How many winters had she asked him to do this very thing? Pull out all of the traps. His answer had been simple then; it was painful now. Most winters, the expense of lobstering in the deeper water was more costly than profitable, and Crockett knew it before he'd ever set out traps that first winter. It was the danger that drew him. Although he could never explain it, even to himself, the risk was something he needed. Very few of the lobstermen went out year 'round, and it seemed like every few years, one of them was lost. Ellen had known this better than he had. Every year she'd waited to be the one to get the news, praying she wouldn't. The one thing he had agreed on was not to take Zach with him in the winter. As much as he would have liked to have had Zach with him, his mother needed him more. She needed to know Zach was home, safe. After all these years, all of Ellen's worrying and praying, it was he who wound up home, alone.

Crockett's thoughts were lost when he felt Jed turn the truck onto the dirt driveway a little sharper than he intended, causing the traps to shift a bit.

"Slow down, boy. We ain't in no damned race."

Jed smiled, glad to hear Gramps' voice. "Sorry, Gramps," he replied, though deep down he wasn't sorry at all.

Jed backed up to the barn door, set the emergency brake, and turned the truck off. He was about to get out when the feel of Gramps' hand on his arm stopped him. Jed turned and looked at Gramps. The long pause was finally broken when Crockett spoke.

"I want you to promise me something."

Jed didn't understand, but then when did he ever, at first? "Sure, Gramps, anything."

"Promise you'll pull your traps out every winter. I don't want you outside lobstering in the winter when I'm gone."

This made Jed chuckle. "Sure, Gramps, I promise. Besides, I'll be too old by then anyway."

Jed shook his head and started to get out again, but Crockett tightened his grip. It was then that the seriousness of what Gramps was saying hit him. Jed looked at his grandfather again.

"I promise, Gramps," he said again. But this time it was filled with feeling. Gramps nodded and released his grip so Jed could get out of the truck.

Jed began unloading the traps, placing them in the barn with the rest. As with everything, Gramps required it be done just so, in neat, even stacks. The traps were five high, with rows twenty deep and ten across. Well, that was how it would be if they'd found all one thousand of them. Still, it was quite a sight looking down the length of the barn at the orderly rows of traps. Jed felt tired just looking at the stacks. Each trap would have to be checked, slat by slat, nail by nail. Plus, there were the bait bags and netting to be gone over. Gramps hadn't said, but he was sure that they would be...

"Hi, boys!" came the sound of Winnie's voice, interrupting Jed's thoughts. "Is that the last of them?" she asked, looking down the line of traps.

"Hey, Winnie," answered Jed. "Yep, that's all of them."

"Looks like you have a lot of work ahead of you this winter. Is there anything I can do?"

"Oh, I don't think so. This is man's work," Jed replied, without even looking her way.

It was a good thing, too. Winnie was giving him the eye. She wanted to help badly, and knew she could. Jed was going to be in this barn working most of the winter, and any chance she had of spending time with him hinged on her being here as well. All she needed was a legitimate reason to be in here, and not just to hang out. Hanging out meant running errands. Run here for this and there for that, make coffee and sandwiches, that kind of thing. Not that she minded doing these things; it just wasn't what she wanted to do most. She wanted to be next to Jed, doing whatever he was doing. To breathe in his scent, watch his body movements as he worked, feel his warmth just inches from her... all the while hoping he'd notice *her* scent, *her* body, her burning desire for him.

Crockett was not surprised by Jed's answer, but he was disappointed. He'd been waiting for this moment, for his chance to help bring Jed and Winnie closer together. He knew how important Ellen had been to him over the years. Not just as a wife, but also as a helper, best friend, and companion. He knew Jed still looked at Winnie as a friend and nothing more. His own son Zach had made this mistake with Deb, and he'd stayed out of it. At the time, he'd felt it was none of his business. That was his mistake. A mistake he wasn't going to make again, or let Jed make, either.

"So, you want to help, do you, young lady?" he said. "Well now, what can you do, and what's your price?" he asked as a way to open up the lines of communication.

"Pay?" said Winnie. "I wasn't asking for any money. I just

want to help."

"Oh, really? Well if you're willing to work for free, then your work must not be any good," said Crockett.

Winnie looked at him, completely dumbfounded. Crockett just stared back at her waiting for an answer. She turned and looked at Jed, who was sweeping out the bed of the truck and avoiding her eyes.

"Don't look at me, girl," he said. "You got yourself into this, you get yourself out."

Crockett knew it was up to him to keep this going. He cocked his head and asked, "Can ya' sew?"

Winnie turned back toward Crockett. "Yeah, I can sew. What of it?" she answered.

Crockett liked to hear her get feisty. It reminded him of his Ellen. Her answer also garnered Jed's attention. The broom stopped moving and Jed stared at Gramps, obviously wondering what would happen next.

"Well," began Crockett again, "all these traps need new bait bags, and the netting needs to be replaced. If you've a mind to, I'll teach you how to mesh twine. The first fifty traps you'll do for free to pay for the learning. For the rest, I'll give you a dollar each, but not until they're all done."

Winnie's mouth dropped open and her eyes got big. She knew how many traps there were. Nine hundred dollars would go a long way toward her savings for college. No one knew it, not even Jed, but she had a dream, too. She wanted to go to school and become a veterinarian.

She smiled. She'd come here hoping to find a reason to just hang around. Crockett was offering much more. He was offering real hope. Suddenly, patching up these old traps gave her a way to patch a big hole in her life.

She stuck her hand out toward Crockett and said, "We have a deal, sir."

Crockett shook her hand, pleased with the arrangement as well. He knew he could get the bait bags and heads made for less, but that wasn't important. The most important thing now was taking care of Jed.

Jed didn't say a word. He had mixed emotions about what had just happened. Oh, sure, he liked being around Winnie, but this was different. It was like she was cutting into his time with Gramps. It felt to him as if her presence were foreign. Still, this was Gramps' place, and his traps, so it was none of Jed's business who he hired. Jed did, however, find comfort in the thought that, if it had to be anyone, he was glad it was Winnie. Of course, it also meant he wouldn't have to do the twine work himself.

Looking up, Jed saw the two of them had moved over to the workbench. Gramps had a twine needle in Winnie's hand already. He was showing her how to fill it with twine.

Jed thought to himself, *The only thing missing from this picture is **Mom***. The word sent a chill through him. Actually, not so much the word, but the image. When he'd thought of his mother before, he saw a silhouette, a faceless, somewhat shapeless image. This time, however, he saw Deb. It was as if a cloudy patch in his world suddenly became clear. All at once Jed realized that, although his world was small, the people in it were irreplaceable.

"Hey, Gramps, now that you have someone else to bother, I'm going to call it a day. See you in the morning. You too, Winnie." Without waiting for an answer, he passed through the barn door and headed home.

Crockett turned to Winnie and saw that she was disappointed not to be invited along.

"Don't worry, girlie, we'll find a way to show him how much you care. Even if I have to hit him over the head with a two-by-four," said Crockett with his best smile.

Winnie smiled back and said, "So this job isn't just about money. Thank you." And she gently kissed him on the cheek.

Crockett felt the warm patch Winnie's kiss left on his old scratched-up cheek of wrinkles. Ellen had been the last one to leave such an impression on his cheek, and his thoughts moved to how much he missed her. How much he still loved her.

CHAPTER 12
Traps Everywhere

Jed picked the next trap off the pile and quickly started popping the bad nails out in a single motion with the cat's paw. He no longer needed to check each nail carefully; he could tell which ones were bad without thinking. Crockett had said, "If there were any doubt at all, replace 'em." At first, Jed had questioned the need to replace all of the netting and bait bags, but as he removed them, many tore or broke away from their knots. If he hadn't removed each one, the ones with problems could have easily been overlooked. Once again, Gramps had been right.

It didn't take Winnie long to get good at making the bags and netting. Gramps watched her closely for the first fifty, then left her to it. He began his own job of installing the new netting in the traps Jed had finished repairing. After a few weekends together, a rhythm to the work developed. Things were going as smoothly as workers in a canning factory. The only time they got held up was when supplies ran low. Now that Jed was driving, Gramps let him go and get the supplies as needed with the truck.

Winnie had gone with him in the past, but she was busy after school today, so Jed asked Deb to go with him. To his surprise, she agreed. It meant closing the bakery early, but Deb had said it wasn't all that busy this time of year anyway; there was always a lull between the fall foliage season and the holidays. In the past, she'd done little projects on the building or equipment, but not this year. This year Deb had decided to keep herself free so she could be around in case Crockett needed her. She also missed having Jed around the bakery and saw this as a chance to spend time with him. The trip to Redman Village would be the perfect opportunity for them to talk.

* * * *

The school bell rang; Jed was ready to run out the door, pick up Deb, and head down the road. Miss Wright however, had other plans.

"Jed, I'd like to speak with you for a moment before you go."

"I'm kinda in a hurry," he answered.

"It won't take long, I promise."

Polly could tell Jed had something on his mind. He wasn't as attentive in class and hadn't participated at his usual level. What she had in mind for him needed to be taken slowly. Today, she simply wanted to plant a seed. Jed sat back down in his chair, his shoulders slumped and his backpack in his lap, ready to be released.

Polly began, "Jed, your writing has improved greatly, and I want you to think about what I'm about to say. You don't need to answer me one way or the other. This is entirely up to you. Okay?"

"Okay."

"Good. I think your writing is good enough to get you into a creative writing program at a college. Have you given any thought to going to college?"

Jed looked up sharply, her words of support and encouragement taking a second to sink in. "College is for rich kids," was his answer.

Polly had anticipated this type of response and was ready for it. "I agree that many of the kids who go on to college do have the financial means, but there are other ways. For example, there are all kinds of scholarships and loans—"

"No loans," interrupted Jed. "Gramps says if you can't pay for it, you don't need it."

This made Polly smile a bit. "It's just one of the options Jed, not a requirement."

Jed thought a little more, then asked, "Who would give me money for college?"

"You'd be surprised where the money might come from. But for now, I just wanted you to think about it. Okay?"

"Yeah, I guess I could do that," he answered. "Can I go now? Deb's waiting for me, and I need to get somewhere before they close."

Polly had accomplished what she'd wanted. "Yes, Jed, and thank you for your time."

Jed headed for the door, but stopped just shy of it. "How long?" he asked.

Polly wasn't sure of the question. "How long for what?"

"If I went to college, how long would it be for?"

"Oh, well, for a bachelor's degree in creative writing, it would be four years. But you could go longer and get a master's degree. It's really up to you."

Jed didn't say any more, he just turned and left. If they were going to make it to the hardware store in time, he'd have to hurry. As he came out of the school's front door, Deb was there with the truck, waiting for him.

"Hi, Jed. I knew we didn't have a lot of time, so I thought I'd come to you."

"Hi, Deb, good thinking. You been waiting long?"

"A bit. Is everything all right?"

Jed got in and started the truck as Deb moved around to the passenger's side. He made his way out of the parking lot and onto the road before answering her.

"Miss Wright kept me. She wanted to talk."

"Oh, did she want anything special?" Deb asked.

"She talked to me about college."

"College?" said Deb, a bit surprised. "I didn't know you were thinking about going to college."

Jed turned toward Deb with a quick glance. Deb was smiling. "I haven't been," he said.

"So it was her idea?" Deb asked.

"Yeah," he answered.

Deb could tell Jed was a little bothered so she let it go.

They made it to the lumberyard before closing. Gramps had called ahead and placed the order, so it was all ready when they arrived. Deb sat in the truck and watched Jed and the clerk load the supplies in the truck. She thought about how fast these last twelve years had gone. Jed was nearly a man now.

When they were done loading, Deb's eyes remained on Jed as he walked across the yard into the office. As she watched, she pondered how much Jed now looked like Zach. The way he carried himself, with his shoulders back and square, his long stride, and the way his arms swung in unison with his steps. She'd heard some of the girls cooing over him at the bakery, and rightly so. How handsome he'd become! Not to mention, he never acted full of himself like a lot of the other boys did. Even though many of these girls would jump at the chance to be Jed's girl, all of them assumed he and Winnie were a couple.

Yes, many a time Deb had made this same trip with Zach as a young girl, in this very truck, to this very lumberyard. It was the reason she'd jumped at the chance to come today. Closing her eyes, she took a deep breath. The smells of the past filled her nose, consumed her mind, and made her heart dance. Even after all these years, she could smell the salt water on Zach's body, hear the warmth of his laughter, and feel his tug on her heart. Deb was startled when she heard the truck door close with the squeaky hinge and the hollow clunk as it met the truck's frame.

"You go to sleep over there?" asked Jed.

Deb smiled, but didn't answer. What could she say—I was thinking about your father? The only man she'd ever loved. Or should she tell him how much she wished Jed were her son? How being in this truck made the past come rushing back to her? No, she couldn't say any of that. Instead she reached into her purse and pulled out a small envelope and handed it to Jed.

"What's this?" he asked.

"It...was your father's. He gave it to me a long time ago and asked me to hang onto it. I've been waiting for the right time to give it to you. This really belongs to you now."

"What is it?" asked Jed again.

"Open it and find out, silly."

Jed gently opened the timeworn envelope. Inside was an old bank passbook.

"Your dad wanted to go to college. He opened this account and used to give me money to put into it. See?" she said, pointing to the names at the top. "Both of our names are on it. It sat in my desk drawer for years. I came across it about a year after you came to town and started putting money in for you. I don't know why, it just seemed like the right thing to do."

Jed looked at the book again, then back to Deb. "I can't take this. It's not my money," he said, holding it out toward her.

Deb pushed it back at him. "No, it's yours. You've earned most of it working for me. Your father would want you to have the rest of it. You've worked hard at the bakery for me, and with your grandfather. If you want to go to college, there should be enough here to pay for at least most of it. If you don't go to college, do whatever you want with it. It's yours."

Jed sat looking at the passbook. Deep down, if he were willing to admit it to himself, the dream of going to college was somewhere inside him, but that's all it had ever been—a dream. He'd never talked with anyone about it. Now, not only was he being encouraged to go, here in his hands were the means to do so. Jed realized his life was starting to take a turn and was about to get a lot better. Scary better. It seemed like a simple thing to say, but what else was there to say? He looked at Deb. "Thank you."

He wanted to say, *I wish Dad were here, too*, but he could tell by Deb's look that she felt the same way. Instead he asked something which had just occurred to him.

"You said my father wanted to go to college. What for?"

Deb's thoughts had returned to the past. When Jed spoke, she saw and heard Zach. "I'm sorry, what did you say?"

"I asked what my father wanted to study in college."

A single tear slid down Deb's soft rosy cheek, finding its way into the lines of her smile. "He wanted what you want...to write," said Deb.

Jed felt the air leave his chest. His heart seemed to stop, then began to race. "Do you have any of his writings?" he asked.

Deb couldn't stop the tears now, and for the first time, her face looked its age. Jed knew if he'd learned anything from life, it was the pain of loving someone. That's why he didn't let anyone in. Love to him was nothing but a bunch of peaks and valleys. As far as he was concerned, the valleys made the peaks only look higher. No sir, love was not for him.

"I'm sorry, Deb, you don't have to answer."

"No, I'm okay. It's just that being here, in this truck, at this lumberyard, has brought back a lot of memories. I don't have any of your dad's writings. No one does. Before he left, he burned everything. I tried to stop him, but by the time I found out where he was, the fire was nothing but ashes, and he was gone."

Deb stopped crying. "You two are so much alike. I worry about you sometimes," she said.

"How so?" asked Jed. The pain had left Deb's face, and was replaced by an expression Jed knew well. The one he had come to love, even if he wasn't willing to admit it to himself.

"History has a way of repeating itself," she answered. "If someone doesn't know their history so as to be mindful of it, the same mistakes can be repeated. I told you a while ago, your father and I were not together in the way your story portrayed. That's only partly true. I did want to be with him, to marry him, but he was focused on his dream. Just like you are now. You may not see it yet, but you are. That's why it took me so long to give you the passbook. I didn't want to make a connection from your father and the past, to you now. Then I realized you have to make your own choices. As much as I want to protect you, I can't. Things will repeat themselves whether I try and intervene or not. It's not up to me, it's up to you."

Jed listened to Deb intently. She had never spoken to him this way. This was more like something Gramps would have said. Coming from her, it seemed to have more meaning, to be more profound.

"What if I asked for your help? So I don't repeat my father's mistakes," he said. "Would you be willing to?"

A radiance returned to Deb's face. Zach had never asked for her help, but maybe she could help his son. "Yes, Jed, I'd like that."

"Good, then we have an accord," said Jed.

"An accord?"

"It's an old-fashioned way of saying we have an agreement."

"Oh, okay," said Deb as she reached her hand out toward Jed. "Shall we cut our palms and shake in blood?" she asked with a playful smile.

"How about a hug?" offered Jed. They hugged, and Deb kissed Jed on the cheek.

With things settled, Jed started the truck and they were off.

Deb was happy she'd decided to come. The relief she felt was like a lobster that had scratched its way out of a trap, just as the trap was being pulled up out of the water. Allowing it to return to its own little patch of ocean.

Jed was slowly adjusting to the idea that college was now more than a dream. It was a choice he could make, if he wanted to. He just had to get used to the idea of being trapped into four more years of school.

CHAPTER 13
Choices Require Decisions

Polly waited patiently for Jed to get back to her about the idea of college. She could tell he'd been thinking about it. In preparation, she'd asked the school's guidance counselor for information on a few in-state schools with creative writing programs. The idea of Jed attending college outside the state of Maine seemed unrealistic to her on two accounts, the first being the cost. And secondly, the very idea of Jed leaving New Ireland was one thing, but to put the state of Maine behind him was too much for her to hope for.

A full week had passed and it was Monday again, the last week of school before Christmas break. As the classroom emptied, Polly noticed Jed wasn't moving. She cleaned up the room as usual, giving him time. After a few minutes, and feeling that his still being there was enough of an invitation, she spoke to Jed from her desk.

"Is there something you wanted, Jed?"

Jed got up and walked toward her. Now that his presence had been acknowledged, he needed time not to find the words, but to arrange them. "I've been thinking about what you said last week."

"I see," said Polly in her best teacher voice. "Have you come to any conclusion?"

"Yeah, I have. I'd like to apply to college, and see what they say."

Polly could hardly believe her ears. It took all the self-control she could muster to keep her professionalism. "I'm very pleased," she managed to say firmly. "Have you considered where you might go?"

"That's the thing. I don't really know how to go about it."

"Well, I'd be glad to help, if you like," she said.

"To tell you the truth, I was counting on it," he responded.

Polly reached into the drawer which held the folder of information she'd gathered and handed it to Jed. "I put this together just in case you were interested. These are schools within the state of Maine that offer an English program in creative writing. The two that I would recommend for you are the University of Maine at Orono and the University of Maine in Farmington."

Jed lowered his backpack onto the floor and sat in the chair next to Miss Wright's desk. He opened the folder and took out one of the forms. It was eight pages long and full of questions. Just looking at it gave him a headache.

"I'm not sure I can do this."

"Well, as I said, Jed, I'd be happy to help. The best thing to do is to find a way to relate the task to something you know."

"I'm not sure I understand."

"Okay, think of it this way. Filling out this application is like lobstering."

"I don't see how," said Jed, even more confused.

"Well, before you can go lobstering, you have to get ready, right? Make sure your traps are in good condition, you have enough rope, and bait. Then there's the boat. You have to make sure it's in good running condition, painted up and all that. That's the first part of this application. Filling out your personal information."

"Oh, I get it now. Then the next part is knowing where to put the traps. How to work things, show them what they want to see," said Jed.

"Excellent. See? You can do this. I knew you could. So take these with you and look them over. Once you decide which schools you want to apply to, we'll fill out the applications together."

Jed had another question, but didn't know how to get it out. Still looking at the information in the folder, he tried to find the words.

"Is there something else, Jed?" said Miss Wright.

"Yeah, kinda. But I don't know how to ask."

"Don't worry about it, just ask," she said.

This made Jed feel better. "I've never been much of a student; I'm not sure I can do four more years."

"It's a fair question to ask yourself, Jed. The only thing I can say is that college is not like high school. When you go to college, you're focused on a particular subject, most of your classes are in that topic. As for the other areas, we have time to work on those once you're accepted."

Hearing this made Jed chuckle. "Accepted...you make it sound like a sure thing."

"I have a lot of faith in you," she said.

"Thank you, Miss Wright, I'll try not to let you down."

This made Polly smile. Then she remembered the other thing she needed to address.

"There is one more thing," she began. "You will need three letters of reference. I can do one, and I've asked Mrs. Welsh to do another. But the last one has to come from someone who is not from the school, or part of your immediate family. They must be someone in a position of standing, an adult, not a friend. Do you know of someone who could write the third letter?"

Jed thought for just a few seconds before it came to him. "Yes, m'am, I do," he answered with a smile on his face.

Polly had not seen such joy on Jed's face before. Seeing it now made her hesitate to approach the last detail. But it needed doing. "The other thing we need to get started on is scholarships. Once we have those done, we'll figure out a way to find the rest of the money."

Jed grabbed his backpack and gently placed the folder into it. Still beaming, he looked at her and proclaimed, "Oh, the money's not a problem anymore."

Polly was taken back a bit by this statement. Just last week he'd indicated that money was a concern; now it wasn't? "I see...did a rich relative show up from nowhere in the last week?" she asked, more than half kidding.

"Something like that," answered Jed. "I talked to Deb after you mentioned this whole thing to me last week, and she told me about some money she'd been saving for me, just in case I wanted to go to college."

"Well, that's wonderful, Jed!" she said. Polly found herself standing up to hug Jed, but stopped just short of doing so. Pleased that her plan to save this one child was working, Polly hadn't realized how attached she'd become. It was more than hope now; it was her dream as much as his. Watching Jed leave did little to diminish her need to celebrate. As quickly as she could, Polly finished cleaning up the classroom, gathered her things, and headed for Mrs. Welsh's office.

Polly softly knocked on Mrs. Welsh's door.

"Come in," came the reply as Mrs. Welsh looked up from her desk. "Good afternoon Miss Wright. What can I do for you today?"

Polly liked the way Mrs. Welsh talked. She was the only one in New Ireland who spoke proper English other than herself. "Good afternoon, Mrs. Welsh. I just wanted to let you know I'll be needing that letter of recommendation for Jedediah Baxter." Although she tried not to, a smile simply would not stay absent from her face.

"Well, that is good news," said Mrs. Welsh with little fanfare. "You must be pleased with yourself for saving at least one poor soul from dreaded New Ireland."

Polly was feeling too good about herself to let Mrs. Welsh dampen her spirits. "As a matter of fact, I am. See you tomorrow, and please don't forget my letter."

She then turned and left before any more was said. She wanted this feeling to last as long as possible. This, after all, was why she'd become a teacher.

* * * *

Jed felt the rush of knowing exactly what to do. He entered the bakery and made it to the counter before the bell hanging on the door stopped ringing.

The sound startled Deb. She knew what her bell sounded like, and most of the time, she could tell who had walked in, just by the sounds they made with her bell. Sometimes, she could even tell what mood they were in. However, this sound had her completely stumped. Before she could look up, she heard Jed's voice.

"Hey, Deb! Could you go to Redman with me? If we leave soon, we'll make it in time."

Deb was again startled—an invitation from Jed two weeks in a row. How could she refuse? "Sure, give me twenty minutes and I'll be ready."

"Great, I'm going to run up to Gramps and get the car. I feel like riding in style."

Deb was excited by the chance to ride in the Corvette. She had never been for a ride in the car. Zach's mother had offered it to them once, but he had turned it down. Now, twenty-odd years later, Jed was not repeating the mistakes of the past. Deb took it as another good sign.

In truth, she had more than twenty minutes of work left. She spent ten of them doing some of it, then went into the back to clean herself up and change. If she was going to be seen in a 'Vette, she wanted to look her best.

Jed was back as promised, and Deb was ready. She'd never understood the need to make men wait as most women did. Maybe that was why they all seemed to have one, and she didn't. There had only ever been just the one for her. *Now Debbie, don't start down that path again,* she said to herself as she brushed out her hair.

It was a mild day for December. In fact, it had been a mild start to the winter with just the occasional snowstorm, nothing serious. At the moment, there was no snow on the ground. The wind however blew every day, and it had been brutally cold, giving credence to the old man's prediction. Deb had dressed up a bit, then put on her new favorite sweater. There was just something about the way it made her feel.

Having waited so long for this ride, Deb slid into the passenger's seat, taking her sweet time and wanting to capture the full experience. Jed did the same when he got in. The car moved forward with the grace of its design and the respect it commanded.

"So," Deb said playfully, "do I get to know where you're taking me, or am I a captive?"

Jed relayed the conversation he'd just had with Miss Wright. Deb was pleased to hear of his decision to apply to colleges, but was still confused.

"That's wonderful news, Jed, but what's it got to do with our little adventure here?" she asked.

"Well, when Miss Wright asked if I knew of anyone who could write a letter, it came to me right away: Miss Black at Redman Village Library. I'm kind of into this college thing now, so I wanted to run right up to Redman Village and ask her."

Deb was surprised by his answer and wondered why he hadn't thought to ask *her*. But then it hit her: *Jed thinks of me as family.* This thought warmed Deb against the cool air of the evening. Even with the top up, Corvettes look nice, but they don't offer much heat.

"Is this the first time you've had the car out since the

night Grampy gave it to you?" asked Deb.

Jed thought for a second. "Yeah, I guess it is."

"I'm surprised you didn't ask Winnie to go."

"I haven't said anything to Winnie about college yet," said Jed.

"Oh, any particular reason?"

"I'm not sure how she'll feel about it, I guess."

"And what about you?" she asked.

"Oh, I'm pretty sure I'd like to go," answered Jed.

"That's not what I mean. How do you feel about being away from Winnie?"

Jed hadn't thought about this. If he went to college, Winnie wouldn't be there. Come to think of it, neither would Gramps or Deb. He'd be alone. This put a new wrinkle on things. Jed quickly decided it would be good to know if he could go, so there was no point in turning around.

"You haven't answered me, young man," said Deb with a touch of strain in her voice.

"I hadn't really thought about it, to be honest. I'm still trying to figure this college thing out. Right now, I just want to know if I can go. So I don't see the point in bothering Winnie with it."

"Huh. I'm surprised. I thought you talked to her about everything."

"I pretty much do, I just haven't about this yet. That's all."

They fell into a thoughtful silence.

As the car turned into the library parking lot, Deb said, "Would you like me to wait here?"

"Don't be silly, I asked you to come."

Jed checked his watch and saw it was 4:45; they'd made it with time to spare.

Upon entering the building, they didn't see Miss Black right away. Then they heard the squeak of the wheels on the cart she used to return books to their proper homes. Jed moved toward the sound with Deb by his side. They found the librarian in the autobiography section. A smile filled her face as Jed and Deb moved around the end of the shelf unit.

"What a pleasant surprise," she said. "I didn't expect to see you before school was out next week."

"Hi, Miss Black," answered Jed. "I do plan to visit next week, but something came up today, and I didn't want to wait till then to talk with you about it."

"I see. It must be serious for you to make a special trip. What is it you need from me?"

"A character letter," said Jed.

"Oh, I'd be happy to, Jed, but in truth, I don't really know you that well. Who's it for?"

"I've decided to apply to some colleges and I need a character reference from someone who's not a teacher of mine, or a relative," answered Jed. "You were the first person I thought of, and I drove straight here to ask you."

Irene glanced at Deb as if looking for some confirmation. Deb smiled and nodded, and the librarian opened her arms, inviting Jed in for a hug.

Much to Deb's surprise, Jed moved in without hesitation. It made her realize that asking for a hug from Jed was something she'd not done. There had been many times when she'd wanted to, but something always made her stop. If she had, would they be closer now? she wondered. Was it her fault they weren't? Watching the two of them embrace, Deb couldn't help feeling a little jealous, and feeling the pain of missed opportunities from times past. How might those small patches have added to the beauty and quality of their lives?

As Jed and Miss Black separated, she gave him her answer. "I'd be happy to write a letter for you. I'll have it ready for you next week."

"Thank you, Miss Black. I really appreciate it," said Jed.

"The honor is mine," she answered. "Now, believe it or not, I have to ask you to leave, the library is closing."

This made Jed chuckle. "I see the librarian is back." Turning to Deb he said, "We'd better get out of here before we're fined."

Miss Black locked the door behind them and watched until the car left the parking lot. She then walked to her desk, pulled out a piece of stationary, and wrote a quick letter, folded it, placed it in an envelope, then addressed and stamped the envelope. On her walk home, she dropped the envelope into the mailbox. A deep warmth from within, emanating from released emotions, protected her from the cold winter air that had descended upon Redman Village with the setting of the sun. Patches were being made. The quilt of life was coming together nicely.

CHAPTER 14
Roads Lead Everywhere

Christmas had always been a confusing time for Jed. It made him feel a little depressed. The kids at school talked about having big meals with their families, and all of them opening presents together. Family, family, family, was all he heard about. For him, Christmas meant more work. Deb worked late into Christmas Eve. Some years she even worked into Christmas morning, baking food for what seemed like everyone in town.

Over the last few years however, things had begun to change. On Christmas night, the three of them, Deb, Gramps, and Jed would have their own tree. Last year, Winnie had come over. They would have a nice meal, open presents, all the things Jed had heard the others talk about. Still, it didn't feel just right. He wondered what it would be like to live with a mother and a father, to have what the other kids in town had. Part of him wanted the big elaborate presents, like his friends. The ones he always received were of a practical nature-clothes, tools, things he needed, not wanted.

Shopping was a tediously difficult task for him. Deb would tell him not to spend any money on her, and Gramps always said he had everything he needed. So he would end up buying them little things. His desire to give them something special was as strong as his own desire to *receive* something special. This year was a little different, though. Seeing Deb wearing the sweater with the lighthouse on it made him realize how much she liked it. She also seemed to be attached to it emotionally. If he could find a similar sweater, maybe she would have the same special feeling for it. Now Gramps, he had been a little tougher to figure out, but Jed finally did. He had always offered to shovel the walkway, but Gramps refused. Jed had noticed something new at the True Value in Redman Village called a snowblower, a gas-powered machine with paddles like an old mill wheel. It scooped up the snow and a blower on the back sent the snow out of a chute.

Jed had talked with Winnie about both ideas, and she agreed they were good ones. She even said he could hide the snowblower at her house, and offered to go with him to find Deb a sweater. Jed was pleased with Winnie's offer to help. He didn't know much about girls. In fact, Winnie and Deb were about the only two he'd spent any time around.

With school being out, and the traps nearly done, they had decided to go during the week, thinking it might not be too crazy with shoppers in Augusta. Plus the weatherman was predicting a big snowstorm toward the end of the week, so they had settled on Wednesday as the day to go. Since the roads were still bare of snow, Jed decided to take the Corvette, even though Deb had offered her truck.

Augusta was about an hour away. Christmas music flowed out of the radio in rhythm with the warm air from the car's heater. Jed stayed focused on the road with this being his first time driving to Augusta. Winnie enjoyed seeing the lights and decorations on the homes along the way. Few words passed between them. The time went quickly, and before they knew it, the city opened up in front of them.

"Have you ever seen so many lights?" asked Winnie.

"Kinda," he said. "On the water at night. It looks like this when the moon is full and reflects off the water."

"Really? I'd like to see that," she said.

"Okay. Next summer I'll take you out."

Winnie smiled to herself. She wanted to say, *It's a date,*

but didn't dare.

Not really knowing where to go, they stopped into a mall that had a Sears store along with a few smaller specialty stores. One of these was a sweater store. Jed followed as Winnie scanned the piles of sweaters. There were all kinds of choices, most of which she quickly moved past. She was on a mission, her eyes narrowed and aimed straight ahead. She was looking at each stack quickly but carefully before moving on, leaving no reason to look back. They were at the back of the store when Winnie finally stopped.

"This is what we're looking for," she announced.

She pulled four sweaters out of the fifty or so sitting on the table and laid them out for Jed to inspect. She picked up each one and held it up for Jed to consider. After a review of all four, she asked, "What do you think?"

"They're all really nice, Winnie. How do I pick one?"

"Well, I started with her favorite color."

"She has a favorite color?" Jed said wonderingly.

"Yes, silly, everyone does. Even if they don't know it."

"Okay, so what is it?"

"Jed, you're such a *guy* sometimes, honestly! She loves blue."

Jed took a closer look at the sweaters, each of them had a different shade of blue in it. As he looked, one stood out to him. It had a design of pies, cakes, and cooking tools.

"This is the one," he said.

"Yes, it is. Good choice," Winnie answered.

Finding the one thing they had come for so quickly gave them time to visit a few other stores Winnie had mentioned. Jed wanted to accommodate any and all of Winnie's requests today, and the last place they stopped was a bookstore. Jed had never been in a real bookstore before. The only one he'd ever visited was the used bookstore in New Ireland, which was only open in the summer, and nothing like this one. Walking into this store provided a very different view. The commercial aspect of posters and displays promoting certain books and authors didn't sit well with him at first. Then he looked at it from a perspective he could relate to, the same way Miss Wright had taught him to approach the college applications. They were like lobster buoys marking the traps, each buoy with its own colors, style, and shape. This he understood. Each poster and display was trying to attract people to a particular book. They were like bait, attracting people into the trap of buying a book. And the authors hoped the buyers would be caught up in their stories.

Jed walked around looking at the displays and trying to imagine his book among them. He came to a table covered with books all by the same author. He picked up one of the books and read the jacket. To his surprise, the writer was from Maine. This writer was traveling the world and writing about it. Not as a documentary, but as fiction. Before Jed could read any more, Winnie reminded him of how late it was getting.

They were halfway back to New Ireland when Jed noticed he needed gas. It was close to 8 P.M., and he wasn't sure anything would be open, but a few miles later, he spotted an Esso station with the lights still on. He pulled in next to the gas pumps. After waiting several minutes for someone to come out, then said, "The lights are on in the garage. I'm going inside. You want to go?"

"Hmm, I'll wait here, if you don't mind," answered Winnie. "It's nice and toasty here."

Jed flashed her a smile. "Sure, you stay warm. I'll be right back."

Jed left the keys in the ignition so that the radio would continue to play for Winnie while he was gone. As he came to the open garage door, he could hear the radio inside playing the same country song he'd left on for Winnie. He could also hear someone moving around, but couldn't see anyone. So he hollered out, "Hello, anyone here?"

His call was answered by the squeaking of wheels. A second later, a man appeared from under a car. He looked around before focusing on Jed.

"Hey, what can I do for you?" he asked.

"I was wondering if you were still open. I need some gas."

The man stood up. He wasn't really tall— 5'9", maybe 5'10"—with a build that was slim and lanky, like a lot of mechanics. The thing that surprised Jed was the absence of any dirt or grease. He was clean-shaven, with not a hair out of place.

The man looked out toward the pumps. "That your 'Vette?" he asked.

"Yeah," answered Jed.

The man started walking toward the car. "How' d a fella your age come by a car like this?"

Jed didn't like the tone the man was using, but he wanted the gas so he said, "It was given to me."

The man didn't ask any more questions as they walked toward the car. Slowly, he walked around the car as if to take in every little detail. Winnie looked out the window at Jed, who just shrugged his shoulders. After the man made his way back around, he spoke again.

"How much?"

"How much what?" asked Jed.

"Gas, boy, how much gas?"

There was that tone again. Jed wasn't sure he wanted the gas anymore, but he still needed it. "Fill 'er up," he said with authority.

The man took the cap off the tank and began pumping.

Winnie's curiosity got the better of her and she stepped out of the car.

"Well, hello there, young lady," said the man.

Winnie smiled and glanced at Jed before responding. "Hi, my name's Winnie," she said with a smile that dimmed the lights shining down from above. "What's yours?"

"Name's Bradley," he answered. He turned to Jed. "Looks like you've got it all."

Jed was still trying to stay calm, but this Bradley wasn't doing anything to help. "What do you mean by that?" he said in a way that hinted at the anger he was suppressing.

"Calm down, young fella. I didn't mean anything by it. All I'm saying is, you've obviously got money in your pocket, this attractive young lady in your passenger seat, and this 'Vette. When I was your age, I wouldn't have wanted for anything more."

"Come to think of it, I was about your age when I first saw a car like this. Yep, you don't forget the first time you see a Corvette."

As Jed half listened to Bradley talk, he watched the cost of this unpleasant stop continue to rise on the gas pump, all the while wondering when it would stop so that he could get out of there. Winnie, however, was listening intently.

"Mister Bradley—" Winnie began.

"It's just Bradley, no Mister, little lady," he interrupted.

Winnie began again. "Bradley, do you remember where you saw that Corvette or who owned it?"

"I sure do. It belonged to a woman who lived in New Ireland."

"Really?" said Winnie. "We're from New Ireland and so is this car."

"Is that a fact?" replied Bradley. "Well, the one I saw belonged to the mother of a friend of mine. His name was Zach Crockett."

At that moment, the pump stopped and Bradley announced, "Looks like twelve seventy-five."

Bradley looked first toward Jed, then Winnie. "Did I say something wrong?" he asked.

Jed was trying to take in what he'd just heard. Had Bradley really just said that Zach Crockett was a friend of his? He had to ask.

"Did you say Zach Crockett was a friend of yours?" This was serious information, and he needed to know the answer.

Apparently picking up on Jed's intensity, Bradley seemed to choose his words carefully. "We were friends as kids. I haven't seen him in fifteen or twenty years now. Why? Do you know Zach?"

Jed's head dropped a bit with this news. He wanted to continue the conversation, but couldn't find the words.

Winnie intervened. "Bradley, this is Jed, Zach's son. And I'm guessing this is the same Corvette you saw back then."

"Well I'll be damned," said Bradley. He stuck his hand out to shake Jed's and continued. "I didn't know Zach had a kid. How is the old boy, anyway?"

Hearing Winnie had brought Jed around. He shook Bradley's hand as he answered, "I couldn't tell you how he is. I've never met him."

"Oh, that's got to be rough. I'm sorry, Jed. If it's any consolation, your dad was a great friend. Then he just disappeared one day."

Before Jed could say anything, Winnie once again stepped in and saved him. "Jed, it's getting late. Could we maybe come back another time and you two could talk then?"

Jed looked at Winnie. He knew she was right, so he fought the urge to continue the conversation with Bradley. "Would it be okay if we came back to talk?"

"Sure enough, I'm here all the time. I'd be glad to tell you what I know about your dad. As long as you bring this lovely lady with you, that is," answered Bradley with a wink at Winnie.

The two men shook hands again, and Winnie gave Bradley a hug. Jed paid for the gas, they climbed back into the car, and drove on toward New Ireland.

Winnie stared at Jed for a while, waiting for him to say something. He didn't. Any hope she had of him picking up on the idea of her being a young lady lost its way in the fog she saw in his eyes.

Jed was deep in thought. He'd gone shopping for Christmas presents, and perhaps gotten the best gift for himself. He now had an itch to scratch, another patch for the quilt that was his heritage.

CHAPTER 15
Getting More than You Give

As much as Jed wanted to get back to see Bradley again, it would be a while before he could. There were other things that needed doing, and as Gramps would say, "Needs come before wants." This sentiment, as well as many other influences whose origin could be found with his Gramps, were now part of Jed's character, part of his very soul.

Plus, Christmas was but three days away now. Since work on the traps had gone so well, Gramps had said they could start later in the morning. Jed took advantage of this free time to pick up the snowblower at the hardware store and take it to Winnie's house. Thank goodness Deb had a truck. The machine was way too big to fit into the trunk of the Corvette. Deb had also given Jed a list of things to pick up. They knew Gramps was always watching the comings and goings on Main Street, so if he saw Jed leave with the truck and return empty, he'd wonder what was going on.

Winnie waved from the living room window when Jed backed into the driveway. She had the garage door open before he dropped the tailgate. Although Winnie was small, she was no wimp. Jed could have carried the box into the garage on his own, but he waited for Winnie to help. Seeing her face light up at the other end of the box took the chill out of the air and the weight off the box.

"I cleared a place here in the back, out of the way," she

said, pulling on her end to lead Jed to the open spot where they could set the box down.

As Jed stood up, he said, "Thanks again, Winnie. I don't know what I would have done without all your help."

"Oh, this was no bother," she said with her special smile for Jed alone.

"It's not just this. I mean going to the city with me, helping with Deb's sweater, and all the work on the traps. I know Gramps is paying you, but you didn't have to do it even then. If you hadn't, I'd have been all winter on those cussed traps. With you making the bait bags and heads...well, you know."

Jed's words touched Winnie. She'd wondered if he'd given any thought to the fact that she didn't need to be spending all of her free time in the cold barn fiddling with coarse twine, whether she was getting paid or not. Still, Jed wasn't saying he knew she was there because of him. Winnie decided not to read too much into what he'd said or hadn't said. After all, wasn't it enough that he'd said *something?* She quickly convinced herself it was.

"You're welcome," she said. "You know I'll do whatever I can to help. So, have you given any thought to when you might pay another visit to Bradley?"

"Yeah, it won't be for a while. I have a lot of things to do before we head back to school, and I'm running out of time."

Winnie was a bit perplexed by this. "Really, I would think you'd be itching to run right back there."

Jed's head dropped down and his eyes seemed to focus on the snowblower box. "Oh, I want to go all right. I've waited my whole life to hear about my dad, so a few more days or even weeks won't matter much. God forbid Deb or Gramps should say more than two words at a time about him."

Winnie could hear the pain in Jed's voice and feel the pain of his unspoken words. "I'm sorry Jed, I didn't mean to pry or be a bother."

Jed lifted his head up and looked into Winnie's eyes. *Pry! Be a bother!* he thought. *How could she think that? Of all the things she'd been over the years, she'd been neither of these.* "Winnie, you couldn't be a bother if you tried. Aside from Deb and Gramps, you're the only person I have in my life. You're my best friend. You mean the world to me." With that, he stepped around the box, opened his arms, and gave Winnie a hug.

Winnie tried to be strong, but her heart won out the moment she felt Jed's arms close around her. How long had she waited to hear the words *"You mean the world to me,"* to have him hug her with feeling for the first time? It was more than she could keep contained. The feel of his arms on her back. The firmness of his biceps on the side of her breast. She couldn't tell if her world was beginning or ending. It didn't matter as long as she was in his arms.

In one way, the moment seemed an eternity, yet when he let go she felt a void nearly equal to the pleasure she'd so desperately longed for. For just the slightest measure of time, her own grip around him had tightened. With the rude awakening of his release, she realized the tightness of her own grip, and let go, hoping Jed had not noticed. Her eyes, however, gave her away, as the residue of tears lay just below them, while more evidence showed itself as dark spots on Jed's light-blue chamois shirt.

"Winnie, you okay? Did I say something wrong?" he asked.

As she looked into his eyes, Winnie saw not the reflection of her own emotions, but the concern of a friend. Clearly she was overcome by his words. But their meaning from his perspective apparently fell far short of her own.

"Oh, you know us girls," she began. "We're always emotional, especially during the holidays." Then she quickly tried to change the subject. "So what else have you got planned today?"

Jed wasn't convinced by Winnie's answer, but he was willing to let it go. "Okay, Winnie, I need to get going. Gramps will be working on the boat as usual. You coming today?"

"Oh, yeah, right." She hesitated, brushed her hair back. "I'll be along in a little bit. I'll need to change and make a lunch first."

"How about we go to Deb's for lunch, my treat," said Jed with a smile and a wink.

Winnie smiled back. "Very funny. You know perfectly well Deb would never let either one of us pay."

Jed offered Winnie another hug. This time she took it for the value he placed upon the embrace, rather than her own.

* * * *

On Christmas night, the softest of snow floated playfully in the air as it fell. Jed couldn't help noticing how it made the scene around him look like the inside of a snow globe. As he drove to Winnie's, he thought back to the other day when he and Winnie had gotten back from lunch at Deb's and Gramps had told Winnie to skedaddle until after Christmas. Even though it had only been a couple of days, Jed missed her presence in the barn, though he didn't know why. Anyway, he was excited to be picking her up for Christmas at Gramps. Just as before, the garage door was open when he backed into the driveway. Winnie had not only moved the box containing the snowblower to the garage door opening, she'd also wrapped it in the colors of Gramps' lobster buoys and put a big bow on it.

Jed got out to load the box with Winnie. His smile was all she needed to know that Jed was pleased by her efforts. The hug he gave her was a bonus. Deep in her heart, she secretly hoped Jed would make a habit of these hugs. Jed noticed the pile of boxes on the doorstep leading into the house. Without a word, he picked them up, while Winnie ran and opened the truck door for him.

Realizing that this would be their only chance to talk alone until Jed brought her home, Winnie found the opening topic.

"Did you remember Deb's sweater?" she asked, then immediately bit her tongue.

Jed didn't seem to mind her checking on him. "It's been under the tree for two days now, MOM!" he said with a smirk.

From there, it was small talk all the way to Gramps.

Deb stood at the door waiting to help lug things in. The smell of turkey, potatoes, squash, and apple pie filled the old kitchen. Even though Jed had lived with Deb for a number of years now, her cooking skills never ceased to amaze him. Gramps was sitting in the rocker, listening to the radio as usual. If he saw them walk by with the boxes, he made no sign of it. Once everything was in, Deb began the festivities.

"Supper's ready, hope you're all hungry," she announced.

Everyone took their place at the table. After a short grace, the plates and bowls made their way around until everyone had a healthy helping of everything. Their silence was compliment enough for Deb. They all knew she'd rather see people eating and enjoying her food than talking about it. Once the meal was done, Jed and Winnie banished Deb and Gramps to the living room while they did the dishes.

When the dishes were out of the way, they gathered around the tree. Each of them took turns opening their presents. When an extra-special present landed in front of one of them, a camera was quickly raised. Deb loved the sweater, and put it right on even though the house was warm enough to smoke haddock for finnan haddie. Gramps looked strangely at the snowblower and didn't say much, but Jed could tell he liked it.

Jed gave Winnie a gold-plated twine needle, but she liked

the words he wrote on the card more:

You are the needle that gives a path to my thread,
which weaves and binds my life complete.
Just as these two are one, so too is our friendship,
in the past, now, and into the future ahead.

Deb gave her a dress which could only be described as a prom gown. As Winnie held the dress up, it screamed to be tried on. It took all her strength to resist and place it back into the box.

The biggest present of all was in the smallest package and went to Jed—two envelopes tied together with a simple blue ribbon. Jed removed the ribbon with as much dexterity as his hands had to offer. He opened the top envelope, took out the simple piece of paper and began reading.

"Read it aloud, please," said Winnie.

Jed read from the note: "I, Jedediah Rumford Crockett, hereby give in whole undivided ownership, my one thousand lobster traps, as well as my lobster boat, commonly known as *Miss Ellen*, to Jedediah Zachary Baxter. I also transfer to Jedediah my state license of fishing rights as provided and set forth by State of Maine law. The aforementioned recipient is my grandson. Effective December 25, 1978."

The room was so quiet, you could hear the snow hit the ground outside. Before Jed could react, Crockett spoke. "This here is a closed topic. There ain't no discussing it. I had that paper there drawn up legal. It's notarized and everything. Now open the other one."

Jed did as Gramps told him. Inside was a check made out to Winnie for one thousand dollars. Crockett spoke again. "That check represents the only debt owed on the boat, traps, and gear. Since Winnie ain't quite finished yet, I couldn't pay her. It's your responsibility now."

Deb had known about the gifts. Crockett had had her arrange things with a lawyer since he couldn't get around that well anymore. She also knew there was one more present left under the tree.

"Jed, would you please pick up that last present and give it to your grandfather? Careful, it's kind of heavy."

Gramps slowly removed the wrapping. Inside the box was a movie projector. Gramps' face flushed with color.

"When I saw this projector, it reminded me of when we used to watch old home movies on Christmas in the past. I thought it would be nice if we could do it again. If you still have the movies, that is," said Deb.

Crockett was taken aback by the gift. It was something he'd thought about getting ever since Jed had shown up, but he just hadn't done it. He'd long ago worn out his own projector watching the very movies Deb had spoken of. He'd done so alone. Deep down, he wanted to show the movies to Jed, but there were also things he didn't want him to see. In part he felt that the less Jed knew about his father, the less likely he was to repeat the mistakes. Mistakes that had indirectly led to Ellen's death, and to his and Deb's lives of loneliness and near solitude. His thoughts were interrupted by Jed's voice.

"Gramps...Gramps."

"Yeah, Jed, no need in yelling, I can hear you."

"Do you still have the movies?" Jed asked.

It took another minute for Crockett to find the strength to answer.

"Yeah, I got 'em," he finally said. "Follow me, boy."

Crockett headed for the kitchen to put on his coat and boots with Jed in tow.

Deb watched patiently. The moment they disappeared behind the closed door, she turned to Winnie. A giddy excitement came full force to the surface as she grinned and said, "Winnie, what do you say we head upstairs and see how this dress fits while the boys are gone?"

Winnie felt her eyes grow as big and bright as the ornaments on the Christmas tree. She grinned back at Deb and wagged her head up and down, unable to form her own words as Deb's excitement transferred itself to her. Deb led her up the stairs.

To Winnie's dismay, the room to the left was bare and bore little resemblance to what she would consider a finished bedroom. The closet had nothing more than a wooden dowel strung between two boards. The floor was of unfinished wood with a small old braided rug in the center. The roof rafters were exposed, and you could even see the ends of the roofing nails coming through the boards. Had it not been so cold, Winnie would have expected to see spiders.

The room to the right, however, was a different story. This room had been finished with the love of good parents. The floor was painted like a big checkerboard, the roofline had been transformed into walls, and a painted ceiling finished off the enclosure. Under one eave was a closet; under the other there was a built-in chest of drawers and a bookshelf. The shelf was still filled with books, and Winnie could see clothing inside the partially open closet door.

Deb set the dress on the bed. She then opened the top drawer and pulled a box out. Smiling at Winnie, she gently opened the box. Inside, there was a strapless bra, a snow-white slip, and a pair of blue high-heeled shoes. For just a moment, Winnie was confused.

"Deb, you had this planned the whole time," she said.

Deb smiled. "Yes, I did, and the only thing I'll enjoy more than seeing your face is seeing Jed when he gets a look at you in this dress."

* * * *

The two men made their way over the path leading to an old barn that Jed had never been in. Had it not been for the recent events in his life, Jed might have wondered what secret surprise lay ahead. Now, he simply expected something new to reveal itself. When they reached the door, Gramps handed him a key ring.

"You open it, would ya?" he asked Jed.

Jed took the key, unlocked the padlock, and removed the chain. It was as stiff from the cold as it was heavy. Had Jed thought about how cold it was, he would have worn gloves. The years of hard labor gave his hands some resistance to the cold, but not really enough. Knowing he was under the watchful eye of Gramps, Jed held the chain in one hand and opened the door with the other. He carried the chain inside and set it on a bench near the door.

The darkness inside the building was denser than the night. Jed started to say he'd go back for a flashlight, when he heard the squeak of a fuse box handle. Slowly, the glow of overhead lights began to illuminate the space. Gramps made his way into the darkness ahead of the coming light.

Jed's attention, however, was focused on an object reflecting the light. As his eyes adjusted, a boat's hull came into view. It looked large inside the barn, as boats always do. Jed guessed it was about the same size as Gramps' *Miss Ellen*. The boat looked new, with no sign of wear and tear from the sea. Realizing Gramps would be looking for him, Jed moved down the side of the boat. As he passed by the stern, he looked back. There was a name, but it was difficult to read in the shadows. As the letters became visible, Jed saw *Debbie May*. He wondered who that was. And whose boat this was....

"Where'd you go, boy? I need them keys," hollered Gramps.

Jed made his way back to the sound of Gramps' voice. "I'm right here, Gramps."

Gramps took the keys and unlocked the storage cabinet in front of him. There, at the bottom, was a leather case.

"That's it," said Gramps.

Jed bent over and picked up the case. This, unlike the

barn door, was not as heavy as he thought it might be. On the way back, Gramps stopped at the stern of the boat hull. He didn't look up, or even at Jed. His voice, when it came, was flat.

"This was your father's boat. He only took it out twice. Once was with its namesake, and the other...well, you know that by now. I had it stored here after he left."

Jed couldn't help asking, "Gramps, if you had this boat just sitting here, why did you give me yours?"

The answer was short and direct. "This boat's cursed."

Gramps picked up his pace and didn't stop at the open door. By the time Jed had secured the door and made it back into the house, Gramps was back in his chair. After removing his coat and shoes, Jed carried the case into the living room and placed it in front of his grandfather.

"Inside that closet is a screen," the old man said, gesturing toward a narrow door.

Jed pulled out the screen and opened it up. Next, he and Gramps set up the projector. It wasn't until then that Jed noticed the girls were missing, but he stayed on task. Finally, everything was in place and ready. Rather than make a fuss, Jed sat down to wait for Deb and Winnie to return from wherever they'd spent the time since he and Gramps had gone outside.

A sense of restlessness quickly began building inside Jed, as he was about to see an image of his father for the first time. If there were still photos, he wasn't aware of them. No one had ever offered to show him one—not that he'd ever asked, either. The closeness of the event, just moments away now, brought about a desire, a longing he'd fought not to have. Jed's knowledge that his father had never known he'd been born had helped him dismiss any feelings of rejection. Would viewing these old movies change things? Would they bring out only good things, or things he wished not to know? He remembered something he'd been told by Miss Wright: "As a writer, the most important thing is the search for the truth. Good or bad, right or wrong, it's the truth you should care about most." Within these words was the answer to his anxiety.

The stairs creaked as Deb came down. Her glee was now beyond her control and clearly visible on her face. She stopped at the bottom of the stairs and proclaimed, "Gentlemen, I present to you Abagail Winifred Hastings!"

Deb gestured dramatically at the staircase, and Jed looked up.

Slowly, a silhouette started down the stairs. The dress looked like it was floating on air. It was white and covered with blue chiffon, which hung from Winnie's shoulders with spaghetti straps. The top was just low enough to display an inch of cleavage. The bottom ruffle stopped just at the knee, creating a full bell which made the dress look shorter than it really was. Winnie's hair was pulled up in the front, but the sides and back had been allowed to fall, tickling her shoulders and neck. The light from the stairs backlit the dress, giving her the look of an angel.

Winnie stood still for a few moments at the foot of the stairs.

The room was silent until Deb finally spoke again. "So, what do you think, Jed?"

Jed was still trying to fully take in the sight before him. "Winnie, you're...you're a woman," he said with amazement.

Color filled Winnie's cheeks and rushed down her neck, contrasting with the soft blue. Words, however, failed her.

"It's about time you noticed, boy," said Crockett just loud enough for everyone to hear.

Jed approached Winnie, but didn't dare touch her for fear he'd break the spell and this new vision of Winnie would somehow disappear. He could see the Winnie he knew in her eyes. That's where the tomboy was safely stored. *Where had this woman been hiding?* was the question running through his mind. Had she been in front of him the whole time, and he just hadn't seen it? Now that he had, he would never again see anything else.

As he stood there looking into her eyes, he could feel his heart leave his chest. In its place was love for Winnie. The kind of love a man feels for only one woman—the one he wants to spend the rest of his life with.

Winnie watched the change in Jed through his eyes, as he stood there looking into hers. She felt his heart join with hers. She knew as completely as he did. At this moment, Jed had fallen in love with Winnie and their two hearts became one. There was no patch to fill, or need for scratching, anymore.

CHAPTER 16
Movie Night, Night Moves

O kay, Winnie, I think he's seen enough. Let's put this dress back in the box before he gets drool all over it," said Deb.

It took a second for Winnie to hear. "Yeah, just a minute, Deb," she said before turning back to Jed. "So, there's a Sadie Hawkins dance next weekend on New Year's Eve. I was wondering if you'd like to go."

Jed didn't know what to say. Seeing Winnie this way changed everything between them. She had always been a friend, but going to a dance? On a date? Is that what she was talking about? But he managed to blurt out, "I think I'm supposed to ask *you* that."

Hearing this pleased Winnie. The idea that he wanted to ask her out was heartwarming. Winnie's mind kept repeating the same thought: *If only I'd known a dress would have this kind of effect, I would have put one on years ago.*

"A Sadie Hawkins dance is where the girls ask the guys," she answered.

"Oh, well, yeah, I'd be honored to go with you," said Jed.

Deb jumped back in. "Good, that's settled. Now let's get this dress put away. You can show it to him again at the dance." She turned Winnie around and gently pushed her up the stairs.

By the time the two of them had reached the top, tears

had filled their eyes. Deb unzipped the dress, and as soon as it was off, Winnie turned around and hugged her. Her strength caught Deb off guard, leaving her short of breath.

"Deb, I'll never be able to thank you enough for this dress."

"You could start by letting me go," laughed Deb.

"Did you hear him say yes?"

"I did," Deb confirmed.

"Oh...you should have seen into his eyes, though! How long have I been waiting to see inside those eyes?" Winnie slumped onto the bed.

"Okay, okay, let's not forget he's downstairs waiting for us," cautioned Deb. "Hurry up and get yourself dressed and back down there." Then she left the room, giving Winnie a few minutes to herself.

Winnie settled down and changed. She took a last look at herself in the mirror. The difference in her appearance was staggering. She'd had no idea how well she'd been hiding herself.

When she made it back downstairs, everyone was ready and waiting. There was an empty spot next to Jed. Even though it was the very place she would have sat before, the slightest bit of hesitation ran through her. As she sat down, her thigh brushed against his, sending a tingle up her side. Winnie thought about all the times they'd sat like this before, and how the innocence was gone now.

"You two keep your hands to yourself," said Gramps with a chuckle as he turned on the projector.

The first couple of movies were older ones. They showed Zach as a small child. If there was any doubt in Jed's mind about his father's existence, it was removed by these images. Jed felt like he was looking at himself on the screen at times, which was not what he was waiting for. He wanted to see the man who had fathered him.

As the current movie was ending, Winnie leaned into Jed

and whispered, "It's getting late. I should go soon."

Crockett might have been old, but apparently he could still hear better than most, and before Jed could answer, he spoke up. "I'll show one more, then I got to go to bed," he said, reaching into the box for one more reel.

"What movie did you pick?" asked Deb.

"The one where I got Ellen the car."

During the movie, Gramps and Deb pointed out one detail after another. Trivial things, but important to someone who was hearing about them for the first time. Jed kept waiting for a look at his father. A younger version of Deb was seen for the first time. Jed thought she looked much the same as she did now. Finally, the car came into view. A man got out from behind the wheel.

Gramps stopped the film. "That's my Zach, your dad," he said.

Jed looked at the man frozen in time on the egg-white backdrop. The quality wasn't great, the image was grainy, and the color had a pastel value to it, but the features of similarity were distinctive. There he was, for the first time. The man Jed could call Dad.

The movie started again, but Jed was still focused on that image of his father. Then he felt Winnie grab his arm and take in a deep breath. He turned to look at her. Her other hand was over her mouth and her eyes were popping out. As Jed stared, Winnie pointed at the screen. Gramps had noticed Winnie, too, and stopped the film again. Jed turned back to face the screen and looked. At first, he couldn't see anything.

Then Winnie spoke. "Who's the other man getting out of the car?"

Crockett took a better look at the image. It took a second for him to realize who it was. He'd forgotten about this part. His face became stiff, his eyes narrowed, but no answer came.

Deb spoke up. "That's someone who was a friend of Zach's."

Her voice sounded strained.

Winnie looked at Jed and asked, "Is that...Bradley?"

Crockett shot out of his chair like a cat being chased by a dog. "How in hell do you know about him?" he asked.

The tension in the room became so stifling, it was hard to breathe, but Winnie managed to answer. "We met him the other night on the way home from Augusta. He has a garage up on Route 17."

"Huh! Well, Deb's a better person than I am. 'Cause as far as I'm concerned, he was no friend of my Zach's," said Crockett.

"Oh, Gramps, you aren't still blaming Bradley for what happened, are you?" Deb said.

Crockett looked toward her. "Why in hell not? If it weren't for him, Zach would be here with us now!"

Jed looked at Gramps. He'd seen Gramps mean, mad, even disgusted, but he'd never seen this look before.

"How can you say that?" asked Deb. "You don't know that for sure."

"'Cause he's the one who introduced Zach to that tramp," said Crockett.

"Tramp?" Jed interjected. "You mean my mother, right? So what you're really saying is, if Bradley hadn't introduced my mother to your son, *he'd* be here now instead of *me*. Not here with *us*."

Winnie's fingers were still wrapped around Jed's arm. Her grip gave way to the power of his muscles as the tension of Jed's words worked its way through his body.

Jed looked at Deb. "I suppose you feel the same way—you'd rather have him here than me."

Deb had long ago come to terms with her love for Zach, and put it in a place which allowed her to maintain her sanity. "People are gifts from God, Jed. They can't be swapped or traded. Each of us is unique. I'm thankful to know and love *both* of you. Just as we've learned through the teachings of Jesus, forgiveness is the root of happiness. You remember Jesus, Jed. What I mean is, today's the day we celebrate his birth. If there's a day to forgive, it's this one."

Jed's arm relaxed; Winnie looked at Crockett. He'd sat back down, and his face had softened. The impact of his words upon Jed could be seen on his face. Crockett then spoke.

"Deb's right, Jed. If someone put a gun to my head and said, *'Choose between you two or die,'* I'd tell them to pull the trigger."

Deb began again. "It's the same with you, Jed." This made Jed look her way. Deb continued. "I know you care for me, but I'm not your mother. I never will be, no matter what. Tonight when you looked at Winnie in that dress, it reminded me of how I've spent my whole life wishing Zach could be here to look at me the same way, but he's not. As happy as I am for you and Winnie, I'm still sad for myself. That's just how things are, Jed. It's how life keeps a balance."

"What do you mean by balance?" he asked, obviously struggling to understand.

Deb smiled. Jed had come back to his senses. "I mean that without evil, there is no good. Without right, no wrong; it's because of darkness that we cherish the light. For one to exist, both must. You're not the bad of what happened with Zach, you're the good. If you don't believe me or Gramps, then look into Winnie's eyes and tell me she sees only the bad."

Jed didn't need to look into Winnie's eyes to grasp what Deb was saying, but he did. He did because he knew Winnie wanted him to. In this moment, the love he'd felt for her earlier that evening moved to a new, deeper level. He might not know it yet, but it would be in these eyes that he'd find his way whenever he became lost. Should he ever need the answer to what his life was about, it would be waiting, safely, in her eyes. All the good, and yes, the bad. Every tomorrow as they became yesterdays. This was the writer's truth Miss Wright had spoken of.

Jed looked away from Winnie and straight at Gramps. "I'm sorry, Gramps. I didn't mean anything by it. It's just been a night full of revelations."

Gramps didn't speak, but Jed knew his apology had been accepted. It was Winnie who seized the moment, and brought the evening to a close.

"Jed, I really need to get home. It's nearly eleven o'clock."

"Sure, Winnie, I'll pick this stuff up and we'll go," answered Jed.

"You two go ahead, I'll get this," offered Deb.

* * * *

Jed was deep in his thoughts. As much as Winnie knew he wanted to be left to them, she needed to talk. "So, I guess now you've got even more of a reason to see Bradley again," she said.

Jed answered softly, "Yeah, I guess."

"I wonder why he didn't mention knowing your mother."

"I was thinking the same thing," said Jed, "but I don't remember saying anything to him about my mother."

Winnie thought for a moment and realized Jed was right. She couldn't remember anything about the conversation that had included Jed's mother.

Her attention was drawn to the box sitting in her lap. The box holding the dress. A new thought came to her mind: *Will we kiss tonight?* Earlier in the evening, she'd been sure of it. But now things felt like they were more back to normal between them. Still, she couldn't help the feeling of anticipation as Jed pulled into the driveway. She sat still and watched as Jed walked around the car to her door. He'd left the car running, so she knew he didn't plan on staying long. They walked silently to the door. Jed stepped inside just far enough to set the gifts down on a nearby table, then stepped back out. Winnie followed him out. She knew he had something on his mind, and waited for him to begin.

Jed looked into her eyes. "Winnie, a lot has happened tonight, including a change in our friendship. But there's one thing that shouldn't change. We've always been honest with each other. I'd like that to continue. On the way here, it occurred to me that you've had feelings for me for a while now. Feelings I wasn't aware of. So, how about from this point on, we try to be both honest and direct. I don't want to play that game where one of us should know what the other is thinking. Is that okay with you?"

Winnie smiled up at him. "Yes, Jed, I agree, and I'll do my best to be direct."

"Good, then I have to say something else that's direct."

Winnie noticed a change in Jed's tone and it sent a chill down her spine. She wasn't sure she wanted to hear what he was about to say after what had taken place at Crockett's. But she knew he was going to say it, so she tried to keep her mind open.

"What I want to say is, I'm not ready to kiss you. I really want to, but I'd like to wait."

To her surprise, Winnie felt relieved rather than disappointed with this news. Perhaps she herself was not ready either.

"I was wondering about that, too. Now I need to fess up with something you said. You're right about me having feelings for you that were more than friendship. I guess I haven't said anything because you never gave me any reason to think you felt we were anything more than friends. After seeing how you looked at me in a dress tonight, I realized that in the past, you saw me as a person and a friend, but not as a girl. So it was me and not you that kept your feelings hidden. So I'm fine with waiting."

She opened her arms for a hug. Since they'd begun hugging lately, it felt natural asking for one, and Jed enthusiastically obliged. Winnie could feel a new level of comfort and desire in his hug.

Afterwards, Winnie went inside and watched from the window until the taillights on Jed's car no longer found their way back through the darkness. She then looked to the sky, found the North Star, and said a thank-you prayer for the best Christmas (and the best day) in her life.

* * * *

Deb worked in silence as Crockett rocked in his chair. She thought about how this evening had a little of everything— good food, friends, family, love, anger. They had certainly run the gamut. In the end, everything had worked out, especially for Jed. He had gotten a secure future with an up-and-going business given to him, a look at his father for the first time, and his first good look at Winnie thanks to Deb's help. In her own secret way, a part of Deb admitted she was jealous of Winnie. *She* was going to get the guy.

Deb herself wasn't all that different from Jed, really. She'd grown up pretty much alone. Her mother had died when she was twelve, leaving her to care for her father. Not that he was any kind of a father to her. He went ground-fishing his whole life, which meant he was gone for twelve to fourteen days at a time. When his boat tied up at the dock, it was the bar he called home. Getting drunk as fast as he could and staying that way until the boat headed back out. But he hadn't always been that way. Deb's mom had died while he was out to sea, and she was buried before the boat ever made port. If it had been a normal trip, he'd have been back in time, but they ran into a large school of fish and chased it for two days past their normal time. Then they had to go into Boston with the fish because they didn't have enough fuel or food to make it back home. This all added up to their being four days late getting back, and two days after the funeral.

From that point on, he'd come in from fishing, step through the door, throw his laundry onto the kitchen floor, and walk right back out again. Deb always did the laundry the very instant he brought it home. His clothes smelled so bad, she could hardly stand it. The next morning, she would get up and make him a big breakfast before leaving for school. Then when she was twenty, the boat came in one night and instead of the laundry bag at the door, there was a knock. It was the captain of her father's boat. He came to tell her that her father had been washed overboard off Cape Hatteras. They'd spent all of the next day looking for him, but never caught sight of him. The only thing they found was his hat.

Debbie cried all night after the captain left, though she didn't know why. Out of obligation, she supposed. Any love she'd had for him had left long before. The next day, Deb buried his hat next to her mother. That was the last time she'd been to the cemetery.

Her own past was why, despite all of the reasons not to, she'd taken Jed in. She knew what it was like to feel alone in the world. Now she realized she'd received much more from Jed than she had given. Having Jed, Crockett, and Winnie was almost like having her own family. This thought was most comforting to her. It also reminded her that Crockett was in the other room. Deb walked into the living room to check on him.

"How you doing in here?" she asked.

"Oh, I'm okay."

"I thought you might have joined me in the kitchen."

"I been thinking about going to bed."

Deb looked closely at him. "You're in some pain, aren't you? Is there anything I can do to help?"

"No, I'm used to pain," he answered.

Deb understood that this meant he didn't want to talk

about it, and she let it go. "We had ourselves quite an evening, didn't we?" she said.

"We sure did. Winnie looked real nice in that dress. It was good of you to buy it for her."

"I'm just glad it worked. What you did for Jed was pretty special, too."

"Not really; he was going to end up with it soon enough. Which reminds me…" Crockett reached inside his sweater, pulled out an envelope, and passed it to Deb. "This is for you."

Deb reached for the envelope, opened it, and asked, "What is this?"

"It's the deed to that piece of land with the blueberries and raspberry patch. As far as I'm concerned, it's been yours for years. This just makes it legal."

Deb was speechless. She hadn't given a thought to what would happen to the land in the future, but Crockett knew how much she depended on it. She didn't know what to say.

"There's a nice spot for a house, too. I made sure the parcel ran all the way to the road so nobody could keep you off it. The surveyors are gonna put the pins in next spring. Don't know if I'll be around to make sure they do it right, but that paper will back you up if there's a problem."

Deb couldn't believe it. A patch of land all her own! A place to build a house, a real house. Deb couldn't help herself. She sat in the old man's lap and gave him a big hug and kiss on the cheek.

Her tear-filled eyes were enough thanks for Crockett. He liked the feel of her head against his shoulder, the smell of her hair. He could not have thought any more of her if she were his own daughter. He felt the pride and joy of doing right by Deb and Jed. She had a patch of land all to herself now, and Jed had a good start toward scratching out a decent living. He could die right now, and that would be okay with him.

CHAPTER 17
A New Year

Jed was nervous. He and Winnie had spent countless hours together over the years, and every day since Christmas they'd spent most of each day working, walking, eating, and whatever else there was to do side by side. Tonight however, was different. This was to be their first date. He caught sight of Deb's reflection looking at him in the mirror. Hopefully, Winnie would look half as pleased. Then again, it wasn't like she didn't know him. One thing she didn't know, though, was how bad a dancer he was. For the last week, he and Deb had been practicing every night. Last night was the first time he hadn't been stepping on her toes.

Deb saw him looking at her. She stepped forward and reached around him.

"I got something for you and Winnie," she said.

In each hand was a small box. Deb motioned for him to take the box in her left hand first. When he had, she stepped around and opened the other box. Inside was a flower for his lapel. It was pale yellow with a blue lacy ribbon. The same color as Winnie's dress. Jed was wearing a black jacket and gray pants. There hadn't been time to go into Redman Village for a tuxedo. Besides, this monkey suit was uncomfortable enough. Deb had found a yellow and blue tie for him as well. Overall, he thought the outfit looked pretty good.

"What do you think?" he asked Deb.

"I'll tell you what. If Winnie turns you away, come get me and I'll go with you," she smiled.

"Thanks for the vote of confidence. Maybe I should just go with you. At least you're used to me stepping on your feet."

"Oh, I think Winnie will be proud to have you stepping on her feet, young man. That girl's smarter than you think."

"If that's true, what's she doing with me?" he said, more than half kidding.

"Because she's smart enough for both of you. A girl knows when she's got the right guy," she said while she attached the flower to his lapel.

This made Jed think. *The right guy.* Was he? Somewhere deep down inside, he hoped so, even if he wasn't ready to admit it. Jed had thought a lot about himself and Winnie this past week. Everything they'd been through and done together. They had a lot of history.

"Deb, do you think tonight will change things for Winnie and me?"

"Things are always changing between a man and a woman, Jed. If you want the truth, I think they changed for good on Christmas."

"Yeah, I guess you're right. How come things never changed between you and my dad?"

Deb had been waiting for this question ever since she'd had the talk with Jed about his story. "I don't really know, Jed. The best answer I can give you is I guess neither of us ever took the chance Winnie did."

"What about his boat?"

"What about it? I only saw it once when he took me out on the maiden voyage."

"Then you know what he named it," said Jed.

Deb was not following. "Jed, Zach's boat didn't have a name."

"Yes, it does."

"And how would you know that, young man?" asked Deb, a bit agitated.

"I saw it, on Christmas. When Gramps and I went to get the movies."

Deb was stunned. She hadn't thought about the boat in years. She had no idea it was still around, let alone right under her nose. Jed had opened a can of worms with this news.

"You mean to tell me the boat is at Grampy Crockett's?" she asked.

"Well, yeah. He has it in the small barn out behind the house. He told me it's been there since Dad left. I'm sorry, Deb, I just figured you knew."

Deb felt the past come rushing back at her. How special she'd felt to be the first person he'd taken on the boat. Oh, how she'd wanted to bust out of her trap and tell Zach how she felt that day, but as usual, she hadn't. Zach was so happy to finally have his own boat. So proud. She just didn't have the heart to make any part of the day about her. So she let him bask in his own accomplishments while she lived in his shadow. Just as she'd learned to do with her father.

"So what did he name the boat?" asked Deb sheepishly.

"*Debbie May*. What else?"

This was a surprise to Deb. She slumped down onto Jed's bed, hands to her mouth.

"You mean you didn't know? You really didn't know?" he said.

Deb just shook her head side to side. No, she didn't know about the boat's name, but she did know what it meant for a lobsterman to name his boat after a woman. All the years of doubt, of wondering and not knowing how Zach felt, left her in that instant. She thought of all the times he'd done or said something when he might have been trying to tell her how he felt, and she hadn't responded. Zach *had* cared for her, and she'd missed it because she hadn't listened to her instincts. If only she'd known....

"Deb, you okay? I didn't mean to upset you. I'm sorry," said Jed.

Deb wiped her eyes. "No, Jed you haven't. I just never knew. Thank you for telling me. You better get going now. Winnie will be waiting."

"I don't think I should leave you right now."

Deb stood up, grabbed Jed by the shoulders, and marched him down the stairs. "Not another word, young man. You go out and have the time of your life with Winnie. Don't make the mistakes I made with your father."

When they got to the door, Jed turned around and gave Deb a big hug. He then said the nicest thing he could think to say: "Thanks, Mom."

* * * *

Jed slowly made his way to Winnie's. Snow had fallen twice since Christmas, and the roads demanded an attentive driver. Having to watch the roads so closely helped Jed to keep his mind off the list of unknown events which might unfold this evening. Not that there was anything new to think about. The same scenes had played through his mind all week, starting with his memory of Winnie in that dress. It was in the thoughts of the future, at the dance, when things went bad in his mind. Be it stepping on her toes while dancing, or spilling something on her dress, or a big fight ensuing at one point or another, they always ended up parting mad no matter how he tried to work things out in his mind. Jed knew it was silly to think this way, that it was just nerves. No one knew him better than Winnie. He might not be willing to acknowledge it, but Jed knew what the source of his negative thoughts was. It was the whole New Year's kiss thing weighing on his nerves.

Winnie's driveway lay before him. As he turned in, the back wheels slid a bit, reminding him of the conditions. His headlights showed the garage door was open, and a light inside gave welcome to the door leading into the house. Jed parked near the opening and headed into the house. An anxious mother met him as he came through the entryway.

To Jed's surprise, Winnie was waiting for him in the living room.

Jed's memory of Winnie in the dress had not retained its full effect. She looked even more perfect standing in the soft light of the living room. No words came forth to describe what he was experiencing.

Winnie smiled at him and broke the awkward silence. "I like the corsage on your lapel. It's a good contrast."

The flower, thought Jed. "I'll be right back," he said as he turned back toward the car.

Mother and daughter looked at each other knowingly, while Winnie's father hid behind the evening paper, pretending to be oblivious to the actions taking place in his own living room. Unlike most fathers on this evening, he had no role. Jed was like a cousin who lived next door, who had always been around. Everyone, including Winnie's father, had seen this day coming. With Jed, there was no need for "the talk."

When Jed returned, he'd regained some of his lost nerve. He handed the box to Winnie and waited as she opened it.

"Oh, Jed, it's beautiful."

"You'll have to thank Deb, she bought both of these flowers," he said modestly.

Winnie was already wearing a full smile, but the honesty Jed showed managed to stretch it a bit more. She had suspected as much. Still, most boys would have taken credit for it themselves. That was one of her favorite things about Jed. He was always himself. There were no games with him. No reading between the lines. Just like they'd agreed.

After a few photos were taken, Jed and Winnie made their way to the car. Jed opened the door for her, and made sure her dress was all in before closing it.

Once the two of them were alone in the car, they felt more comfortable and the conversation flowed a bit better.

The dance was being held at a local resort called Water's Edge, a place where the locals never entered unless they were invited or worked there.

"I'm really looking forward to seeing the Water's Edge. I've never been inside," said Winnie.

"Yeah, me neither," added Jed.

"I just know the food is going to be great, and the decorations, and the music. Can you believe we're going to have a live band playing music for us to dance to?"

Jed had tried to forget about the dancing part. He was nearly as worried about that as the kiss. At the resort, there was a big welcome sign, and the driveway was illuminated with lanterns right up to the main entrance. The lighting was so bright, it looked like noontime in the summer. Jed pulled the car up to let Winnie out near where a man was standing. He wondered how far away he'd have to park. He watched as the man opened the door for Winnie, and was surprised when the man then walked around the front of the car. Jed just wanted to park and get back to Winnie.

The man opened Jed's door and held his hand out. After a moment, the man spoke.

"It's my job to park the car, sir. This is your ticket. Bring this to me when you're ready to leave, and I'll go get your car."

Jed thought about his words for a second. He'd heard of this. It was called valet parking. Jed handed the keys to the man and joined Winnie on the sidewalk. Although it was cold, Jed watched as the man drove away to park the car. Not until he saw the valet walking back did Jed become comfortable again.

"Can we please go in? I'm kinda cold," Winnie said.

"Sure, Winnie, sorry I made you wait."

"Oh, that's okay, you're worth the wait," she said with a smile and a squeeze of his arm.

Jed's heart responded to Winnie's touch warming him from bow to stern. They walked arm in arm toward the door.

Just inside, there was a set of steps, with a ramp on the side. Jed felt Winnie's gentle yet persuasive tug toward the ramp. He wondered if this was an indicator of how the evening would go. It was he who should be leading her around the dance floor tonight, but would he be?

The hallway was wide and carpeted, with a high ceiling. The walls had a dark finish which consumed the light. It gave Jed the feeling of being deep under water where the light barely reached. In a strange way, the ambiance relaxed him. He felt as if they were on the water, and Winnie was his boat, there to protect him. The music filled the hall and increased in volume as they walked toward the ballroom.

Jed stopped just short of the point where people inside the open double doors could see them. He turned toward Winnie to find her looking at him. In her eyes, he saw the moment. It was one of those moments that come along only a few times in life, offering a fork in the road. Not so much a defining moment, but a choice: A choice to move things in a new direction, or continue on the same path. Jed took Winnie into his arms, leaned in, and their lips met with the apprehension of a first kiss, seeming to draw back while moving forward at the same time. The scent of Winnie's hair and perfume filled Jed's nose, bringing out a passion from deep within him.

Winnie's heart raced. Her breath caught in the pit of her stomach. She felt Jed's lips part and his tongue touch hers. The intimacy created by their tongues touching sent warmth throughout her body.

It was a single action, lasting just a few seconds and yet a lifelong memory was born. Forevermore, this would be known as the best seconds of Winnie and Jed's young lives. As their lips parted and they returned to reality, another couple passed by.

"Way to go," said the man.

"It's about time, you two," said the woman.

Winnie and Jed just smiled at each other. With the first kiss out of the way, they relaxed and enjoyed the evening. Although surrounded by people all night, they didn't notice. They only stopped making eye contact long enough to kiss.

After a few hours, they decided to leave. Outside, they were welcomed by a coat of new-fallen snow. Everything was covered in white. Not a single scratch could be seen.

CHAPTER 18
Spring Ahead, Fall Back

As winter continued, Jed and Winnie became even more inseparable. January turned into February, and February into March. Work on the boat moved at a slow and steady pace. In part, this was due to Gramps doing less and less work as time passed. His time was spent instructing Jed in the proper methods of boat repair. Jed was trying hard to learn, too, a task he found to be difficult at times with Winnie there working on the traps and well within sight. Always available to provide a distraction, whether she intended to or not.

Deb loved seeing the two of them sitting together on one side of the booth at the bakery. She'd even stopped reflecting back to her missed opportunity with Zach. She was just happy for Jed and Winnie.

By the start of March, Jed had forgotten about his college applications, but Winnie hadn't.

"Jed," she asked, "have you heard from any of the colleges yet?"

The question caught Jed off guard. "No, I guess I haven't. Why?"

"Well, are you still interested in going?"

Jed thought about her question. He did want to, but he didn't want to leave Winnie. "Well, not without you," he finally said.

This made Winnie smile. "Thank you for saying that, but you should go."

"What would you do if I did?"

"Well, there's something I haven't told you. I've applied for college as well," she said.

This surprised Jed. "That's great, Winnie. What for?"

"I want to be a veterinarian."

Jed knew that Winnie liked animals. Her being a vet made sense to him. "Where have you applied?" he asked to show support, yet fearing the answer.

"Well, a few places, but where I really want to go is UMO."

"That would be great; then we could be in school together."

"So you wouldn't mind me going to the same school?"

"Mind?" Jed took Winnie in his arms and gave her a long kiss, then said, "I can't think of anything I'd like better."

Winnie smiled. "I'm really glad to hear you say that, because I got my acceptance letter in the mail yesterday." She took out the letter and showed it to Jed.

As he read and she watched, neither of them noticed the mailman enter the bakery. Deb took the mail from his hand, then handed one of the envelopes back to him. The mailman walked toward Jed and Winnie, who were still lost in their own world.

"Mr. Jedediah Baxter?

"Ah…Mr. Jedediah Baxter?" he repeated.

Jed looked up. He so seldom heard his surname, it always sounded funny to him. "Yes, I'm Jed Baxter."

"This is for you," said the mailman.

Jed still had Winnie's letter in one hand as he reached for his with the other. As he put it on the table, Winnie set her envelope next to it. Except for the name and address, they looked the same—both were from UMO.

Not wanting to miss the moment, Deb made her way over

to their table. Jed sat there looking at the envelope. He made no move to pick it up. Winnie and Deb waited patiently. Finally, Winnie said, "Are you going to open it?"

Jed sighed. "Yeah, I was just holding onto the moment for as long as I could."

"What moment is that, dear?" asked Deb.

Jed looked up at Deb, then across to Winnie. "As long as I don't open it, there's hope, but once I do, there's no going back."

"Would you like one of us to open it?" Deb offered.

Jed looked up at her again. "Would you mind?"

Deb smiled and picked up the envelope. As carefully as she could, she opened it and pulled out the letter. Jed thought she would read it aloud, but she didn't. After she'd finished, she put the letter back into the envelope, and handed it back to Jed. He was mystified, and it showed on his face.

"I said I'd open it. If you want to know what it says, you can read it for yourself. I've got work to do."

Deb then turned and walked away. Nothing in her appearance or actions gave him a hint of the letter's contents. Jed looked toward Winnie.

"Don't even think of asking," said Winnie. "I opened mine. That was hard enough. You can open your own."

Winnie's words had a calming, reassuring effect on Jed. He smiled, kissed her, and said, "Thanks, I don't know what I'd do without you." Jed fished the letter out of the envelope and began reading aloud.

Dear Mr. Jedediah Baxter:

After careful review and consideration, we are pleased to inform you that your request to become a student at the University of Maine, Orono's English Department, as a member of the fall Nineteen Hundred Seventy-Nine Class, for the pursuit of a Bachelor's Degree in Creative Writing, has been approved.

Furthermore, due to the quality of your application, and the writing samples you submitted, along with your letters of recommendation, we are pleased to inform you that a scholarship is being offered.

At your earliest convenience, please contact our office to confirm your interest in committing to this offer.

The rest of the letter was a blur to Jed. As he looked at Winnie, he saw the tears in her eyes and fought to keep them from his own.

Deb had returned to the table without the two of them noticing. "Congratulations, Jed, I'm proud of you," she said as softly and caringly as any mother could.

Both Jed and Winnie looked up at her. Winnie reached out, handing Deb her letter. Deb read it while the tears already hanging on the edge of her eyelids dropped, one by one, as she blinked in an effort to clear them. Before she'd finished, Deb had sat down in the booth across from them. When she finished, no words were needed to express how she felt.

"You know who else would like to hear this news?" she asked.

Jed thought for a second, then it came to him. "Miss Black. Thanks for reminding me." He looked at Winnie and said, "Do you want to go? I'm ready if you are."

"I'd love to go, but I need to tell my parents," she answered. "Deb, is it all right if I use your phone?" Waiting for an answer wasn't necessary, and Winnie trotted off to make the call.

"Well, actually," Deb said to Jed, "I was thinking of your grandfather."

Jed gave her a puzzled look.

"Your grandfather is a graduate of UMO," Deb said.

"Gramps has a college degree?" said Jed, somewhat amazed.

"Actually, he has two," answered Deb. "He has a degree in agriculture, and one in marine biology."

Jed had had no idea. Knowing this, however, was not enough to overcome the desire now burning within him. Other than Miss Wright, Miss Black was the one who had been the most helpful and supportive in his desire to go to college.

"Thanks for telling me, Deb. I can tell Gramps tonight, but I want to go now and tell Miss Black."

Winnie returned. "They said it was okay."

Deb looked at Jed. "You're right, Jed, go ahead. Drive safe. I'll see you two later."

Deb watched them leave. Her own excitement was tempered by the weight of Crockett's secret. *Don't wait too long to tell him*, she thought.

* * * *

Winnie and Jed planned out their college futures as the miles passed under the car's tires. The day's news filled them with a joy and comfort, which stretched into the future. The trip to Redman Village went quickly despite the fact that Jed was driving slowly. The lights inside the library were in full glow when they pulled into the parking lot.

Irene was at the front desk and saw them as they arrived.

Winnie grinned and said, "Hi, Miss Black, I've got something I want you to see," and handed over her envelope.

Irene opened it and read the letter. She was pleased. "Congratulations, and thank you for sharing this news with me, Winnie. It was very nice of you to come all this way."

Winnie was obviously excited and trying to hold it in when she said, "Thank you, Miss Black."

Irene could tell there was more. Just as a book would offer hints to the mindful reader, people do as well. "Okay, what else is up, you two?" she asked.

Winnie looked at Jed. At this point, she was on her toes bouncing up and down. Without saying a word, Jed pulled out his envelope and handed it to Irene.

Once again, she opened and read a UMO acceptance letter. However, her timid nature failed her this time, and she said enthusiastically, "Jed, I'm so happy for you, and a scholarship as well!"

She came around the desk and gave a big hug first to Winnie and then to Jed. "You two are going to have a wonderful college experience together. Come, let's sit down and talk."

They moved to the nearest table to sit, and Irene continued the conversation.

"You know, there's a writer who's just recently become recognized for his work. Perhaps you've heard of him. His name is Stephen King, and he's a graduate of the University of Maine at Orono."

Winnie and Jed looked at each other with blank expressions, then looked back at Irene.

"No? Well then, have you heard of the movie *Carrie*?"

"Oh, yes, I have," said Winnie.

"Yeah, me too," said Jed. "It's a horror movie about a girl who kills her classmates."

"That's Stephen King's story," said Irene. "He wrote the book. And do you know what the amazing thing is?"

Winnie and Jed were both completely engrossed now, but before Irene could answer, Deb entered the library. Irene looked up upon hearing the door. Jed and Winnie's eyes followed her stare.

"Deb," said Jed, surprised. "What are you doing here?"

As Deb came closer, it was clear that she had been crying. "Jed, it's your grandfather. He's on his way to the hospital."

"What happened?" asked Winnie.

Deb sounded as though she was choking on the painful news she had to deliver. "He's sick, he's been sick for some time now. Please, can you drive us to the hospital?"

Jed was already up and moving. "Come on, let's get going. You can tell me the rest on the way."

The three of them left so quickly, the letters remained on the table. Irene picked them up carefully. Before she put them away, however, she made copies for the letter she would mail tomorrow. For now, it was time to lock up and head home to get her car.

Walking down the sidewalk on this early spring evening, Irene couldn't help but think that as a new patch scratches out a place to grow, an old one must move aside.

CHAPTER 19
Taking the Bad with the Good

Deb, Winnie, and Jed sat in the visitors' area waiting for news.

"Deb," began Jed, "can you tell me what's going on?"

Deb was now in the situation she'd known she would eventually be in; she'd dreaded it ever since Crockett had first told her of his condition. She didn't want to break her promise to him, but it was time Jed knew. She sighed. "Jed, your grandfather hasn't been well for several months now."

This information hit Jed like the wave of a mean tide broadside to a boat. Once it strikes, there's nothing you can do but wait and see whether the boat will right itself or turn over. Jed, however, was stronger than any boat. "What do you mean?" he asked.

Deb gathered herself and said, "It's cancer. He's got cancer, Jed."

If asked, Jed wouldn't be able to explain it, but Deb had said the word he was thinking. He glanced at Winnie, who was pretty much a wreck. She was just sitting there between him and Deb, starring into space. Their words were passing through her without registering.

"How long has he had it?" he asked quietly.

"I don't really know," answered Deb. "He told me last fall, about the time the boat was taken out of the water."

Jed thought back to that time. How he'd thought then that it seemed funny Gramps hadn't said anything in advance about taking the boat out. Then there was Gramps offering to have Winnie make the new bait bags and heads for the traps. Jed thought about all the work he himself had done on the boat instead of Gramps. Gramps had never let anyone touch his boat or traps before then. He should have suspected something before now; he should have known.

"Jed, he made me promise not to tell anyone," said Deb. "Until now, I've kept this God-awful secret."

Jed looked at her. He wasn't mad, or even upset, he was just hurt. Hurt by not having been trusted to know, to maybe not mattering enough to know.

Deb spoke again. "I want you to know, not telling you hurt me as much as my knowing. More, even."

Jed heard her words, but they didn't make it through the fog clouding his mind. He'd already begun to blame himself for not seeing it sooner. Christmas came to mind. Why hadn't he seen it then? It was plain as day now. That's why Gramps had given him the boat and all the traps. That's why they were doing all the work on the boat and gear. Gramps was making sure everything was in tip-top shape before…

"How long?" he asked.

Deb seemed not to hear him.

"How long does he have?" asked Jed again.

She looked at him. "Less than a year was all he told me."

After that, none of them could think of anything to say, so things got quiet. All they could do now was wait to hear something from the doctors. Jed looked up at the clock—7:30 P.M. They had been waiting for almost three hours, and Jed thought that someone should have talked to them by now. Restless, he stood up and walked around. Winnie got up with Jed, matched his stride, and slipped her hand into his. Jed felt her hand in his and understood it was her way of saying, *I'm here for you.* He turned to look at her and managed a smile.

"Why don't you call your parents and have them come and get you?" Jed suggested gently.

"Thanks, Jed. I should call them, but I'm not going anywhere." She squeezed his hand, then headed for the pay phone.

Jed walked back over to Deb, sat down, and put his arm around her. Deb leaned into his embrace. "I'm sorry," she whispered.

Jed tightened his hug. "You don't have to be sorry, Deb. It couldn't have been easy for you, knowing all this time and not being able to say anything."

Deb was comforted by Jed's words. She kept forgetting how mature he was for his age. Instead of sitting here with her, he could have gotten mad and run off to do God-knows-what, but not Jed. He was right where he should be—right where he *needed* to be.

"Any word yet?" said a voice from the doorway.

Jed looked up. He was surprised to see Miss Black coming into the room. "No, nothing yet.... Thanks for coming."

Irene sat down. "There's something I haven't told you, but I'm not sure this is the time or place to do so."

"Well, if it's bad news, I'd just as soon you keep a lid on it," said Jed.

Irene smiled just a bit. "No, it's not that kind of thing. I'm kind of related to Mr. Crockett."

Jed had thought he was done with surprises today. Apparently not. "I'm not sure what you mean," he said.

"It's a little complicated, but let me try and explain," Irene said. "My mother was a second cousin to his wife. So it's only by marriage that there's a connection."

"I'm still confused," said Jed. "Do you know my Gramps?"

"Only through my mother; we've actually never met."

"So did you know me before I came in that first time?"

asked Jed.

Before Irene could answer, the doctor came in.

"Jed Baxter?" he called out.

"I'm Jed."

"Mr. Crockett is resting," stated the doctor. "We've given him something for the pain, and he seems comfortable. As for his long-term prognosis, I'm afraid it's not good."

"How long does he have?" Deb asked.

"It's not the cancer that concerns me," answered the doctor.

"Then what does?" asked Jed.

"His mental state. With treatment and medication, he could have another year, maybe more. But he's refused all treatment to this point."

"Why would someone do that?" asked Deb.

"When people get to his age, sometimes they're ready."

"Ready for what?" asked Jed in frustration.

"To die," answered the doctor.

This Jed understood, and so, it seemed, did the others. Somehow, everything that had taken place over the last several months now made perfect sense. Gramps was getting ready to die. All the work was to get things ready for Jed, not himself.

"Can we see him?" asked Jed.

"If you like. Just so you understand, though, chances are he won't know you're there. Even still, no more than two of you at a time," advised the doctor.

Irene spoke to Winnie. "Why don't I give you a ride back to the library so you can get Deb's truck for her?"

Deb got her keys out and handed them to Winnie and said, "You may as well head home with the truck. There's no sense in all three of us sitting here for who knows how long. Jed and I can ride back together."

Winnie looked at Jed. He had a different idea. "How about you go get the truck, then come back here for Deb, and you two ride back together?" Jed could see that neither of the girls wanted to go. "Deb, I don't think Winnie should have to drive back alone, and you have to get up early. Nothing more can be done right now."

"Jed's right." said Irene. "I'll come back to be with him here. And he's welcome to stay overnight with me if he'd like."

Deb glanced from Jed to Winnie. "What do you say, Winnie?"

Winnie nodded and took the keys from Deb, then turned to Jed. "I'll see you when you come out." With a hug and a kiss from Jed, she and Irene left.

The doctor led Jed and Deb to the ER area where Crockett was being monitored. Redman General was not a large hospital, but it didn't need to be. Fortunately (and unfortunately) it had an outstanding cancer center. Cancer seemed to be a large part of life here.

The doctor opened the door and reminded them not to stay too long. Jed and Deb moved in slowly and the doctor left.

A soft light above the headboard was the only illumination in the room. As Jed looked at the old man in the bed, he saw Gramps in a new way. He'd never seen Gramps lying down, or even with his eyes closed, that he could recall. For the first time, Jed could see how old Gramps was. As he himself had become stronger and more vibrant, Gramps had headed in the opposite direction.

Jed looked around the rest of the room and saw that it was empty. There was no window, just bare walls and a lot of medical equipment. The room felt lifeless. The only indication of any life at all was the monitor sitting below the light, just above Gramps' pillow. A single red beacon of light flashed in rhythmic fashion. A single IV tube was attached to Gramps' arm, that and a wire for the heart monitor.

"He looks so peaceful," Deb commented.

"Yeah, he does. How long do you think he'll have to stay here?"

"I don't know. We'll have to ask the doctor tomorrow."

Tomorrow. This word had a new limiting meaning for Jed. Before now, he'd never considered the idea of there not being a tomorrow. How many more tomorrows would Gramps have? Clearly there were far more yesterdays in Gramps' life than there were tomorrows.

Jed and Deb stood in the room, silent and motionless, until a nurse came along announcing the close of visiting hours. Knowing nothing could be done, they offered no argument and simply left.

Deb slipped her hand into Jed's and leaned into him on the way back to the visitors' room. Jed gave no sign of retreat from her weight against him. Instead, his hand enclosed hers with more strength than she'd expected. She felt Zach's presence reach out to her again from within. And over the last several years, Jed had become much like his grandfather. Strong in body, mind, and spirit. Deb knew she could not love Jed more had she given birth to him herself. As they walked, she grew stronger through his example.

When they reached the waiting room, Winnie was there.

"Miss Black went to the store. She'll be right along," said Winnie. "How did it go?"

"He's asleep like the doctor said," answered Jed.

"Well, we'd better get going," said Deb. She knew Jed didn't need them in the same way they needed him, or each other.

"Jed, do you want us to wait until Miss Black comes back?" asked Winnie.

"No thanks, Winnie. It's getting late. You two should get going."

After another round of hugs and kisses, the women left.

Jed looked for a comfortable spot to sit and wait for Miss Black. He settled into a corner that provided a full view of the room. It occurred to him how quiet it was. On the way in, he'd read the sign over the door: "Main Entrance / Emergency

Entrance." He had thought it would be busier. A few minutes passed and Jed heard the automatic glass door slide open. He looked up expecting to see Miss Black, but it was a man. His face was turned away from Jed, but there was something familiar about him. The man moved with an efficiency that only comes with practice and knowledge of one's terrain. Watching him reminded Jed of the lessons Gramps had given him on the water. How to see the water move in a channel with the tide. How its color changes value and becomes darker when rocks are under the surface. "You have to be looking to see, Jed," Gramps would say. "Not just with your eyes, but with your mind as well. The eyes see everything; it's the mind you have to train. When you look at water, if you're not looking with your mind, all you'll see is what you think water should look like, instead of what is real and right under your nose."

Jed's thoughts were interrupted when he heard his name.

"Jed? Jed, is that you?"

Jed looked up to see Bradley standing there.

"I thought I recognized your car out in the parking lot," said Bradley. "What brings you here?"

Seeing Bradley brought back Christmas night and Gramps reaction to Bradley's image in the home movie. Jed didn't want to be rude, but he didn't want to disrespect Gramps, either. "My Gramps is sick," he heard himself answer. "What about you?"

Bradley held up his left hand. It was poorly wrapped with a clean rag. He heard Bradley chuckle. "You'd think after all this time, I'd know better than to stick my hand into a running engine, or at least get better at putting bandages on my own injuries."

"Is it serious?" asked Jed.

"No, occupational hazard is what the doc always says. How about your grandfather?"

Jed didn't really want to give too much information. "I'm not real clear on things yet," he managed to say, feeling this was more truth than lie. But he was getting pretty uncomfortable. Fortunately, Miss Black chose that moment to show up. Jed excused himself and walked over to meet her.

"Any news?" she asked.

"No, I haven't seen the doctor again. I doubt I'll know anything more till tomorrow. May as well head out," he said.

As they turned to leave, Bradley called out, "Hope everything's okay with old man Crockett."

Something about Bradley's tone set Jed off. He turned and stepped toward Bradley with determination. He didn't stop until he was nose to nose with Bradley. "What's that supposed to mean, calling my Gramps an old man?"

Bradley smiled. "Easy, boy. I never had any trouble whopping your dad's ass. I'm sure I wouldn't have any trouble taking care of you with just one good hand."

The nurse on duty came out from behind her glass enclosure with a needle in each hand. "All right, boys, that's enough. I can take you both out with these needles. Bradley, you march yourself right over there and sit down. And you, young man, I believe you were leaving."

"Yes, ma'am," said Bradley. He grinned at Jed. "You were saved by the dingbat, boy."

"Bradley!" said the nurse.

"Oh, I'm just having a little fun," he answered.

Jed didn't say a word. He turned and stalked out the door, followed closely by a dumbfounded Miss Black.

Bradley watched them leave, then started hounding the nurse for information. It wasn't long before he found out what he wanted to know.

* * * *

As the girls started down the road, Deb came to: this was the first time since Christmas that she and Winnie had been alone together. Although the circumstances were not ideal, it was an opportunity to get better acquainted.

"I'm sorry you got caught up in all this," said Deb.

Winnie looked her way. "I'm not," she said. "I want to be here. Wait; that didn't come out right. I didn't mean…"

"I know what you mean," said Deb, interrupting her. "I'm sure Jed's glad you're here. I know I am." Deb felt like it would be okay to dig deeper. "Things seem to be getting more serious between you two lately."

Winnie lowered her chin for a second, then raised it smiling. "For him, it's lately. I've been serious for a long time."

"I know you have," answered Deb. "It takes boys longer to recognize things like this. I guess it's because they're taught to hide any feelings they have. Except for anger, of course. Not that Jed's been angry all that often."

Winnie looked thoughtful for a moment, then nodded in agreement.

"I'm afraid he's going to take Grampy's passing hard. They've gotten quite close since the day of the puffin," said Deb.

Winnie was reminded of Jed's story, of how Jed and Crockett had found each other. How he'd been left at Deb's by his mother, and how the two of them had met on the breakwater. Every time Jed needed someone, somehow, in an odd way, a stranger was there for him. Jed's life, it seemed, was full of scratches and patches.

CHAPTER 20
And Now...

Much to his surprise, Jed actually got a decent night's sleep at Miss Black's house. This was the first night he'd spent away from New Ireland, and one of the few sleeping somewhere besides his little room at Deb's, since being left there by his mother. When he was younger, and with his mother, it had seemed at times, like they slept in a different bed every night.

The little alarm clock on the bed stand read 4 A.M. Jed thought about getting up, but felt it might be too early. He lay there thinking about everything, and nothing at all. His thoughts were interrupted by the smell of coffee making its presence known. Jed took the hint. Throwing his clothes on, he followed the scent.

The dawn light showed him the way through the maze-like hall and elongated rooms of the Victorian home. Miss Black had propped the swinging door to the kitchen open. Jed could see her moving around with rhythmic movements. He stopped short of the door to watch for a minute. It reminded him of how he watched Deb like this sometimes. It always amazed him to see how well a woman could make her way around a kitchen. Miss Black went about her work without thinking. She reached for things without looking, already knowing they were there. The moment she spotted Jed, she stopped.

"Good morning, Jed," she said. "Did you sleep well?"

"Morning, Miss Black. Yeah, I guess I did."

"I think we're past the formalities at this point. Please, call me Irene," she said with a smile. "We can't get into the hospital until seven, so I thought we'd have something to eat and you can take a shower if you like. Have a seat, breakfast is almost ready."

Irene made small talk hoping to keep Jed's mind off his grandfather for a while. She knew the outcome would more than likely be grim and wanted to keep it at bay for as long as possible. As they finished up, Irene reached for the bag she always used to carry things back and forth from home to the library and pulled out a book. Handing it to Jed, she said, "I took the liberty of signing this book out for you. It's the first in a series written by the same author, and I thought you might relate to his writing."

Jed took the book, looked at the cover, read the jacket flaps, and flipped through the pages. "So if I understand it right, this is a story about a young man who leaves his small town to travel the world," he said. "I think I saw a new book by this writer at a bookstore in Augusta a couple of weeks ago."

"You might have. There are several more novels in the series. If you like this one, I do have more of them at the library."

"Thanks, I'll give it a try," said Jed. "Thanks for the breakfast, too….if you don't mind, I'd like to take that shower now."

He took a long hot shower. Having not been inside many houses, he found himself looking at every aspect and detail and comparing them to Deb's house or Gramps. Both of those had been built with needs in mind rather than any wants. This bathroom was bigger than his room at Deb's. The walls were papered with a river scene, instead of just being whitewashed. The fixtures in the tub matched those on the sink, there was a cover over the shower curtain, and the toilet seat cover had a rug on it that matched those at the base of the toilet and in front of the tub.

He'd found out during breakfast that Irene had been born in this house and had never lived anywhere else. Jed couldn't imagine what it must feel like to have spent your whole life in one *town*, let alone in the same house. Despite this fact, he could see that Irene and he had two things in common. They both felt alone much of the time, and both longed for the past. For Jed, it was so that he could somehow, some way fix his life, while for Irene, it was to relive it. She was totally alone now that her mother was gone—no parents, siblings, or relatives of any kind. It was from this void that the two of them connected.

Deb was up at her usual time. After giving some thought to the day, she decided not to open, feeling it was more important to head back into Redman Village and be with Jed and Crockett. She placed a simple sign on the door: CLOSED DUE TO FAMILY ILLNESS. Not that anyone would be surprised at her being closed, or need to be told why. The Open/Closed sign was still swinging on its thin chain inside the door as Deb climbed into her truck.

Despite the early hour, the town was filled with life. Fishermen on their way to the shore, other shop owners getting ready to open. Life in New Ireland had little to do with daylight. There was always plenty of work and little time for sleep. As Deb passed the edge of town, she sped up. Leaving Jed in Redman Village last night had created an uneasy feeling within her, stirring a sense of urgency about getting back to him.

However, her truck had a mind of its own. The temperature had dropped to an unseasonable low overnight, creating a layer of frost on the windshield, and the truck was taking its sweet time removing it. *I should have started the truck ahead of time*, Deb thought. The frost-covered windshield made her think about how unclear the future was in Jed's world right now. She wished it could be as simple as turning on a little heat to clear things up for him.

Jed had decided to head out despite Irene's warning that he would not be able to see his grandfather until visiting hours started. As he walked through the doors to the hospital, he was reminded of his encounter with Bradley the night before. Why had he lost his temper so easily? It wasn't like him to do so, and what did he really care what Bradley thought, anyway?

Jed stopped at the nurses' station. He didn't see anyone at first, then a nurse came through the hallway door behind him. She walked past him and into the nurses' station as if he wasn't even there. As Jed looked the room over, he saw there was no one else around.

"Visiting hours do not begin until seven, young man. You can have a seat and wait if you'd like," the nurse said.

"Yes, ma'am, I know," said Jed. "Would you be able to tell me how my grandfather is doing?"

"Does your grandfather have a name?"

Jed felt a little silly. He'd forgotten he wasn't in New Ireland where everybody knew him and his grandfather. "Sorry about that, ma'am. His name is Crockett."

The nurse looked up at Jed. She came around to face him. "I'm sorry to tell you this, but your grandfather passed away just before four A.M. this morning."

Jed was speechless. The doctor's words from last night came back to him. Had Gramps given up? For the first time in his life, had Crockett actually given up? The very thought of this upset Jed. He just couldn't believe his grandfather would give up on anything, let alone life. Life for Jed was still new. It would be many years before he'd understand the kind of love that connected a man and a woman through and past death... how the desire to be with your love, your life partner again, can be stronger than life itself when one's time is short.

Not too long ago, he would have taken Gramps leaving personally, thinking that, like his mother, Gramps had left him behind by choice—because someone else was more important than him. But not now. Now he knew differently. His love for Winnie had shown him that there were different kinds of love. No one kind of love was more important than the other; they were just different.

Jed didn't see Deb come in. One look at him told her what she needed to know. She walked straight to him, stepping between him and the nurse. The nurse slipped away while Deb locked eyes with Jed. Taking his hand, she led him to the seats. They sat quietly for a few minutes. Irene arrived shortly thereafter.

"Jed, did you get to see him?" asked Deb.

He looked her way. "No. I didn't get to tell him about college, or even say goodbye. Now he's gone....I can't believe he's gone."

The three of them sat there consoling each other for some time before the nurse returned.

"Excuse me," said the nurse. "I know it's a difficult time, but we need the next of kin to do some paperwork."

Jed stood up, "That's me."

"Follow me, please," said the nurse.

Irene watched as Jed and the nurse walked away. Something didn't add up to her.

"Debbie, I'm confused about something."

"About what?"

"Where are Jed's parents, siblings?" she asked.

"Crockett is the only family Jed has other than his mother. And she made her choice years ago," answered Deb.

"Do you mean to say he really is abandoned?"

"Yes, his father and I were...close some years back. I guess his mother thought if she left him with me, I'd make sure Jed reunited with his father."

"Why didn't you?" asked Irene.

"He's been gone for years. In fact, he has no idea Jed even exists."

Irene had one more question to ask, but before she could, Jed and the nurse returned. Neither looked happy.

"Is there another next of kin?" the nurse asked.

"Is there a problem?" Deb said.

"You must be of age to claim a body. This young man is not. Or rather, he can't prove that he is."

"I'm sorry, there isn't. What happens now?"

"The deceased becomes a ward of the state. You will need to contact an attorney. I'm sorry, it's the law." With that, the nurse returned to her duties.

Jed was still in shock, so the coldness of the nurse didn't register. He was trying to stay focused on the job at hand, as Gramps would have wanted him to.

"Deb, do you know an attorney?" Jed asked.

"Your grandfather had contacted one a short while ago. I have his name. He has an office here in Redman Village. Why don't we see if he's in. Maybe he and Gramps prepared for this."

"I need to get over to the library and open up," said Irene. "I'll catch up with you later. And I'm very sorry about your grandfather."

"Thanks for putting me up last night, and for breakfast," said Jed.

"It was my pleasure. You're welcome anytime," answered Irene.

Jed and Deb took the truck to the lawyer's. They pulled out of the parking lot and headed downtown. They didn't notice Bradley parked across the street, waiting for them to leave. As soon as they were out of sight, he drove over to the hospital. He calmly walked up to the nurses' station and asked to see

Mr. Crockett. The news was exactly what he was expecting to hear, and he knew just what to do with this little patch of information. It had been a long time coming, but finally, he had his chance to scratch an old itch.

CHAPTER 21
Crockett's Launching

It was still early in the morning when Deb and Jed made their way onto Main Street. Compared to New Ireland, Redman Village took a little longer to wake up.

"What's the name we're looking for?" Jed asked.

"Ashley Walters, Attorney at Law," answered Deb.

They rode up and down Main Street three times before they spotted the name on a recessed wooden door set between two granite posts. Deb parked the truck and they walked to the door, half expecting it to be locked, but it wasn't. The stairs were wide and steep. A single bulb at the top of the stairs provided the only light. At the top right, was a door with Ashley Walters' name on it. Deb turned the handle and pushed the door in. The room was nearly all covered in mahogany, from the wall panels, to the trim, to the fireplace mantel. Even the floor was made of mahogany parquet squares. This place was all business and very intimidating. As Jed and Deb were trying to take it all in, a well-dressed woman sitting at a desk spoke.

"May I help you?" she asked.

Deb opened her mouth to speak, but Jed beat her to it. "We're here to see Mr. Walters."

"And what is the nature of your business?" the woman asked.

"We're here on behalf of his client, Jedediah Crockett," answered Jed.

Deb was surprised by Jed's manner. He seemed very comfortable. His speech was clear, with a strong tone. Just like his grandfather. A sense of pride welled up within her.

"Is there a reason Mr. Crockett is not here on his own behalf?" was the woman's next question.

"Yes, he passed away this morning," Jed said.

"I see," said the woman. "What is your relationship to Mr. Crockett?"

"I'm his grandson."

"Have a seat, please. I'll let Mr. Walters know you're here."

Deb and Jed moved toward the chairs that were placed around an oval table. The chairs were also mahogany, and the cushions were covered in deep brown leather. Deb had made deliveries to Mr. Walters' office in New Ireland. That office was a very unassuming place, and couldn't have been any further away in decor from where she sat now. She couldn't imagine what kind of money it took to acquire a place like this, let alone maintain it. Having her own place, Deb knew the costs of a simple business owner. Then a thought entered her mind. *How did Mr. Crockett know this man? Where had they met?* Before an answer could be formed, the woman returned.

"Mr. Walters will see you now," she said, her arm extended toward a doorway with no door.

Once they had entered, the woman reached for a latch hidden in the door casing and slid the pocket door closed behind them. This room was smaller and much simpler in style. Deb and Jed looked at each other and relaxed a little, feeling more comfortable in these surroundings.

Behind an unassuming small oak desk was an even smaller man. Even though he was sitting, Deb could tell he was no more than five feet tall.

The man looked up at the two of them. Immediately, he put down his pen, took off his glasses, stood, and came around the desk to greet them.

"Welcome to my office. Though I'm sorry we must meet under such dismal circumstances," he said as he moved toward them with his hand extended.

Deb's assessment had been correct: the man was short. Although advanced in years, he was in excellent shape. He offered a firm handshake and stood with shoulders back, chest out, and not a hint of a potbelly. His three-piece gray pinstriped suit fit him just as the tailor had obviously intended.

Mr. Walters motioned to a seating area. "Come have a seat over here. I hope my reception area wasn't too overwhelming for you. You see, I serve a number of clients, some of whom judge a man by such trivial things as the façade you saw out there. It also helps to keep the undesirable clients away. Over the years, I found my greatest pleasure in representing people like Mr. Crockett." There was a pause before he continued. "I'm sorry to hear of his passing. You said it happened early this morning?"

"Yes, sir," Jed answered. "At about four o'clock. He had cancer."

Walters looked directly at Jed. "Yes, I know he did. So you're Jed. I've heard quite a bit about you lately. Your grandfather thinks—or thought, as the case is now—very highly of you."

At a different time, this comment might have pleased Jed, but not today. Today he was somewhere between shock and mourning. "Do you mind my asking, sir, how did you come to know my grandfather?"

"Not at all, we went to college together at UMO. We were roommates for four years there, before I went on to Harvard Law School. In fact, I'm your father's Godfather."

Jed perked up a bit. "You know my father?"

"Not really," answered Walters. "I've met him a few times, but that was before he was even your age now."

"Do you know where he is?" Jed heard himself asking. Grasping for something positive to balance against his grief.

The lawyer looked hard into Jed's eyes. "No, Jed, I don't. But I've spent a good deal of my free time looking for him over the last seventeen years at your grandfather's request. Despite my efforts, I've yet to come up with any information. But that's not why you're here today, is it?" he said, shifting the conversation back to the needs of the present.

Jed felt the desire to drop his head in disappointment, but he wouldn't give in to it. "No, sir, it's not. The hospital says I can't claim my Gramps because I can't prove my age. Can you help?"

"Yes, I can. Your grandfather took care of everything. I have the papers all ready for the hospital." He opened a large folder that was sitting on the table and handed Jed a smaller one. "You'll find all you need in there."

Jed couldn't help noticing the size of the bigger folder, but his upbringing prevented him from inquiring. As if reading his mind, Walters smiled and said, "The answer to your question is yes."

"What question?" asked Jed.

"This entire folder is about your grandfather. He's quite wealthy. The property in New Ireland is just one of several he owns. There are also stocks, bonds, and other assets as well. The bottom line here is that financially you have nothing to worry about, ever. But that's not what's important at the moment. We need to take care of your grandfather's service first."

Walters reached back into the thick folder and pulled out a second folder. "Your grandfather left very specific directions as to how and where it was to take place. Here's a copy for you."

Jed took the folder, but didn't look at it. "So, after the... service, then what?" he asked.

"We'll get together in my New Ireland office sometime next week and start the process. Because you're a minor, there is a legal process, which will take time. Given the preparations made by your grandfather, I don't anticipate any problems."

"Jed, I mentioned earlier that your grandfather had a

great deal of respect for you. I meant that sincerely. Losing his son and his wife had taken quite a bit out of him. Our talks took on a very somber tone for many years after. All he wanted to talk about was the past. When you came along, he perked up again. It was like we were back in college. Everything was about you and the future. Even when he was here planning for the inevitability of this day, there was nothing sad about it."

"I'm not sure how much you know about your grandmother, but she was quite a woman. If your grandfather hadn't seen her first...well, that's water under the bridge, as they say."

"I don't know anything about my grandmother," said Jed with interest.

Walters took a deep breath. His eyes looked through Jed and into the past. "Ellen was one in a million. Your grandfather had an unlimited future. He could have gone anywhere and done anything he wanted. He chose love."

"The night he told me he was marrying Ellen and moving to New Ireland, I kept him up all night talking about it. Not because I wanted to talk him out of it, I just wanted him to be sure he understood what he was giving up. He never wavered."

"A few years later, he started talking with the local accent. When I asked him about it, he said it was necessary to adapt to the local culture for Ellen's sake. Because of his background and education, the townspeople were shunning them, even though they'd known Ellen all of their lives. So he started talking with an accent and talking to people the way they had become accustomed to. After that, things got better. Still, I can only imagine what your grandfather *might* have done with his life."

"Whatever pain life may have provided him was more than balanced with pleasure. Having you around these last years was, I think, his greatest pleasure. I'd never seen him happier in his life than the time he had with you. It was my honor to be his friend, Jed. I'll do everything I can to help you through this and into the future."

* * * *

Five days of the paper calendar had hit the floor since Crockett's passing. It took Jed this long to make all the arrangements, the biggest of which was to get the boat back in the water. Winnie stood by Jed, tolerant of his painful silence, watching as he stared into the bottomless pit of depression, struggling against the desire to leap headfirst into the abyss. She had seen this side of Jed's personality before. This was different, though. Before, it was his mother's absence he fought with. The why of it; the endless not knowing whether she would ever return. Crockett's passing had created a new void in his life, one that others would be happy to fill if Jed would but open the lid just a crack. Jed, however, was like the granite that made up the shoreline of New Ireland. He never gave way. Instead, he stood fast, cold and emotionless against the abuse of man and nature. All Winnie could do was play the part of a passive lighthouse, offering a light in the darkness, a beacon in the fog.

Today, however, was an overcast but calm day. Crockett had stated that he didn't want a church service or a gravesite. A simple service was performed at the blueberry field on the backside of the house. The wind was off the water. As Jed let some of the ashes trickle out of the urn, they were carried across the plants below the crest of the hill. From here the procession headed to the harbor. Every boat was there ready to carry any and all mourners who wished to go. They left the dock with Jed's boat in the lead, while the others fell in behind just as ducks do. On Jed's boat were Deb, Winnie, Mr. Walters, Miss Black, and Miss Wright. Not that Jed really noticed their presence. He was focused on his duties, moving with a sense of purpose through the details left in his grandfather's will. Driven by the love and respect he felt. There'd be no tears from his eyes to stain the boat's deck. Crying simply wasn't his way.

At the end of the channel where the water opened to the ocean, and with Rock Island in sight, Jed slowed the boat, turned toward the others, then cut the engine. Above, the sky was cloud-filled, but offered no threat of rain. The water had a green tint to it, much like a fish tank in need of cleaning. The lobster buoys took on a gray-scale hue under the overcast sky, their colors appearing faded from the lack of light. The license numbers embedded in the buoys brought a finality to their gravestone look for the impending ceremony. All the boats cut their engines when they saw Jed turn. The only sound was the waves lapping against the sides of the boats as if Crockett's mistress of the sea was impatient to welcome her long-awaited lover. Finally, the man known as Jedediah Rumford Crockett would be hers, ever more.

Jed walked to the stern of the boat with the urn in hand. He took the top off and spoke in a strong voice. "Gramps spent part of his life in the blueberry fields, and the rest out here on the water. It was his wish that his ashes be spread over both. He didn't want to be trapped in a box deep in the ground. He wanted to be free to roam over all that which he loved and held dear. In the future, when you look at his blueberry field, or out onto this harbor, remember him as a man who took nothing from anyone, and gave far more than he ever asked for."

Jed bent over the stern and slowly tipped the urn. As the gray ash hit the water, it disappeared. The only disturbance occurred when a small chunk of bone parted the water with a *ka-plunk*. A sound which would ordinarily go unnoticed could be heard in this moment by the occupants of the furthest boat. What took only seconds felt like hours to Jed. His fingers ached from fear of dropping the urn. His back strained from the weight of the responsibility, and his head pounded as blood rushed violently toward it, emptying his heart. With the urn finally empty, Jed stood up and turned to face the bow of the boat.

Suddenly, something strange and wonderful took place.

Two puffins landed on the roof of the wheelhouse, side-by-side, and stared at Jed. Granted, puffins land on lobster boats all the time when they're around, but it was a good three months early for the flock to arrive. Even then, you never saw a pair off the island together. Somehow, Jed knew that one of the puffins was the very same he'd saved that day. The one Gramps had said was his Ellen. The second one gave Jed a look which told him who it was. It was his grandfather. Jed could no longer hold back his grief. A smile crossed his face like a sunrise, while his boisterous laughter filled the harbor like a morning fog. Gramps was where he belonged—with his Ellen once again. His ashes may have been claimed by the sea, but not his heart, nor his love.

Jed made his way to the wheelhouse while the others looked on with shock—not because of the unexpected puffins, but because of Jed's laughter. Their reaction didn't bother Jed, though. Still grinning, he fired up the engine and headed back toward the docks. The two puffins rode the boat nearly all the way in before flying off. As Jed watched them fly away, an idea came to him. This was his boat now, and it should have his name on it. *From now on,* he thought to himself, *this boat will be known as* Two Puffins.

As the other boats made their way in, the water in the harbor took on the look of a quilt made of patches where the wakes of the boats met and were redirected. The clouds parted and color began to reflect off the water. Although the effect of the clearing sky only scratched the water's surface, the result could be seen all the way to the horizon.

CHAPTER 22
The Business of Death

Back at Deb's Bakery, where a celebration of Crockett's life was being held, Ashley Walters looked around the room. *This is why I keep an office in New Ireland*, he thought. Here, right now, everyone in town was remembering Crockett. Some liked him, others not so much, while others couldn't stand the man. Still, all of them respected the man for who he was and what he had meant to the town.

Ashley knew that in a town this small, each person had a role, a part in its culture, and when a person died, a piece of the town was lost with them. No one could take the place of the person who had passed. Even if they wanted to, they couldn't. Because it wasn't just the person who died that was missing. It was the person they'd become, as well as the child they had once been. It was the history, the years they'd spent living in the town. When it came their time to leave, life moved on, taking away the thoughts and feelings others had had about them. Oh sure, there would be stories told and times remembered, but this would change, too—because history is recorded by how and why a person is remembered, rather than by who they might truly have been, or what might really have happened. That's the way it's always been, and always will be.

A feeling came over Ashley and he began to consider what he himself brought to the town, what his role was. Was he just a lawyer to these people, or was he one of them in his own unique way? The answer came to him before the question finished forming in his mind. It wasn't for him to ask or answer; it was up to them and what they thought. It only mattered if they decided he'd been important to them. Ashley chuckled to himself, then made his way discreetly around the crowded room.

He was there for both personal and professional reasons. As there was no point in putting things off, he quietly made an appointment in his New Ireland office the next day with all parties of interest, for the reading of Crockett's will. Once this was accomplished, he left. For all the things he didn't know, there was one thing he did know: he was an outsider here, and he always would be. He understood that if you hadn't been born here, you weren't *from* here, and you never would be. A fact he and Crockett had discussed many times in the past, as neither were from here.

* * * *

Jed read the sign on the door: "Ashley Walters, Attorney at Law." Deb and Winnie stood on either side of him, waiting for him to enter. The simple act of opening the door was harder than Jed had thought it would be. The idea of turning the doorknob captivated him. Gramps was gone, this he knew. So why did it feel like he should stop trying to bail out a boat sitting at the bottom of the Atlantic? Yes, he knew why. Because doing so was acceptance of the truth, of his reality. What if the woulda, coulda, shoulda's started to creep into his mind? Did he really have to go in? His grandfather wasn't in there. So why go in at all?

Despite these thoughts, Jed knew he had to see the attorney. Somewhere deep inside him was the understanding that opening this door somehow made Gramps death final. Jed took a deep breath and reached out. As he did, Deb placed her hand on top of his. She'd sensed his troubled mind as any mother would. Together they squeezed the knob, turned it, and pushed open the door.

Inside, they were met by the same woman from the office in Redman. The room was clean and bright, but had a much more relaxed feeling. Instead of a mahogany theme, it was weathered gray wood and nautical fixtures. What caught Jed's eye were all the paintings of lobster boats. Upon taking a closer look, he realized they were the boats of New Ireland. He was searching for Gramps' boat when a voice broke through his daze.

"'Bout time you showed up."

Jed turned toward the sound. Sitting against the opposite wall was the town manager and a man named Albert Eaton, who ran the lobster co-op, and between them sat Irene Black. Jed wasn't sure which of them he was more surprised to see.

"Hi," said Jed. "I didn't know anyone was waiting."

"Don't let them ruffle you, Jed, they haven't been here that long," Irene said.

Before anyone else could speak, Walters stepped out from a room in the back.

"Good, good, everyone's here," he said without addressing anyone in particular. "We can get started. Would you all please step into the conference room....Jed, I need you to go first."

Jed stepped forward with Deb and Winnie in tow. The others stood up and followed. As Jed stepped into the room, he saw what he'd been looking for out in the waiting area. There on the back wall was a large painting of Gramps' boat. It was in a blue frame with a line of gold in the center, and a light accented it from above. As Jed looked at the painting, he could feel the salt water on his face, and smell Gramps' scent in his nostrils. A tightness gripped his chest, his eyes began to burn. Just when he thought his emotions were going to get the best of him, Winnie took his hand into hers. Instantly, Jed felt his muscles relax and the tears dry up. He felt Winnie's gaze on him, but couldn't look her way. If he looked at her, the sense of calm her hand offered would be lost in the seduction of her eyes. For the first time, Jed felt he had some sense of what Gramps must have felt for his wife. That power of having someone in your life more important than yourself was a difficult emotion to control, and Jed didn't like not being in control.

"That's my favorite one," Walters said. "I've done better paintings, but that was my first real attempt at watercolor. When I presented it to your grandfather, he told me he had the real thing to look at every day, so I should keep it. That gave me the idea to paint all of the boats in the harbor. I've spent more than a few years doing just that....ah, but I digress."

"Let me begin by thanking each of you for taking the time to come in today. Rather than keep everyone here for the entire reading of the will, I think it would be best if we take care of the non-family items first so that you can be dismissed. If there are no objections, we'll begin."

Walters sat down at the table, picked up a stack of papers, and started to read.

"I hereby bequeath my two-acre waterfront lot to the town of New Ireland, along with funds to establish a public park, boat ramp, and dock so that all may have access to the harbor. As for my shares in the Lobstermen's Co-op, I hereby bequeath them to the Co-op so that they may be used to raise funds for research and development, thereby ensuring a future for the generations of lobstermen still to come. I hereby bequeath the sum of twenty-five thousand dollars to the Redman Library for the building of a new wing dedicated solely to writers with origins in Maine."

The lawyer set the will down and said, "This concludes the non-family portion of the will. I ask that these parties please depart at this time. I will be in contact with you within the next few days to complete the transfers of these gifts. Again, I would like to thank you for your time."

Given the reputation Gramps had, Jed knew that many of the townspeople would be surprised when the news of these gifts got out. With the exception of Miss Black, the people in the room however, had known Crockett well and were not surprised in the least. The town manager and Albert Eaton shook hands with Walters and Jed as they left. It was clear from their faces that the gifts were greatly appreciated and would be treated with the respect and honor they deserved. Irene Black asked Jed if it would be okay for her to stay. Jed sensed that this was important and told her she was welcome.

Walters opened a file cabinet and pulled out a folder that was several inches thick, then began again. "The rest of the estate, with one exception, is of course left to you, Jed. As I mentioned the other day, the overall estate is considerably more substantial than you know. Your grandfather made investments in real estate and the stock market over the years, and did quite well for himself. In fact, there's enough money for several lifetimes here in New Ireland."

He then turned to Winnie. "The exception I mention is for you, Miss Hastings. Mr. Crockett thought a great deal of you. He was also aware of your interest in becoming a veterinarian."

Winnie was in complete shock. She had not given any thought to the possibility that she might be mentioned in these proceedings. When Mr. Walters had asked her to be here, she'd assumed it was to support Jed. Her love for Jed's grandfather rushed over her like a fog moving into the harbor on the coming tide.

Walters pulled a file from the folder. "There are two things for you. The first is a college fund, but before you get too excited, it's a reimbursement fund. You get the money at the end of each school year for classes you pass with a grade of B or higher, but you'll have to find the money to get started on your own."

"The second item also has a condition. Assuming you become a licensed veterinarian, you have a place to set up your practice." He pulled out a photo and a deed to show her.

"Mr. Crockett is the owner of this abandoned building on Main Street, and someday, with a lot of studying and hard work, it can be yours."

Winnie's cheeks glistened, wet with tears she didn't know were there. Out of this loss had come a gain she could not have imagined. Her joy was stifled only by the hint of guilt it carried in balance. She wanted to speak, but words could not find a path through the fog.

Walters continued. "Deb, you've received your inheritance already, but I felt it should be a part of these proceedings for the record. Jed, Deb has been deeded the land with the raspberry patch and the old blueberry field, which consist of ten acres more or less. It was Crockett's wish that she have this land as a way to show his gratitude for all she's done for you."

Then he handed the rest of the folder to Jed. "This is a copy of everything for you to look over when you're ready. There is one legal matter we need to go over now however. There is a question as to your age. I've been doing some research to see if I could come up with a birth certificate. At this point I've not been able to. If you're not of legal age, that being eighteen years or older, then here in the state of Maine, you cannot take possession of an estate. The estate will have to be left open until such a time as we can establish your age. We will also have to place a public notice for sixty days to be sure there are no other heirs. While that's going on, I'd like to recommend that we take measures to have Deb become your legal guardian. Given the history and facts of the case, it shouldn't take more than thirty days for the state to grant the approval. Once your age can be established, we can begin transferring the assets into your name."

"Does anyone have any questions?" Ashley knew there should be questions, and that there would be in time, but hearing none now, he shook everyone's hand, then walked them out. Irene had asked to use the bathroom and remained behind after the other three left. When she came out, there was a short meeting between her and the attorney.

No words passed between Deb, Winnie, and Jed as they walked back to the bakery. Deb wondered how Jed really felt about her becoming his legal guardian, but wanted to give him some time. She also wondered about Winnie, and how she was doing accepting her new-found wealth. It had to be a shock to have your dream become an attainable reality in such an unexpected way.

When they reached the bakery, Deb spoke. "You two coming in?"

Jed looked at Winnie. "I was thinking of walking the breakwater. You want to come along?" he asked.

Winnie's smile was answer enough, and the two of them headed for the place where they'd met. The one place they always seemed to end up when life asked more of them than they were ready to give or receive. It was their patch of comfort where they could scratch privately, without being watched or judged.

CHAPTER 23
The Old Becomes New

Jed and Winnie sat in their booth at Deb's. More than thirty days had passed since the reading of the will and there had been no news from Ashley Walters' office.

"Do you think you'll hear from the state today?" asked Winnie.

"I don't know, I hope so," said Jed.

The bakery hummed with activity, but the two of them were in their own world as usual. Even the townspeople had begun to see them as a couple—not to mention seeing Jed as a man. The fishermen talked to him as one of them instead of just some kid. Jed's words were heard and welcomed. It was as if they were looking to him as the one to fill his grandfather's place both in town and on the water. This change in the way Jed was viewed had not however been missed by Winnie. She took her supporting role seriously and did what she could to help Jed keep from being overwhelmed. That was one of the advantages of living in a small town with a working harbor; you grew up fast. Fast and sometimes hard.

Deb secretly swelled with pride when she heard the way the men were talking about Jed in the bakery. It made her realize how difficult and complex life had become for Jed. In many ways, he'd become a man, and yet he couldn't prove how old he was. The changes in Jed's life had also impacted Deb's.

Jed no longer had time to pitch in at the bakery, so Deb had hired some help. She was always rooting for the underdogs in life, and even in a small town like New Ireland, it didn't take her long to find a new one.

His name was Richard Rank. He was tall, skinny, and really smart. A lot of the kids didn't give him the time of day because things didn't seem to ever go quite right for him, and he was constantly asking questions. That was the one big difference between him and Jed. For every word Jed had never uttered, Richard had said ten. Even though it had only been a couple of weeks since Richard had started, Deb kept reminding herself a change wasn't ever all good or all bad. But as these things seem to go, Deb was about to eat her words, or at least chew them for a while.

Deb looked up to see Ashley Walters walking in. He had a different look about him. Somehow he looked…less businesslike. He was in a suit as usual, but his face seemed to lack the intensity Deb had come to expect from their past encounters. She made her way toward him.

"Hi, Mr. Walters," she said.

"Good day, Deb. I have some news for you and Jed," the lawyer said, pulling a letter from the inside pocket of his suit.

"Well, Jed's sitting right over there," she answered.

She instinctively grabbed a coffeepot so she could fill cups on the way. So instinctive was this action, Deb didn't even ask whether a mug needed to be filled. She just filled the ones that needed filling, and left the others as they were. If she was in doubt, a quick glance at the person's face was all that was needed.

Jed had also seen Walters come in. Gramps had taught him to sit facing the door. His grandfather's words rang in his head: "Always try and be mindful of what's going on around you, and face the world head-on."

Jed motioned Walters to come have a seat, and Deb stood

at the end of the table. She rarely sat down while the bakery was open. Jed had asked her about it once and Deb had said she didn't want to set a bad example. It was a while before he'd understood what she'd meant. Everyone in town worked hard, and they came to Deb's because she did the same. Jed had thought how funny it was that the one thing which helped her business might have hurt her personal life.

"We received the approval of your guardianship from the state, which is good because I've still not found anything to provide proof of age," Walters said.

"So what does this do, or change?" asked Jed.

"Well, not a great deal, really, I'm afraid. It more or less gives legality to what's been in place for a number of years. The estate will still need to remain in escrow for now."

"So, what—?" Deb said.

The bells on the bakery door rang out and interrupted. A coldness entered the building. The hustle and bustle of the crowd stopped. Dead silence filled the void. The next sound cut through the air like lightning splitting a tree.

"There's my boy, right where I left him!" said a woman's voice.

Deb dropped the coffeepot. It was the first time in twenty-plus years that she'd done so. It hit the floor with a crash, but no one noticed. They were all mesmerized by the person who'd just entered. Jed turned toward the voice in disbelief.

"Mom, is it really you?" he heard himself say.

"Of course it's me. I told you I'd be back, didn't I? Well, here I am! Come here and give your mother a hug."

Winnie watched as Jed stood up and hugged this strange woman. *Could it be? Is this really Jed's mother?* she thought. One look at Deb and all doubt was gone. Never had she seen such pain in Deb's face. It was as though the pain had a life of its own. A life which could not be denied. As Winnie looked at Deb, the pain transferred itself into her. As the pain became her own, Winnie knew that nothing good could come of this.

Deb couldn't move, couldn't speak, couldn't feel anything except the pain of the past pulsing through her. Like a whip, each strike was worse than the last, and yet there was a numbness in between the blows. How could this woman just walk in, demand and receive Jed's affections? Had Jed really missed her? Had Deb not done anything for him all these years? Had she missed something? Her mind was screaming to leave, but her body wouldn't respond. All she could do was stand there and stare at Jed's face. That face which was illuminated in a way Deb had never seen before. Why had she never seen that look in Jed's face as she'd looked into his eyes over the years? Yes, this was his mother, but she had left, had actually abandoned him years ago. How could...? Deb's head was spinning as she tried to listen through her own thoughts.

"You came back, you really came back," said Jed. "I can't believe it. I mean, I wanted to, and I had always hoped you would, but now you're really here."

"Let me get a look at my boy," said Jed's mother. "Well, you turned out pretty well I'd say. Guess your grandfather took good care of you." She paused for a moment. "I was sorry to hear about his passing. You must be lonely living in that big house alone."

"I don't live at Gramps, I never have," said Jed.

This news seemed to disturb Jed's mother. "Well, where *have* you been living?" she asked.

"I live here, with Deb. I wanted to stay here so you could find me when you came back," answered Jed.

These words hit Deb with a greater force than seeing *her* again. Had Jed stayed simply in hopes that his mother would return for him? Did he have no feelings for her at all? The pain Deb now felt was the same she'd had when Jed's father left. All of her past regrets and missed chances filled her mind. How clear it suddenly was now. She'd done the very same thing with

Jed that she had done with Zach. Sure, the loss of Crockett had moved her to reveal a few things, but it takes years to develop trust in a relationship. Deb had wanted Jed to see her as a mother. Not as a replacement for the one who'd left, but a better one. Showing emotion was something Deb had stopped doing when Zach had left. Without realizing it, she'd done this with Jed, as well. Even though he'd filled her heart with love again, she never let it show. Just like a lobster sitting in a trap, the way out was the same as the way in. Ah, but once inside, the opening looks too small, impossible to fit through. That's what Deb's heart had become, a trap for others' love, while she couldn't see a way to let her own love out.

Winnie's eyes moved from Jed, to his mother, to Deb. She wanted desperately to do or say something, but what? She knew nothing about this strange woman. Her eyes drifted back to Jed. He was beaming. She was reminded of an early morning out in the boat with him. The sun sat on the horizon, the sky and water filled with its rays, shrouding everything with light. It was impossible to know where one began and the other ended. Even though she knew better, the feeling overtook logic, caused her mind to wander and her heart to race. As Winnie looked at Deb, she saw this same feeling. Deb's eyes were fixed on Jed. Her chest was moving up and down with each breath. Seeing this reminded Winnie of something her mother had told her years ago, when she'd started to develop as a woman. Boys and yes, even men, would begin to look at her differently. "Males are obsessed with breasts," her mother had said. "They can't help themselves from staring at them."

Winnie looked around the room at the men. Her mother had been right: almost every man in the room was staring at Deb's chest, obsessed with her breasts. They could care less how she was feeling, or what she was going through. They were thinking of themselves. That was one of the things Winnie loved about Jed. He wasn't like that at all. Even now, Winnie was sure Jed was happy to see his mother, but not just for selfish reasons. She was sure it was also because he was happy to know she was alive.

Winnie's focus turned back to Deb and what she could do for her. But it was Ashley Walters who ended the moment that had entranced them all.

"Excuse me, Jed. Am I to understand this person is your biological mother?" he asked.

Everyone turned toward the attorney. His presence had been forgotten in the shock of the reunion.

"Yes, this is my mother. But what did you mean when you said *biological*?" asked Jed.

"It means she's not your guardian. Right, Mr. Walters?" interjected Richard, who had joined the group unnoticed.

People glared at him; he never seemed to know his place.

Walters looked first at Richard, then at Jed. "This young man is correct. That's what this document means. By order of the State of Maine, Deb here is the legal guardian of Jedediah Baxter."

"See, told ya," said Richard.

"Oh, I think not. I am Jed's only mother," said the woman now holding Jed like a possession.

"I understand your position, Miss...I'm sorry, we haven't been properly introduced. My name is Ashley Walters, I'm the—"

"I don't care who you are, you have no right to tell me anything," said Jed's mother.

"You can challenge the state's order," said Richard, butting in again.

Deb had now regained her bearings. "Okay, Richard, you've helped enough. Back to work."

"What is he talking about?" asked Jed's mother.

"That's what I've been trying to explain," said Walters. "We were unable to locate any of Jed's relatives. We also have not been able to establish proof of Jed's birth. Therefore, we petitioned the state for Deb to be appointed his legal guardian as a method of resolving Mr. Crockett's estate."

"Well, what's wrong with his father?" asked Jed's mother.

Deb felt the pain stab her again. Just hearing this woman refer to Zach was unbearable. Still, she was compelled to ask, "Do you know where Zach is?"

"Isn't he here in New Ireland?"

Jed looked at his mother with a face full of questions. "I've never met my dad," said Jed. "It was years before I even knew who Gramps was."

Suddenly, Jed's mother understood the difficulties Jed had endured since she'd left him that day. No words needed to be said. It was on her face for all to see. The ache a mother feels when she realizes she has caused pain to one of her children cannot be described with words. Like the emptiness of a page before a writer begins to fill it, it is just *there,* staring back at you. She had somehow assumed Jed's father was here and would look after him when she left. She looked at Jed with a true mother's eyes.

"So who took care of you for all these years?" she asked quietly.

Jed looked from his mother, to Winnie, to Deb before answering. "Well, lots of people, but it was Deb who raised me."

Jed's mother looked at Deb and could see without question this was true. But why? What was in it for her? If Zach had married her, as she'd assumed, it would have made sense. A quick look at Deb's left hand showed no evidence of a ring ever having been on her finger. Knowing Deb was a forever kind of woman, if she'd ever married, the ring would still be there. Then it hit her.

She looked deep into Deb's eyes and said, "So Jed's the

only known heir to Crockett's estate, and now you're his guardian. You know he's not eighteen, so now you have control over everything that really belongs to Jed."

Then she turned to Walters and snapped, "And I bet you're in on it. Well, I'm going to get a lawyer and fight you two on this."

She took Jed by the hands. "I'm sorry, Jed. I didn't expect this to happen. But don't worry, I'll fight for you. Let's get away from these people right now."

"Where will we go?" Jed asked.

"To your house, of course. Possession is nine-tenths of the law."

Jed had waited too long for his mother to come back. He couldn't let her go. They walked out hand in hand. He felt like his life was a fishing net. Just when you get one patch fixed, it scratches the bottom and a new hole rips open.

CHAPTER 24
"Oh, What a Tangled Web We Weave..."

The thought of how or why his mother had shown up at this particular time had not entered Jed's mind. But then, how could it? His mind was filled with the joy of having his mother back in his life. There could be no wrong, no blame, in his mind or heart for her. And he was completely oblivious to the pain his abrupt departure had created in those left inside the bakery. All the waiting, wanting, longing, aching he'd kept bottled up for years seemed to end with the arrival of his mother. The questions now were: Was having her back worth everything he had? Everything he'd become? What about that which he could become? Had all of this now changed?

None of these thoughts were a part of either Jed's conscious or unconscious mind. Instead, he was like a kindergartener on the first day of school, ready to receive and accept any and all information as the gospel truth.

The next voice Jed heard brought him back to earth a bit.

"Hey, boy, ain't you gonna thank me?"

Jed looked past his mother for the source of the voice. To his amazement, there stood Bradley. He had the same smile as when Jed had first seen him. This time, though, Jed's mind did ask the question, *What's he doing here, and why?* The answer was obvious.

"Bradley's the one who got ahold of me and told me about

your grandfather's passing," said his mother.

Jed remembered the last time he'd seen Bradley—at the hospital. Had his past emotions gotten in the way of thinking Bradley was able to do anything good? He remembered believing Bradley had no right being there. That they had almost come to blows there in the waiting room. Standing next to his long-lost mother, Jed had a different view of the man. Perhaps he'd been wrong back then.

"I don't know how to thank you, Bradley," said Jed. "How did you find her?"

"Well, after you stopped into the garage that night, I got to thinking about your father, then your mother. I wondered if I could find her. So I started making calls to some old friends, and they made more calls. It wasn't until after Crockett died that I heard back from one of my friends about a place I might find her. It was a ways off, but I hadn't been on a road trip for a while, so I struck out to see if she was there. Sure enough, she was. I told her about you, and about the old man dying."

Jed's mother interrupted. "I wanted to come right away, but I had to take care of a few things before I could leave. Bradley was a big help with that, as well."

"Well, anyway," said Bradley with a teasing smile, "if you really want to thank me, you could sign over the title to the 'Vette."

Jed didn't hear him, though. His focus was back on his mother. "It's okay Mom. None of that matters now. How long can you stay?"

His obvious need made her smile. "Oh, honey, I'm here for good. We've got plenty of time to get caught up. Let's go to the house so I can get settled. I'm tired and want to rest."

Jed didn't really feel right going to Gramps' house. But he also didn't want to do anything that would give his mother a reason to become upset, so the three of them climbed into Bradley's car and drove off. Jed didn't even glance back.

Inside the bakery, looking out was a town that now saw the boy Jed still was instead of the man he was becoming. A man would never have let any woman, including his mother, push him around like that. While most of the people returned to their meals and conversations at the departure of the car, there were three who could not.

Deb's emotions moved from shock to controlled anger. Years before, she had stood by and done nothing as this woman entered her life and took away the man she loved. The only man she'd *ever* loved. Because she had not acted, Jed's father had left. This was a mistake she wasn't going to make again. Jed might not be her child, but that wasn't going to stop her from acting like his mother. Even if he did have a real one. This time, she was going to fight, not for her own sake, but for Jed's. If she were going to lose him, then it was going to be because of something she *did*, not something she *didn't* do.

"Can she do what Richard said?" she asked Ashley Walters.

He was pleased to see in her eyes what he'd hoped for. Deb had the look of a woman with resolve. A woman who was devoid of doubt, ready to do the right thing for someone else, whatever the price to her personally.

"Yes, Deborah, as the boy's biological mother, she can challenge the state's order. If I might explain..." said Ashley.

"Please," said Deb.

"The order was issued not with *your* interest in mind, but in the best interest of Jed. If it can be shown that there is a better way to provide for and protect Jed's interests, the state has an obligation to consider it. Should Jed's mother challenge the order, the state must go through the process of a hearing to consider her rights."

"If she does, what kind of a chance do you think she has?"

"I can't lie to you, Deb. The state seldom rules against a parent in these hearings. However, the difficulty she will have, based on my experience, is to prove that leaving Jed here was in his best interest at the time."

"What about all the years I've taken care of him?" asked Deb.

"That was your choice, Deb. It will have no value in a courtroom. Unless Jed should speak to what you've done and what it means to him. Then, it would have value, if you see what I mean."

"Yes, I think I do understand. The state is only interested in hard facts. Thank you," she said.

Ashley nodded and continued. "There is another area of concern here, as well. If Jed is still a minor and the state reverses the order, thereby giving guardianship back to his mother, she will control the assets Jed's been awarded in the will."

Ashley could tell by Deb's face that this bit of information did not sit well with her.

"Should this happen," he went on, "it could affect you and others. Including you, Miss Winnie."

"How so?" asked Deb.

"Under the conditions I stated previously, she could contest Mr. Crockett's will on behalf of Jed, whether he wants her to or not." He shook his head. "I'm afraid we've taken a significant step backward in the process."

"How can she contest the will? It has nothing to do with her," said Deb.

"You are correct, Deb," said Ashley. "But as Jed's legal guardian, she would have the right to act in his best interest as she sees fit. Since Jed is the only known heir, she could argue that he's entitled to *everything* in Mr. Crockett's estate. Based on what Jed has been through, it would be a compelling argument, one that a judge could easily be convinced of."

"Excuse me," Winnie broke in. "I don't mean to sound selfish. But you said this could affect me."

Ashley had been waiting for Winnie to speak up. There

were certain things he needed to know about her if he were going to consider taking the case on. "Yes, Winnie, I did. If she does challenge the will, it will mean that the building Mr. Crockett left you would be in question, and, I'm afraid, the money for college, as well."

"Jed would never do that," said Winnie with an air of confidence.

"Perhaps not, but, as I said, Miss Winnie, it would not be up to him as a minor. Now, I have a question for you two. If Jed's mother does move forward on the events as we've discussed, do you want to fight her, and if so, would you want me to represent you? I don't want you to answer right now. Take some time to think about it."

Deb said, "Wouldn't it be a conflict of interest? You already represent Jed."

Ashley was pleased by this question, as it showed him that Deb was already thinking about fighting. "That's a good question, Deb. The answer is no. Because I don't represent Jed; I represent Mr. Crockett's estate. Besides, under the circumstances, representing the two of you in defense of the will is acting in Jed's best interest as well as Mr. Crockett's, as far as I'm concerned....well, you two think about it and let me know."

With that, Ashley got up to leave. As he did, Deb asked one more question. "Is there anything we can do now?"

"You could find that birth certificate. That would be an enormous help."

The two women watched him disappear. No words passed between them, but their pain had a common thread. Jed had finally become comfortable as a citizen of New Ireland. Any doubt of that had been erased by the way he had handled his grandfather's passing. With his mother coming back, things were changing just when life had become settled, something Jed could depend on. Why did she have to show up now? Or for that matter ever?

Finally, Winnie said, "I can't believe Jed just walked out like that."

Deb turned to face her. Tears were balanced on Winnie's eyelids like a glass overfilled with water. "He didn't walk out, Winnie. She took him. Give it a few days and things will be better, you'll see."

Deb held her arms out and Winnie leaned into them wishing they were Jed's.

Would everything be fine in a few days? she wondered. *Does Deb really believe that?* Winnie hoped Deb was right. She hoped Jed's mother would find a reason to leave, and soon.

"Do you think we should try and talk to him?" she asked, even though she knew the answer.

"No, honey. Give him time to come to us. He needs some time with his mother whether we like it or not."

Hearing this helped Winnie feel a little better. She tried to remember the last day she'd spent without seeing Jed at all, but none came to her. The very idea of a day without Jed tore open a patch within her heart and created an itch she could not reach to scratch. Only Jed could do that.

CHAPTER 25

"When First We Practice to Deceive"
Sir Walter Scott

Jed woke up on Saturday morning not knowing where he was at first. Then he realized he was in Gramps' house. He'd stayed here now and again over the last few years, but it had been a while. In fact, other than checking on the house, he hadn't spent any time inside since Gramps had passed. Suddenly he remembered why he was there. His feet hit the floor. The clock read 3:47 A.M. It wasn't likely his mother would be up this early.

They'd spent the rest of the previous day and evening talking. Not about anything important. They both knew that would come later. Besides, Bradley hadn't left until after nine, which was past bedtime in Jed's world.

He walked toward the window facing Main Street. The light in the bakery was on already. There had been a moment last night when Jed realized he'd just walked out of the bakery without a word to Deb, Winnie, or Mr. Walters. He felt bad about that and hoped they understood.

As Jed looked around for fresh clothes, it hit him that all of his things were still down there, above the bakery light. He looked again and could see Deb's shadow moving around.

Dressing quickly in yesterday's clothes, Jed started down the stairs. Halfway down, he met the aroma of coffee. At the bottom, he could see light coming from the kitchen. He slowly stepped into the room and found his mother busy at the stove. She didn't see him at first, giving Jed a chance to watch her. She moved like a woman who was used to this type of work. There was a flow, an air of confidence in her movements. Jed had seen this in Deb many times. This feeling was different somehow. Not just because it was his mother, either. It was there, deeper.

Within seconds, Jed was able to identify it. This wasn't *work*; she was expressing her love by making breakfast for him. A rush of emotion swept over him, like when you turn a corner where a strong wind hits you in the face and takes your breath away. No one had ever made breakfast just for him—well, except for Gramps. Deb had never done it, he was sure of that. Somewhere deep inside, this gesture made its way into Jed's heart. This was a thing he believed only a mother would do, could do.

"Morning, Mom," he said. "You're up early."

His mother turned toward him. She had a smile on her face that warmed him to his core. "Have a seat. It's almost ready," she said, motioning to the table.

He hadn't noticed that the table was set for the two of them. Plates, glasses, coffee, even the silverware had a napkin tucked under it. Before he had a chance to move, his mother put her arm around him, and nudged him to the table. All Jed could think was, *This is what having a mother is really like. This was what had been missing from his life. No one could make a person feel this way but their mother.*

It was in this moment, by virtue of such a simple act, that Jed forgave her. The past didn't matter. Answers to important questions didn't matter—like, why had she left him? Where had she been all these years? And why had she shown up now? These and all the other questions that had been bouncing around in his head were gone. She was his mother, and more than anything, he wanted to be her son. To be treated like a mother's child, to know unconditional love.

Jed sat down and ate the first meal ever made for him and only him.

* * * *

Deb stopped to look out the window at the house on the hill. She could see the kitchen light was on. She felt bad that Jed was there alone, making his own breakfast. The urge to go up to the house forced her to lean forward, but her feet stood their ground. Once again, she found herself fighting the instincts of a mother. Now that Jed's biological mother was here, she wondered if her self-imposed rule of keeping a distance had been the right course of action. Just as when making muffins, you can over mix the batter, Deb had felt she should be mindful of getting too mixed up in Jed's life. It was too late to fret about it now. The muffins were in the oven, so to speak.

Deb turned back to the abyss of endless work. Most days she didn't mind, and today she did so thankfully.

* * * *

Jed ate slowly as a way to make the moment last. He should go out today and check his traps, but he didn't want to leave for fear she'd be gone when he got back. It was a fear he'd carried all his life, one he had not come to terms with as of yet.

"Don't you have to get going?" she asked.

"Yeah, I kinda do," he agreed. "Will you be here when I get back?" Jed couldn't believe the words had come out of his mouth. He looked away in embarrassment.

His mother put her arms around him and gave him a hug and a kiss. "It's okay, I deserved that question." She caressed his cheek with her hand, looked him straight in the eyes and said, "Yes, son. I'll be here."

Jed could see and feel the meaning of her words. She would be here when he got back. "Thanks, Mom, I'll see you then."

She watched as he put on his boots and coat. Just as he got to the door, she asked, "Any idea when you'll be back, son?"

Jed stopped, turned, and said, "I should be home by two," then left with a smile.

* * * *

Winnie looked at the clock: 3:47 A.M. Jed would be up by now. She had planned to go lobstering with him this morning, but wasn't sure after yesterday. *I know,* she thought, *I'll go see if Deb needs any help.* She was out of bed in a single motion, the way young people do without thinking and older people think about, but can't do anymore. There was no point in taking a shower if she was just going to get all sweaty, she thought, but discipline and habit got the better of her, and a few minutes later she was in the shower.

Nearly every time Winnie took a shower, she was reminded of the day she'd first met Jed. The way the two of them had sat there in their birthday suits, so innocent, so naïve that day on the breakwater. Winnie watched the soap slowly move down her breast and build up before finally cresting the nipple—only to gather again at her navel, then divide in two and follow her hips as a way to prolong its path and move ever so softly down her slender legs. The wishing and wondering what Jed would think now was ever-present, replacing the naïve while the innocence remained. Like all the females before her, she was at that time when the little girl in her was fighting for its life, as the woman slowly, painfully emerged and innocent ideas became heated thoughts and desires.

The water suddenly lost it heat. Its coldness brought Winnie out of her trance and her pace quickened. Within minutes she was making her way down the road. This was her favorite time of day. When the sun was just coming up, everything was fresh and new. By the time she reached Deb's, her spirits were high and her mind was free of despair. The smell coming from inside was one she didn't recognize, though it was somehow familiar.

"That you, Jed?" Deb called out.

The question made Winnie feel a little sad. "Sorry, it's just me," she answered. "Is Jed here?"

Without answering, Deb turned back to what she'd been doing. Winnie joined her. "I came to see if you would like any help this morning," she said.

Deb forced a smile. "You're always welcome here, girl, you know that."

Winnie smiled back. "What is that smell?" she asked. "It's like I know it, but can't remember what it is."

Deb flipped over the dough ball she was kneading and pounded it with her fist a few times and flipped it again. Winnie could feel the force of Deb's blows vibrating the counter as she leaned against it.

"It's bear claws you smell," answered Deb. "It's been quite a while since I've made them. I hope I remembered the recipe correctly."

Bear claws, thought Winnie. *Jed's favorite. Deb really is hurting over what happened yesterday.* "So he's upstairs?" said Winnie as more of a question than a statement.

This time Deb answered, but still didn't speak. She stopped kneading the dough and turned toward Winnie. Her face was covered with little clumps of dough where her tears had mixed with the flour. Winnie pulled out the towel that was tucked into the string of Deb's apron and began to gingerly wipe them away. Deb let her head rest on Winnie's shoulder.

Years of doubt had been seeping out of her all morning. Although this wasn't the type of help Winnie had intended, it was what Deb needed, and Winnie was clearly pleased to be the one to provide it. Several minutes passed in silence as Winnie gently wiped tears and flour from Deb's face. They were both women who loved the same man. Granted, each was a separate and different love, but neither was more powerful than the other. This bond allowed things to pass between them by the touch of their bodies and souls. Words were not needed.

This connection was interrupted by the smell of something that was cooked to the better side of done. Deb broke away and ran to the oven just in time to save the bear claws. She set them on the counter to cool for a few minutes before applying the glaze.

"I know that smell. It's bear claws," said Jed as he came through the back door into the kitchen.

Deb's old habits stayed true and forced her to contain her surprise and pleasure in seeing him.

"You'll have to wait a few minutes, I just took them out and they're not glazed yet," she said.

"Oh, I couldn't possibly eat one now. Mom made me a big breakfast this morning and I'm stuffed," said Jed.

No sooner had the words left his mouth, than he was sorry for saying them. He'd made it sound as though he was rejecting Deb.

"Well, if you don't want any, I'll just toss them out. They're overcooked anyway," said Deb, not looking at him.

She reached for the tray, but Jed caught her wrist. "I didn't say I didn't want them, Deb," he said, forcing her to look him in the eye.

It was then he noticed the faint white rings left behind by the clumps of flour Winnie had wiped off. Jed knew this was the moment he'd hoped for.

"I'm sorry about the way I left yesterday. I hope you can understand and forgive me."

Deb felt her own heartbeat as it pulsed against Jed's grip. She wanted desperately to tell him no, she didn't understand. How could he just dismiss her without a single thought after all she'd done? But she couldn't say it.

"It's okay, I understand. After all, she is your mother," she said, trying to force a smile that wouldn't come.

Jed, however, was able to smile. "Thanks, Deb. I only hope Winnie will be as understanding."

"Well, here's your chance to find out. She's out front."

Jed made his way to the front of the bakery. Winnie was standing with her back to him. He wanted to walk up behind her and put his arms around her, but he thought better of it and spoke instead.

"Morning, Winnie, you still want to go lobstering today?"

Without turning around, she answered, "I don't know. What if you decide to leave? Then I'd be stuck out there on the water."

Jed had expected her to say something like this. Even though the words were mean, the tone was not. He walked up behind her, placed his hands on her shoulders, and whispered into her ear. "I'm sorry about walking out without saying goodbye yesterday. I was in shock over seeing my mother after all these years. Please forgive me."

Jed could feel tension in Winnie's shoulders. With her back to him, he could smell the shampoo in her hair, and noticed it was damp. He had his answer. She would not have showered before going out lobstering with him.

"I'd really like you to go," he began, "but I understand if you don't want to."

"It's not that I don't want to," she answered. "It's just that I'm helping Deb now."

Jed knew there was no point in pursuing the matter any further. Winnie had made up her mind, and she still hadn't turned around and looked at him. He'd hurt both of them yesterday and felt bad about it, and yet he knew how important he was to the both of them. This made him feel a little better.

Realizing any further attempts to sway Winnie would just anger her, Jed gave up on the idea.

"Sure, I understand," he said. "I was thinking of going into Redman Village after I get in. Would you like to go with me then?"

Winnie's heart screamed, *Yes, yes!* But young love is complicated. It's always looking for something and feeling unwanted without it. Once again, she answered in a defensive manner, "I've got something I need to do."

This time, however, her words had a different effect. She felt the weight of disappointment in Jed's hands on her shoulders. As he lifted them and walked away, Winnie thought twice about her answer.

She turned and said, "Jed, would you call me before you leave, just in case I can get away?"

Jed stopped and looked back. Winnie had the slightest hint of a smile. "Sure, thanks for the second chance."

Deb had tried to listen but couldn't hear. The look on Jed's face, though, told her things had gone well. As he walked through the kitchen, she handed him a bag with four bear claws in it.

Winnie returned to the kitchen, and after a minute of silent work, Deb spoke to her.

"So, did you two patch things up?"

Winnie smiled. "Kinda," she said as she scratched her shoulder.

CHAPTER 26
Wake of a Turning Tide

Jed had a rough day on the water. Nothing seemed to be going quite the way he wanted, which caused everything to take longer than usual. He knew it was partly because of Winnie's absence. She'd been out with him pretty steadily this spring. So much so that they'd developed a rhythm much like Jed had had with Gramps. Jed thought about how hard it must have been for Gramps working alone all those years. Then again, he'd lived alone for so long, maybe it didn't make any difference where he was. Jed knew that feeling of solitude and loneliness.

As these thoughts rattled around in his head, a new one formed and brought a warmth to him. Like the warmth a person feels when they hold a new baby for the first time and realize how precious and fragile life truly is. The way Jed felt now, having his mother back, must have been how Gramps had felt when Jed came into his life. He thought about how having his mother back made him feel connected to the world. It was a feeling like none he ever remembered having.

By the time Jed got back to the dock, it was after two o'clock. If he were going to Redman Village, he'd have to hurry. But there was still work left, work that other men weren't faithful to. Jed, however, stayed true to his grandfather's teachings and finished all the work properly. Little things like making sure everything was clean, and in its proper place. He also got ready for the next day by making sure he had plenty of bait bags ready for use. Next he'd check over the engine and other equipment to be sure everything was in good shape. The last thing he wanted was to break down out on the water and have to call the Coast Guard for help. "They got better things to do than rescue lazy fishermen," Gramps would always say.

Once he finished, he headed straight for Deb's. He was done with his shower and in his room getting dressed before it hit him. He should have gone to Gramps, but then all of his things were still here at Deb's so he figured it was okay.

Things were quiet in the bakery. He found Deb and Richard cleaning up, but no sign of Winnie.

"Hey, Deb, is Winnie around?" he asked.

Deb looked up from the table she was wiping. She half expected to see him still in his lobstering clothes and smelling of salt water and fish bait. The sight of him all cleaned up and wearing fresh clothes pleased her. She knew it meant he had come to her place without thinking. At least he still looked at the bakery as home.

"No, she left a while ago, honey. I think she was hoping to go with you to Redman Village. Give her a call if you'd like."

"Thanks, I think I will. Oh, I took a shower; I hope that's okay. I plan to move my things up to the house tomorrow," said Jed as he turned toward the phone.

Her pleasure at Jed's thinking of the bakery as home died as quickly as it had formed. The idea of him moving out had not occurred to her. She wished it hadn't now.

Jed dialed Winnie's number. She answered on the second ring.

"Hi there. Forgive me yet?" he asked.

"You're late, I've been waiting for you," she said.

"Sorry; I didn't have my helper today. Guess you have to blame her."

"Very funny. Are we still going?" she asked.

"You bet. I'm at Deb's. I'll get the car and pick you up."

"Okay. I'll start walking to save us some time. See you in a bit."

* * * *

Jed's mother was in Crockett's office when she heard Jed come in. She quickly pushed things aside and closed the door. However, she failed to notice a small journal that had made its way out of the office and onto the floor next to the bookcase in the living room.

"Hi, Mom, I'm home," said Jed just the way he had heard them say it on old black-and-white TV shows. The few seconds it took her to answer sent a chill filled with prickly pain through him. He'd waited so long to say these words. So long waiting to hear a mother's voice answer. In this smallest moment of time, the idea that she'd left him behind again managed to encompass him, body and soul. Then she answered. "How's my boy? Did you have a good day fishing?"

All was right again with the sound of her voice. "It's lobstering, Mom, and it was fine."

She hugged him and gave him a wet kiss on the cheek.

"Why, you're all cleaned up! Where have you been, young man? Out with some girl?" she asked.

These words would cause rebellion in many teenage boys, but they were music to Jed's ears. "No, Mom, I took a shower at Deb's. All my stuff is still there so it made sense to wash up there." Jed knew this was a white lie, but for some reason he couldn't tell his mother he'd gone there instinctively, without thinking.

"I see. Well, perhaps we should collect your things and bring them here this very second," she suggested.

"I would, Mom, but I was planning a trip to Redman Village today. I told Deb I'd stop in tomorrow and collect my things."

The idea of waiting didn't sit too well with her, but the fact that he was doing it tomorrow and had told that meddling Deb so, pleased her. "Sure, son, tomorrow's fine," she said.

"Thanks, Mom. Do you need anything in Redman Village?" he asked.

She was happy that he asked, and happier still that he was going to be gone a while longer. She needed time to clean up the mess she'd made. "No, dear, but thanks for asking. How long will you be? I've missed you and want to spend time with you," she said to help cover up any sign she might have given of delight that he was leaving again.

"Well, I'm not sure, Winnie's going with me. We'll probably eat something for supper before we head back. I'd guess about seven. Is that all right?"

"Yes, dear, that will be fine. Why don't you bring...what was her name again?"

"Winnie, Mom, her name's Winnie."

She smiled and placed her hands on his cheeks. "Why don't you bring Winnie by so I can meet her?"

"Sure, Mom. I really need to get going, though. The library closes at five and that's my first stop."

At this point she was just happy he was going and didn't really hear him say *library*, or she might have balked. "Okay, dear. See you later. Have fun."

Jed smiled and kissed her, grabbed the keys to the Corvette, and left. She watched from the kitchen window to be sure he'd gone before returning to her work, the true purpose of her return to New Ireland.

Winnie had walked nearly all the way to Deb's and was feeling a little cross with Jed's tardiness.

"Sorry, I had a visit with Mom," he offered as the reason for his delay.

Having momentarily forgotten about his mother being back, Winnie gave him a seductive smile with her eyes. "Me too. I should have thought of that."

Jed returned her smile a bit awkwardly, the art of looking seductive was still somewhat of a mystery to him. "There's nothing to forgive," he said.

"So, where we going?" asked Winnie, as if she didn't know.

"Well, the library of course. Then I thought we'd get something to eat."

"Oh, where?"

"Your choice," he answered. "And I was thinking of inviting Miss Black. If that's okay with you...."

Winnie was pleased to be asked for her opinion. "I think that's a wonderful idea."

The conversation during the rest of the trip reverted back to the usual, school and the idle events of New Ireland. Before they knew it, the library was in front of them. As they got out of the car, Jed said, "Oh, Mom invited you to visit when we get back, she'd like to meet you."

Winnie had received such invitations from others, but somehow the words sounded funny attached to Jed's voice. Her first thought was of the day before. Why hadn't his mother wanted to meet her then? She decided not to make a big deal about it.

"Sure, I'd be happy to meet your mother," she answered as they reached the library door.

The library was busier than it had been during their previous visits. Miss Black didn't see them at first, as she was reading to a group of younger kids. Jed and Winnie decided to look around while they waited. Just before closing time, Miss Black came over to them.

"I thought I saw you two come in a little bit ago. Can you stay after I close? It's been a busy day and I could use your help," said Miss Black.

"We'd be happy to, right, Jed?" answered Winnie without waiting for his answer.

"Good, I'll work on getting people out the door. Though I do enjoy it when we have such a busy day."

Within ten minutes, the library was empty and the three of them were busy picking up books and putting them back on the shelves. Most of them were children's books, which surprised Jed.

"I didn't know there were so many books written for kids," he said.

"Didn't you read as a child?" asked Miss Black.

"No, but that reminds me of why I came. I wanted to return the book you gave me to read, and check out the next one in the series—and I have some big news."

"Do tell," said Irene.

"My mother came back. She's in New Ireland right now, at Gramps' house."

"Well, that *is* news! I'm very happy for you, Jed."

Feeling a little left out, Winnie interjected. "Miss Black, we were wondering if you'd like to go out to eat with us."

"Oh, that would be delightful," she said.

While picking up, Winnie and Irene had consulted and agreed they were in the mood for steak. They decided that Bill's Beef House was the place, so they headed in that direction. The meal was full of pleasant talk. While they were waiting for the check, Winnie excused herself and gave Miss Black a look that said she wanted company. The two of them made a trip to the ladies' room while Jed waited for the check.

Winnie was pleased to see that the restroom was empty. Before she could speak, Miss Black did.

"So, what is it you need to tell me?" she asked.

Knowing there wasn't much time, Winnie got right to it, revealing the complications which had accompanied the arrival of Jed's mother. Including the possibility of the library not receiving its share of Mr. Crockett's estate. Miss Black took the news in her typical sedate fashion. She thanked Winnie for the information and said she would plan accordingly.

They returned to the table, where Jed was ready to go.

"I'd ask what you two were going on about in there, but I know you won't tell me, so why bother?" he said, trying his best to look grumpy.

"Well, I'm glad to see you know your place," Miss Black teased. "Now, if you'd please, I'd like to go home. I have some correspondence that needs tending to."

Winnie snuggled up to Jed. "We need to get going, too. Your mother will be looking for you."

Jed turned to look at Winnie. "You mean *us*," he said.

Winnie answered with a smile as they walked out of the restaurant.

* * * *

Jed's mother met them at the door.

"Well, aren't you two the cutest couple," she said by way of greeting.

"Mom, this is Winnie," said Jed.

Winnie held out her hand and said, "It's a pleasure to meet you, Ms...."

"It's Constance, Constance Baxter, but just call me Connie, dearie. No need for formalities here."

"Okay, Connie. Thanks," answered Winnie, letting her hand drop back to her side.

Winnie lasted an hour before she felt uncomfortable and wanted to leave. On her way back from a quick trip to the bathroom, she noticed the small journal on the floor next to the bookcase, and picked it up. She was about to set it on the bookcase, when she noticed a patch of tape coming off it. She scratched off the residue under the tape and found a date written there. Inside the front cover was the name Ellen

Crockett. Recognizing it as a journal written over fifteen years ago by Jed's grandmother, a dangerous thought entered her mind. No one was looking, so she tucked it hastily into her back pants pocket. She knew it was wrong to take the journal, but she couldn't help thinking there might be something in it that could help. Since she still didn't know what to think of Connie, she wanted to keep it a secret.

During the ride home, she thought about telling Jed, but feared he might tell his mother about it. Besides, she reasoned, there might not even be anything in it. She decided to read it herself first. That way if there were something important in it, she'd have a reason to show them the journal. If not, well, she'd find a way to return it without anyone noticing.

Once Jed was back home, he couldn't wait to hear what his mother thought about Winnie.

"So Mom, do you like her?" he asked.

"Well, I'm not sure. It seemed like...oh, it's not for me to say, honey," came her answer.

"No, really, Mom. I want to know," he persisted.

Connie gave a reassuring smile and said, "I'm sure it's nothing. She seems like a very nice girl. I just felt like she was..."

"Was what, Mom?"

"Well, like she was hiding something from us," she finally said reluctantly.

Jed thought about this for a few minutes. *Would she, could she, keep something from him?* He wondered. His mother interrupted his thoughts.

"Jed, honey, I'm sure it's nothing. After all, I just met the girl."

Jed smiled, "Yeah, I bet you'll feel differently once you get to know her better."

"Me too," she smiled back.

"Well, guess I'll go to bed. 'Night, Mom."

"Bed, so early?" she pondered.

"You have to remember, I'm an early riser."

Connie said no more. She was far too pleased with herself. With one simple comment she had created doubt in her son's mind about a girl he clearly thought a lot of. Her power over Jed was building quicker than she'd thought it might, and this was just the beginning. Before long, she'd be scratching patches in all aspects of his life. This was going to be easier than she'd originally thought.

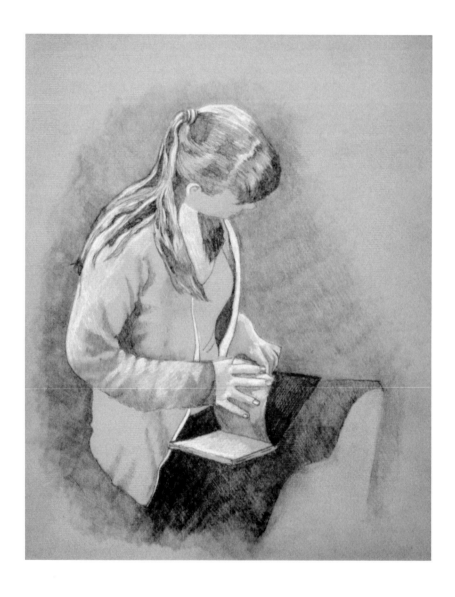

CHAPTER 27
Do I Really Know You?

The guilt of taking the journal without telling Jed kept Winnie from looking at it for a week. Eventually, curiosity got the better of her, and she slowly convinced herself she'd done the right thing by taking it. Reading it, however, turned out to be difficult, as Ellen had a small, looping cursive style of handwriting. It took a few more days of studying Ellen's writing before Winnie could recognize the letters and begin making sense of the entries. Then there was the dating system. Winnie finally figured out that Ellen had entered the year at the beginning, then the month. From there it was just the days of the week, but no dates. So instead of just reading an entry here and there, she had to start at the beginning so she wouldn't lose her place. Winnie decided to keep her own journal based on the entries she read, while adding a date to the days.

While Winnie was playing the role of investigator, Jed's mother was refining her role—the one where she was Jed's only advisor with any influence. Since Jed had moved his stuff out of Deb's, Connie had made sure he hadn't had a reason, or a chance, to go see her. It was time to bring this to Jed's attention.

"So Jed, how's Deb doing?" she asked one evening.

"I don't really know. Haven't seen much of her lately," he said before filling his mouth with another helping of mashed potatoes.

"That's strange," she said.

"What do you mean?"

"Well, it's just that she claims to care about you and to have taken care of you all these years, but the minute you move out…oh, it's not for me to say."

"Mom, you're always doing that. You know I want to hear what you have to say."

"Well, if you insist, dear. It's just that I would think she'd be checking in to see how you're doing. If she really did care, that is."

Connie could see that he was thinking, perhaps wondering for the first time why he hadn't heard from Deb, so she decided to push another button.

"I bet I know what it is," she said. "She likes boys in need. Once you got older and didn't need her anymore, she got that new kid, what's his name?"

"You mean Richard?"

"Yes, isn't the main reason Deb hired him—because he's not well liked and needed someone? At least that's what I've heard."

My God, thought Jed, *she's right. It never was about me, it was always about her, and what she needed. Why didn't I see it? Wait. . .why do I care? My mom is here now, that's all that matters.*

It was working. Her plan was coming along nicely. She could tell by the look in his eyes.

"Jed, honey, I want you to know something." She held his face in her hands to be sure he was listening intently. "I really thought your father was here to take care of you. I left you at Deb's because I was sure he'd find you there. Had I known he wasn't here, I never would have left you. I did it because I thought he could offer you a better life than I could at the time.

It must have been awful for you having to live in that attic all those years. I am so sorry. Can you ever forgive me, son?"

Jed listened. These words were the exact one's he longed to hear. How could he tell her he'd already gotten over that hurdle? His grandfather's advice gave him the answer: "Keep it simple."

"I have, Mom."

"Thank you," she replied, then added, "I'm just glad she didn't try to adopt you."

With these words, Jed's face turned white and he nearly choked on his food.

"She was given guardianship over me by the state," he said.

Connie's face clouded over and she said, "When?"

"The day you got here. The man who was at the bakery that day, he's a lawyer. That's why he was there. To give us the news."

"I don't understand," said his mother.

"Well, when Gramps passed away, he left most of his estate to me, but there's no proof of how old I am, so as a way to help move things forward, Gramps' lawyer, Mr. Walters, said Deb should be made my guardian."

"Then what?"

"I don't know. We haven't spoken about it since."

"Well, is that what you want, for Deb to be your mother?"

Jed couldn't believe she even needed to ask. "You're my mother," he said with a hint of anger in his tone.

Connie stood tall and said firmly, "If you want, we can fight this. I know a lawyer who could help us."

Jed's head was spinning; he didn't know what to think. Mr. Walters had been very professional and helpful. Even though he was still a teenager, Jed felt he could tell when someone was trying to be tricky or play him for a fool. It was part of the defense system he'd developed over the years. Mr. Walters had not given Jed any feelings of distrust toward him, but then neither had Deb, for that matter. So had he been fooled? Was he being played? The possibility just didn't sit well in his mind.

"Maybe we should meet with Mr. Walters and see what the next step is. I mean you are my mother. A piece of paper won't change that," said Jed.

Connie was prepared for this. In the short time she'd had to reconnect with Jed, it had become clear to her that he was not easily fooled. Jed had learned to rely on himself and become a good judge of character. The only real influence she had was his desire for her presence in his life.

She went over the words looking for a place to work from.

"Jed, you said they did this because there was no proof of your age," she said.

"Yeah, Mr. Walters said he couldn't find my birth certificate."

"Well, I'm your mother. I know when you were born, I know how old you are. I'm all the proof you need. You don't need a piece of paper for anything, they do. Now that they have it, we need to fight for what's rightfully yours. It's not fair, I know, but it's how these things work. Trust me, son. I know I don't deserve it, but I'm asking you to just trust me on this. Can you do that?"

Jed looked into his mother's eyes. Within them, he saw a kind of pain he knew all too well. He himself had given that look in the hope that others would see him for who he was and give him a chance. No one had until the day that puffin had shown up. That day his Gramps had given him a chance, and from then on they were inseparable. Jed remembered the way he'd felt on that day so long ago, when a single connection changed his life for the better. Having a family, even if it was just one person, had made him feel like he had value, that he was somebody. Jed also remembered reaching out to Deb that day thinking it might matter to her. Looking back now, he couldn't point to any place or time in his memory where things had changed between them. No, the change was with his grandfather, his family. That's what he wanted with his mother. She deserved that, and so did he.

He gave his mother a reassuring smile. "Of course I trust you, you're my mother. We'll do whatever you think is best."

Connie smiled back. "Thank you, son. I'm going to give Bradley a call right now. He's the one who knows the lawyer. We don't have a moment to lose. I'll bet they've even talked about us doing this and have a plan, but don't you worry, son. I won't let them take what's rightfully yours."

Jed watched as his mother went to the phone. Bradley? Now that was someone who gave off signals of mistrust. Jed thought about this while his mother was on the phone. He remembered meeting Bradley at the garage; things had seemed okay then. *So where was it? Oh yeah, at the hospital.* Jed thought about the fact that Bradley had been hurt, and he himself was dealing with the thoughts of his grandfather. Maybe it wasn't mistrust but misunderstanding that Jed had felt. After all, his mother trusted Bradley.

Connie returned with a piece of paper. "Okay, I've got the lawyer's name and number." Then she let her eyes and head drop as if something were wrong.

"What is it, Mom?" Jed asked.

Without looking up, she answered, "While I was talking to Bradley, he mentioned something you need to do...Oh, I can't ask you that," she said, breaking off her sentence. This was the true test. If Jed would go along with this, she knew he was hers.

"What, Mom? You can ask me anything."

Connie warmed inside, but didn't let it show. "If we're going to do this, really do this, you can't go to Deb's or talk to her anymore."

She watched for Jed's reaction. Seeing none, she added, "Same goes for Winnie, too."

This brought a reaction. Jed's eyes got big and he leaned toward her, like an animal getting ready to pounce. "I know you have feelings for her, son, but we need to keep things to ourselves. Anything you say to her, she's going to tell Deb. If you think about it, you'll see that I'm right."

Jed did know this. Winnie had grown as close to Deb as he was. He had never imagined life without either one of them, let alone both. This was going to be harder than he'd thought. This was their senior year. There was the prom, graduation, and all that stuff to share with Winnie.

Then a completely new thought cropped up. Maybe Deb would not fight it and would just give up her guardianship rights.

"Mom, before we do this, can we ask Deb to simply give up the guardianship? Maybe she won't mind."

Damn it, thought Connie. *This kid's smarter than I thought.* She knew refusing to do this would make her look bad. After going over the different scenarios in her mind, she said, "Okay, son, we'll do it. You may as well have Winnie there, too. But if they want that Mr. Walters there, then we need to have our lawyer come. I'm going to call him now."

"Thanks, Mom."

Jed liked the idea of getting everyone into the same room. He'd seen Gramps do this with the Lobstermen's Co-op to settle disputes. Things would get hot and heavy for a while, then clearer heads would prevail and a solution which worked for everyone would present itself.

Jed was sure that, given the chance, his mother would see that Deb and Winnie weren't bad people, but ones who truly cared for him. This would also give the two of them a chance to see how much his mother loved him and that she was only looking out for his best interests.

Yes sir, this was a great idea. The more Jed thought about it, the more pleased he became with himself. This was the perfect way for them to patch things up without scratching each other's eyes out.

Jed's mother came back from the phone. "Okay, Jed. The lawyer thinks that idea of yours is a good one. If it works, great, and if it doesn't, it will show that we tried to work things out before taking any legal action. So go ahead and set it up. It's perfectly fine."

CHAPTER 28

The Needs of the Many
Rest in the One

After Jed called her, Deb had spoken to Mr. Walters. It was decided that the meeting should take place in the bakery rather than his office. "Keep it simple and light," he had said. "Don't get into a confrontation, just listen to what they have to say and report back to me."

The day was Sunday, first thing in the morning. That was a quiet time for the bakery because it was against the law to go lobstering on Sunday. The men who had families stayed home with them, leaving only a few customers to contend with. One of them was an older man by the name of Gus Blood. Gus was a loner, not by choice as much as by desertion. Calling Gus a big man didn't quite get the job done. He was all of three hundred pounds and about six feet tall. He wore clothes that most people wouldn't use for rags. Even though the people of New Ireland had found occasions to gift Gus clothes in the past, no one had ever seen him wear any of them. He just kept patching up the ones he had whenever they were scratched or torn. Even the hat he wore was the same one he'd been given as a kid working at the old sardine canning company, which had long since closed. If you didn't know the name on the hat, you'd never be able to read it through the sweat and grime: New Ireland Canning Company. The only hair anyone had ever seen on his head was sticking out from underneath that hat. Then there were his teeth. The front ones up top, had been knocked out by his father one night when Gus was sneaking back into the house after a party at the quarry. The bottom ones were there, marred with tobacco stains from years of chewing. But none of this was the reason people avoided Gus. It was the smell. He gave off the stench of clam flat's baking in a hot August sun.

Usually Gus didn't give much attention to the events and happenings around him. He'd long ago resigned himself to his world of solitude. This morning, however, he took notice of Jed when he came into the bakery. The woman with him looked a might bit familiar. He was too far away to hear anything, but there was something about her. As he ate, Gus stared and pondered.

There was a second person of interest at the bakery that morning as well. It was Irene Black. She'd come in early and tucked herself in at the table diagonally across from where Deb had planned to have them all sit. At the last minute, Mr. Walters had called and asked her to be there as an observer. Deb was in on it, but they didn't want Jed or his mother to know. Mr. Walters felt it would be good to have someone there who wasn't so emotionally attached to the meeting's agenda.

The air had a thickness to it, much like a business meeting where there's a lot riding on the outcome, and indeed there was. Jed was the first to speak.

"Thanks for doing this, Deb."

Deb smiled, thinking this was a good beginning. "You're welcome, Jed," she replied. "It's nice to see you again, Connie." She didn't really mean it. After all, how could she? This woman had done so much damage to her life.

"Why thank you, Deb, you too." Connie was being polite, but Deb didn't trust her.

"So, what is it you two wanted to talk about?" asked Deb.

Jed looked at his mother, then turned to Deb. "Well, we've

been talking about how you were named my guardian the same day Mom came back…"

"Yes, that was quite a coincidence," interrupted Deb as a way to make it harder on Jed, despite the fact that it made things just as difficult for her. But that's what Mr. Walters had advised her to do—challenge Jed to gauge his level of commitment.

"Yeah, well, anyway, Mom and I were hoping you might be willing to give up your rights of guardianship over me. Since, you know, now that Mom's here, I mean," said Jed.

He hadn't expected to be this nervous. It wasn't like he didn't know who he was talking to. If anything, it was his mother he knew the least. He sat still without speaking, waiting for Deb's answer. Would she say no? Was his mother right?

"Well, Jed," began Deb, "it's not that simple. This is all tied into your grandfather's estate. I don't dispute the fact that Connie's your mother; nothing can change that. But I have to consider what your grandfather would have wanted." She looked at Connie and said firmly, "No offense, Connie, but I don't think he would want you to have any influence over his estate."

Connie couldn't be still any longer. "So your answer is that you want to keep control of my son so you can get your hands on what's rightfully his."

"No, Connie, that's not what I said."

"No, it's not, but it's what you're up to," Connie snapped. She turned to Jed. "We're wasting our time here, Jed. She's not interested in what *you* want. I think she's made it quite clear."

Jed turned to Deb. "Are you saying no, Deb?"

The look on Jed's face was the same one Deb had seen on his father's the last time she'd been with him. Was history repeating itself? Deb tried to keep her emotions in check, but it was a battle she was losing. She glanced at Winnie for help.

They had previously discussed a question, and this was the right time to ask it.

Winnie said, "Connie, do you know where Jed's birth certificate is? If we had that, it would be a big help and might even clean up this whole mess."

This question caught Connie and Jed off guard. Why hadn't they thought of this? Connie could feel all eyes were on her. She needed a way out of this predicament, an answer that would put the burden of proof back on Deb. Fortunately, she had one. And it was the truth.

"No, I don't," she answered. "I sent it to Jed's dad years ago."

"You mean to Crockett's house, where you are now, right? Or do you know where Zach is?" Deb asked.

Connie was visibly upset now. She looked straight into Deb's eyes and said, "I told you what I did. That's not what we're here about. Are you going to give up your rights to my son or not?"

With renewed strength, Deb looked at Jed and answered, "I'm sorry, Jed, I can't. Not just because of Crockett's estate, but because I think it's in your best interest as well."

Jed didn't know what to think. Was Deb really after Crockett's money? He found that hard to believe, but did his mother know more than she'd told him so far? It did make sense for her to have the birth certificate. She was his mother, after all.

"Let's go, Jed, we're done here," said Connie.

Jed got up to leave, his thoughts still swirling. Part of him wanted to stay, but most of him needed to be with his mother. Jed had turned halfway toward the door when Winnie spoke to him.

"Jed, could I ask you something else?" she said. "The money I was promised for helping to rebuild the traps, I could really use that right now for my college tuition."

Connie placed her hands on Jed's face as she'd become accustomed to doing. "You see, son? Do you see now? All they care about is the money."

As much as Jed was beginning to believe his mother was right, on this particular point she was not. Winnie had done the work and was due the money as promised, not by him, but by his Gramps. He had to speak up for Winnie on this.

"She's right, Mom. She is due the money. Gramps made the check out before the work was done, just before he passed away."

Connie glared at Winnie. "You want it, come and get it."

Turning to leave, she grabbed Jed by the hand and led him out of the bakery as if he were a little boy.

Winnie quickly reached for his other hand and placed a note inside.

Irene Black had listened well and had clearly heard Connie's comment on the location of the birth certificate. This was something she was sure Mr. Walters would want to know, and quick. To be sure Jed wouldn't see her, she decided to sit still just a little longer. It was a good thing she did. As Deb and Winnie were trying to collect themselves, Gus made his way over to them. That was another surprising thing about Gus: for a big man, he was quiet on his feet. When he spoke, he was even quieter, so the only people who heard were the ones he wanted, and no one else. But Irene's occupation as a librarian had helped her to gain a very astute level of hearing.

"Was that there Connie, Jed's mother?" Gus asked Deb.

"Yes, Gus, it was," she answered, nodding slightly.

"Hmm, thought so. Be mindful of that one. She's a clever devil," said Gus.

This comment made Deb wonder. "Have you seen her before, Gus?"

"Sure enough have," he responded, "but it was a long time

ago, before the boy come along. Well, I got to get going. Heed my words. Don't be puttin' your trust into that she-devil. She's a man-eater that one is. Worse than any shark or demon in them there waters."

Before Deb could say another word, Gus was gone.

Irene Black made her exit shortly thereafter.

* * * *

Jed slipped Winnie's note into his pocket on the way back to the house. As soon as they arrived, he went into the bathroom to read it.

Jed, I need to see you. Meet me at the breakwater lighthouse today at three.

Love, Winnie

As much as he wanted to keep the note, Jed thought better of it and flushed it. The thought of his mother finding it made it too risky to keep.

The day passed slowly. At two o'clock, he piled some gear into the truck and told his mother he was going down to check the boat and do a little work. He'd try to be home in time for supper.

Jed took the gear aboard the boat, then drove over to the breakwater. He saw Winnie's bike there and put it in the truck without thinking. The walk out took about twenty minutes, as the breakwater was a mile-long stretch of granite blocks. It always amazed him to think about doing this kind of work with nothing but horses and brute labor. He'd often wondered what it would have been like to live in that era.

Winnie stood on the deck of the lighthouse watching Jed make her way to her. She'd had all day to think about what she would do and say, and still she wasn't ready. Prepared, yes; ready, no. This was one of those times when a woman had to make a choice and stand by it. Looking down the long stretch of granite, she could see only a few people on the rocks fishing. Hopefully, no one would come along and spoil her plans.

About halfway there, Jed saw Winnie. His stride lengthened and his steps quickened. He reached the base of the lighthouse and looked up to find her gone. Up the steps he went. A walk around the lighthouse offered no sign of her. Then he noticed that the door was ajar. Sticking his head in, he called, "Winnie, you in here?"

A tug on his arm brought the rest of him inside. Behind him, the door shut, leaving him in blinding darkness waiting for his eyes to adjust. Although he couldn't see anyone, he could hear breathing. So he said again, "Winnie?"

"Yes, Jed, it's me."

"What are we doing here?" he asked, reaching out toward her voice.

But she had positioned herself beyond his reach purposely. Now that the moment was here, all doubt left her. She knew this was right.

"Jed, a lot's happened lately," she said into the darkness. "I know you're confused. You're wondering who you can trust."

"I'm not wondering about you Winnie, I trust you."

"Thank you, Jed. I'm glad to know you feel that way. I brought you out here to prove that you can always trust me. That I'll always be there for you, and most of all, that I love you."

She lit a match and started to light the candles she'd placed around.

After several began glowing, Jed's eyes saw something they could not believe. Winnie was naked. He spoke not a word as she finished lighting the candles. Had he been able to take his eyes off of her, he also would have seen the nest she had made.

When the last candle was lit, Winnie spoke again. "Do you remember the day we met out here as kids and I was dressed just as I am now?"

"I remember, but Winnie…"

"I knew then, you were the boy for me. We're not kids anymore. I'm ready to be a woman, Jed, and you're the man I want. The only man I've ever wanted. When I thought about where I would want to do this for the first time, this was the only place that came to mind. I've thought about this for a long time, Jed. Have you ever thought about it?"

What a silly question, thought Jed. Of course he had. Many times since he'd seen her in that dress coming down the stairs at Gramps' house.

"Jed," Winnie's voice came into his thoughts. "You do want to do this, don't you?"

The look on Winnie's face showed her concern. Instinctively knowing that words were not the way to answer her, Jed began taking his clothes off, just as he had years before. Winnie stood back and watched as the clothing came off. As he finished, she lay down and reached for him, and Jed obliged.

Slowly, lovingly, a boy became a man and a girl reached womanhood there in the dim light of a late spring afternoon, just as it has been written in love stories through the ages. Had either of them looked up, they would have seen two dark patches in the lighthouse window, scratching around for a good view.

Puffins are not a curious bird by nature, but then these were no ordinary puffins.

CHAPTER 29
A Time for Confessions

As word of the impending trial spread, people began taking sides, as they often do. Not that anyone had enough information to make a rational decision; it was just human nature. The hard part was that Deb's business began to feel it. The people who had sided with Jed and his mother no longer stopped at the bakery, including the person who supplied Deb with her eggs. Thankfully, Richard's mom had hens and agreed to supply Deb the eggs she needed. It also could not have come at a worse time. Most of the locals were busy with spring chores and getting their work done to go fishing, or clamming, or, lobstering like Jed. Had business been the same as in past years, it would have been just enough, but now there were days when Deb barely broke even. If not for the supply of eggs, Deb would have let Richard go, but she was glad to have him there, talking obsessively on the days when business was off. It was nice to have the distraction.

On many days, she found her mind bouncing between the impending trial and the memories all of this had brought back. She was thinking more and more about Zach these days. How all of this would not be happening if he were here. How differently her life might have turned out if he had stayed around. She had managed to create a feeling of contentment with her work for years. When Jed had shown up, she'd learned to love again. Granted, it was a mother's love for her son rather than a woman's love for her man, but it still provided her with the opportunity to do something she'd stopped doing when Zach left—to have feelings for another human being. Until Connie showed up and took Jed away, she had not realized how strong her feelings were. Now, with business so slow, Deb had far too much time for feelings and regret.

Just when Deb thought she couldn't take any more, the summer people who came early every year to stay for the season started showing up and the bakery regained its busy atmosphere. Most of the summer folks didn't really care one way or the other how the trial might turn out; they were just happy for the excitement. They found the reaction of the townspeople humorous. It was, of course, the talk of the town, to the point where it took on a life of its own.

* * * *

Winnie stood on the steps of Crockett's house. She'd decided to wait a while before going to see Jed about the money she was due for working on the traps. Because she'd been given the money for college in Crockett's estate, Winnie hadn't applied for any scholarships. She would need to apply for a loan now in the hope that things would be worked out somehow. In the meantime, if she didn't send a deposit soon, college would have to wait another year.

In a time when Winnie had thought she'd be shopping for a prom dress and looking forward to all the hoopla of graduation, she instead was trying to find a way to save her dream. When her feelings were down, she'd dig out Ellen's journal and read a few pages. Having made it almost all the way through the little book, she knew she'd need to find a way to return it soon. It had been two weeks since she'd seen Jed, other than passing each other in the school's hall. Connie's words still stung when she played them over in her head: "All they care about is the money."

Before Winnie could knock on the door, Jed opened it.

"Hey," he said.

"Hi," she said. "I've missed you."

Jed's head dipped a little. "I'm sorry about the other day, at the bakery."

Winnie could tell he was sincere. She reached out her arms, inviting him in. Jed stepped out onto the stoop and wrapped her in his arms.

As they stood there lost in the warmth of each other's arms, the open door gave away their unplanned, unexpected embrace.

Connie had been upstairs when she heard someone arrive. After waiting a minute to see if Jed would call her, she made her way downstairs. She entered the kitchen to find Jed missing, which surprised her until she saw what was going on outside the door. *This isn't good*, she thought to herself. *Something has to be done, and quickly.*

"Are you planning to kidnap my son?" said Connie with just the right balance of sarcasm and humor.

Winnie lifted her head from Jed's chest and peeked over his shoulder. "Hi, Connie."

"What can we do for you today, dearie?" asked Connie.

Winnie let go of Jed and looked into his eyes. "I was hoping to get that check today, if it's okay. I really need to send my deposit to Orono before I lose my place."

Jed nodded. "Sure, I'll go get it for you."

Jed walked back into the house and Connie stepped out. She looked Winnie up and down. "It seems you have plans for my boy."

Winnie knew Connie was playing her, but today, however, she wasn't going to take it. "We're close, if that's what you mean," she said with authority.

"Well, if I were you, I'd worry about college and forget

about him," said Connie.

"Thank you for the advice, Connie. As you can see by my visit today, that's exactly what I'm doing."

"I'm glad to hear it. It's a relief to know you'll be able to get over my son," said Connie.

"What do you mean, get over him? He'll be at school with me," said Winnie. She didn't like the way this conversation was going.

"Oh, I'm sorry to be the one to tell you, but we'll be leaving as soon as the trial's over. Jed won't be attending college anywhere near here. There are much better schools out there, and I want the best for him. In everything."

Winnie felt her insides empty like a drinking straw finding the bottom of a cup. Jed's not going to Orono? He's leaving, forever? Could this be possible?

Before she could find words again, Jed was back with her check.

"Here it is, Winnie," he said, passing it to her. "Sorry you had to wait so long for it. Things have been…what am I saying? You know what I've been going through. Maybe we could get togeth—"

"Jed," interrupted his mother. "Remember we discussed this."

Jed's face lost its glow. "Sorry, Winnie, we'll have to wait for this mess to be sorted out before we can spend time together again."

Winnie was angry now. "Oh, I see. Well, why don't you give me a call when you get your mother's permission to come out and play. That is, if I have time for you."

With this, she spun around and stomped off.

Winnie stomped herself all the way to Deb's. Once inside, she didn't stop until reaching the kitchen. Deb followed her in.

"What's the matter, honey? Did Connie refuse to give you your money?"

Winnie was too upset to answer, so she yanked the check

out of her purse to show Deb. The force of her action knocked her pocketbook off her shoulder, spilling the contents onto the floor. Winnie and Deb bent over to pick her things up. Richard was also there and was the first to notice the journal.

"Hey, what's this? It looks old," he said as he picked it up.

"Please, Richard, may I have that back?" asked Winnie firmly.

Richard handed the journal to her and she clutched it against her breast. She knew now that she'd have to reveal her secret.

Deb couldn't help but notice the emotion Winnie had attached to the tiny book. Knowing Winnie as well as she did, Deb wondered why she'd never before seen a possession that seemed so important to Winnie.

"Winnie," said Deb, to be sure she had her attention, "this book seems special to you, but I don't remember seeing it before. Have you had it a long time?"

Winnie let out a long raspy breath and revealed the details of her transgression.

"It's not really mine, it's Ellen's journal. Ellen Crockett's."

"Where did you get it?" asked Deb.

A look of guilt came over Winnie's face. "I saw it on the living room floor at Mr. Crockett's, and took it." Her head dropped down so that her lips came to rest on top of the book.

Deb was stunned. It wasn't like Winnie to do something like this at all. Surely there was a good reason for it, at least in her mind. Rather than ask her, Deb took a minute to try and think why Winnie might have taken the journal.

Richard was already there with the answer. "Hey, I bet there's information in there about Jed. Maybe even about his mother," he said.

Winnie looked up at him. "That's what I was thinking when I took it," she said.

"So have you found anything?" asked Deb.

"I'm not sure. There is one entry I've been wondering about, though."

Before she could get another word out, they heard a voice from behind them that sent a cold chill through the room. It was the last person they expected to hear, and the last one they wanted to hear at this moment.

"I can't believe it. Mom told me and told me and I just wouldn't let the thought enter my mind and take hold. Why, Winnie? Why would you take anything from my grandfather's house? You would have been the last person I would have ever expected. I can't believe it, I just can't believe it."

Winnie began shaking. The worst possible thing was happening. Jed had found out. Caught her red-handed with the evidence. She had no words, no defense for her act of impropriety. Instinctively, she grasped the journal with both hands. Still on the floor she stood on her knees with the journal held out. No one moved, not even Richard.

Jed's eyes never left Winnie. It was as though a part of him were looking for a reason, a purpose that would allow him to forgive her. To pick her up and take her into his arms, to tell her it was all right. But he didn't.

"You keep it if it means that much to you," Jed finally said, breaking the silence. "It's the last thing you'll ever get from me."

Jed turned to go before his anger got the best of him. Deb reached out and put her hand on his shoulder. He stopped.

"Don't do this, Jed," she said. "Don't walk out like this. Stay and talk it through. Call your mother and have her come down if you want, but please, Jed, I beg of you, don't walk out now feeling this way. Because if you do, everything you are could be destroyed forever. Please, Jed, don't do this."

Without turning around, without hesitation, he answered her plea with a few simple words: "I'm not the one doing this, you two are."

Deb watched as Jed left the bakery for what she believed would be the last time. Winnie didn't move until she heard the bells ring on the door, then she hit the floor simultaneously with the closing door. Drained from the flood of emotion, she began to cry uncontrollably. Deb knew this feeling. She'd been through it herself with Zach. There was nothing anyone could do for her. Winnie would have to cry it out. However long it took was how long it would take.

Deb looked at Richard and said, "Richard, honey, could you call Winnie's mother and ask her to come down here? Then close the bakery for me. We've got more important things to do today."

Deb knelt down and wrapped herself around Winnie. "Go ahead and cry, honey, cry all you need to."

When Richard returned after calling Winnie's mother, he noticed the journal had fallen out of Winnie's hands and lay off to the side. He picked it up and set it on the counter, then went out front to close up the bakery. Winnie's mother came. Deb explained what had happened, and they walked Winnie out to the car together. After they had cleaned up, Richard saw that Winnie had left the journal behind, and he started to read it. Deb noticed he was doing so. Even though she knew it was in part wrong, she understood why Winnie had taken the journal in the first place.

"How's the reading going?" she asked Richard.

Richard looked up. "It was a little difficult at first, but I've got it now," he answered. "I think Winnie might have been onto something. Do you think I can take this home to read? There might just be something in here. It's the right time period. See here, there's a patch of tape scratched off."

Deb took a deep breath and exhaled. "Why not?" she said. "I can't imagine things getting any worse."

"Okay, see you tomorrow then."

* * * *

Back at the house, Jed walked in to find Connie sitting in Gramps' rocker and giving it a workout. He stopped in the middle of the floor and looked at her with anger flaring in his eyes. She stopped rocking.

"You were right, Mom," he said. "I can't trust or believe them. It's just you and me."Connie got up and hugged him. "There, there, son. Mommy will make it all better. Don't you worry."

CHAPTER 30
A Search for the Truth

When Richard arrived back home, he read the journal straight through. These types of things had always interested him for some reason. Reading small tidbits about the lives of others from the past seemed to give some comfort in his own. Despite his young age, he'd come to realize that for many people, their true purpose didn't reveal itself until later in life.

The next morning he read through the journal a second time. Doing so with an eye toward any hint of a clue that might help Deb with her case. She'd been better to him than anyone else ever had, and he knew she was not the person Jed's mother was trying to make people believe she was. Near the end of the journal, he did notice one particular entry. He wondered if it was the same one Winnie had referred to. His inquiry would have to wait, however, as it was time for school and he wanted to return the journal to Deb's on the way. Before he left, he wrote down the entry so he could study it again later.

* * * *

Jed sat in his seat at school looking around. Thankfully, he had not seen Winnie yet this morning. He told himself he wanted to keep it that way, although deep down, he knew differently. Seeing Winnie would please him, if only to see that she was all right, even though he was still upset with her. For some reason, Jed had chosen not to tell his mother about the journal. He knew what she thought of Winnie, and hearing about it would have pleased her, of this he was sure. But somehow it just didn't seem right.

Polly Wright looked around the classroom. Priding herself on being an astute teacher, she tried each morning to take notice of any change in the behavior of her students, especially her favorites, a category in which Jed and Winnie were most definitively members. It had been easy to see the tension between them over the last couple of weeks. Today, however, Jed appeared to be under a great deal of stress, and Winnie was nowhere in sight. Another student walked in with the absentee list, and Winnie's name was on it.

There were a few more minutes before class started. Polly called Jed up to her desk.

"Jed, is everything okay? You seem a little distracted."

"Yeah, I guess."

This was the type of answer Polly had expected. She, like everyone else, knew what was on Jed's mind. She herself had given him some slack because of it.

"I see here that Winnie's absent. Is she feeling okay?"

Jed thought for a moment. He could see what Miss Wright was after. He also had noticed how people had been treating him since the news of the trial broke. In the past, it would have been unacceptable to use this to his advantage, but his mother's presence had begun to have an influence.

"I don't know. We're not really allowed to see each other because of the lawsuit and all," he answered.

"I see," said Polly with that tone teachers have, giving one the sense they disapprove. "Well, I can just check in with her mother later. Thank you, Jed. You may return to your seat."

Jed wanted to ask her to tell Winnie he missed her. That

he'd even forgiven her for taking the journal, but he didn't, or perhaps couldn't. Just as he'd picked up the phone last night only to come up a number short in dialing. Or rode by the house with every intention of stopping, only to pass by.

Jed didn't know it yet, but he was no longer the Jed of old. The Jed of New Ireland, the lobsterman, the boy who grew up at Deb's, that Jed was no more. Nor was he the Jed who had helped the puffin that morning so long ago. He was much less now. At some point, he had stopped being Jed and had become simply Connie's son. Proof of this came in a conversation with Miss Wright.

"Jed, how are your college preparations coming along?"

Rather than tell her the truth—that he wasn't going now—as he would have under his grandfather's guidance, he chose his mother's method and said, "I'm working on it."

"I see," said Polly. She wasn't really surprised, as she had noticed an overall lack of interest toward the future in Jed lately. Since she wasn't ready to give up on the one she wanted to save, she made an offer. "If you're in need of any help, I'd be glad to do what I can."

There it is again, thought Jed, *That ray of hope, of unconditional compassion. Why did she keep doing that?* Jed turned to face Miss Wright so that what he was about to say would be as clear as being on the water with visibility to the horizon. "I've got my mother back; she's all I need."

This statement did set Polly back. In her eyes, Jed had always seemed like a loner. Even his relationship with Winnie had its limits. Jed's words made her wonder how this could have changed so quickly, with such conviction. Before Jed had reached his seat, the story he'd written about the puffin filled her mind. She dug out the copy she'd made from her desk. Something had told her to make a copy, and she'd read it several times since.

This time as the class was reading, she read it while trying to imagine how a young boy would feel. Living day after day with no family, believing he was alone in the world, only to find out, after years of feeling alone, that he had a grandfather, and everyone in town knew it but him. And just as he becomes comfortable with this relationship, his grandfather dies. Even though he knows he's dying, he doesn't tell you. So once again, the only relative he knows is gone, leaving him alone again. Then, out of the blue, his mother shows up. *Why now?*

Polly felt her chest tighten, so much pain at such a young age. It was clear to her now why Jed had grabbed onto his mother so quickly, so definitively. With so much pain and negativity, it must have seemed like a miracle to have something positive happen. Asking why she had shown up now must have been the last thing on his mind or in his heart.

Polly wondered if anyone else had come to this same conclusion. She'd heard the talk around town. Being a teacher, Polly had been careful to stay neutral. However, this didn't mean she couldn't get involved, or help.

* * * *

Others may not have come to the same conclusion as Polly, but they had chosen to help. Some did so consciously, while others were drafted into service. One of the volunteers was, of course, Irene Black. She had reported to Ashley Walters the events of the bakery meeting she'd attended. The one aspect in which Ashley had the greatest interest was not even part of the event, but the conversation which had happened accidentally after the meeting was definitely of interest. Ashley wanted to know more about this Gus fellow.

Irene had been, if anything, overly explicative as to the

tone and nature of Gus's presentation to Deb. How he'd been so careful to make his comments private and intimate. Ashley felt it was vital to the case for him and Gus to speak. Years of practicing law had given him a feel for the subtle things that were often missed by others. Lawyers were sometimes arrogant in believing they were more important than the facts of a case. Something told him that Gus held one of the undiscovered facts on which a case like this could hinge.

More importantly, Ashley still wanted to find a copy of Jed's birth certificate. Even though he knew its presence could work either for or against the case, the ability to prove Jed was not a minor would take the matter out of the court's hands and give it back to the family where it belonged.

Irene left the meeting with Ashley feeling she had contributed greatly to the cause. In both a direct and an indirect way. As a librarian, she led a quiet, somewhat uneventful life. Being involved in the lives of others helped to fulfill her own life, which had its own void not unlike Jed's. Since her mother's passing, Irene had felt her own loneliness in the world. Having her level of involvement increase and become more important in Jed's life was very gratifying. However, she couldn't forget her other commitments. It was time for another correspondence. Time to get back to the library.

* * * *

Polly had decided to visit Winnie's house rather than call. Since it was a small town, having a teacher take such a personal interest was not uncommon. This was part of the reason she'd chosen to teach in a small community. The ability to have a personal relationship with the students was important to her. Just knowing the impact she could have on a student's life gave value to her own.

Much to her surprise, Polly arrived to find Richard at

Winnie's house, and the two engaged in conversation. As Polly had expected, Winnie was visibly upset and crying. As soon as the two of them saw her, they clammed up. Polly explained the reason for her visit, and relayed her earlier conversation with Jed.

Richard and Winnie looked at each other as if confirming a prearranged agreement. Winnie turned to Polly and said, "If we tell you what we're talking about, you have to promise not to tell anyone."

Polly, thinking it was some kind of high school kid thing, agreed. Winnie then confessed taking the journal from Jed's house. Then she explained how and why they and Deb believed Jed's mother was just after Jed's inheritance, along with the property and assets willed to others. But most importantly, she told Polly about the clue revealed in the journal.

"Here, I wrote it down," said Richard.

Polly took the slip of paper and read it.

A package from Jed's mother arrived a few days ago. I've tried to open it several times, but I just can't. Last night I showed it to Jedediah. He couldn't open it either. This morning he took the box with him. When I asked what he was going to do with it, he said, "I can't have this in the house."

Then I asked if he didn't want to know what was in it and he said, "That woman took too much from us to even think about giving anything back." He came home tonight without it. I asked him what he'd done with it and all he would say was he'd taken it to where it belonged, to its origin.

Polly read the words a second time. The word, which stood out for her, was *origin*.

"What do you think the word *origin* means?" asked Richard.

Polly looked up at him. "I'm not sure. But it usually means *beginning*, *roots*, or *birth*." Then it hit her. Her face flushed as a prickly tingle ran up her spine. She looked at the two of them. "Do you think he tossed it into the harbor?"

Winnie and Richard didn't have to answer. She could tell just by looking at them that they'd had the same thought. Then a new thought came to mind. "This entry, was it written before or after Jed came here to live?"

Neither of them was sure. As they thought about it, they came to the conclusion it must have been written before Jed had come to town. Both of them remembered Jed's arrival, but neither had any memory of Mrs. Crockett.

"Well then," began Polly, "I'd have a hard time believing Mr. Crockett would have tossed away the only possession connected to his grandson. From what I understand, they became very close over the last ten or twelve years."

Winnie began to pucker up again before saying, "Richard and I were thinking that since no one knows where Jed's birth certificate is, it might be in that box."

Polly knew how much Winnie cared for Jed. Even now, when he was clearly upset with her, all she wanted to do was help him.

"Then the thing we need to figure out is what Mr. Crockett meant when he used the word *origin* so we can find this packet," said Polly with determination.

They all agreed to give it some thought. Richard thought of asking other people if Crockett had ever mentioned the packet, or had used the word *origin* in a way that might provide a clue. Each of them knew the potential importance this little patch of a journal entry was that Winnie had found and Richard had scratched down onto paper. But they would need to hurry, as time was not on their side. The trial was starting soon. A trial, which would profoundly affect not only Jed, but all of them.

CHAPTER 31
In the Hands of Others

It was the morning of the trial and Jed had not yet met his mother's lawyer. They'd agreed to meet at a small restaurant an hour before the trial began to go over things. Jed knew the lawyer had tried to get the case to a jury trial, but the judicial system didn't allow for it. The state believed this type of case should be private between the individual families. Allowing one's peers to interject their morals and values on others was not seen as good judgment in these matters. Instead, the state wanted to have these types of cases heard by a judge whose role was that of a facilitator looking for the best solution for the situation. Ideally, judgment was made in the best interests of all. There was, however, one cardinal standard: if a child was to be separated from a parent, particularly the mother, it was not done so lightly. This seemed to be the key to the case for Jed's mother.

Being an early riser, Jed had been down to the harbor to check on his boat before his mother was up. Even now, he had to fight the urge to walk into the back door of Deb's. The event of the day ahead caused Jed to, without thought, go into the barn holding his father's old boat. He didn't need to turn on a light. Instead, he let the lines of the boat show him the way. He'd heard the old fishermen talk about the life in a boat, how after just a short time on the water, a boat developed a personality. Some were strong and good while others, not so much. The important thing was to know and understand this spirit. That way you'd know how the boat would react in all situations, and you could react accordingly. Boats can turn quickly or slowly, needing more or less room to do so. They may sit low in the water or high, and they may even list or lean to one side or the other. Knowing these things about your boat's spirit and personality could mean the difference between life and death on the water.

Jed ran his hands along the sides of the boat, then climbed up onto the deck. He walked all the way around, with his hand on the rail. He stepped into the wheelhouse to rest his hands on the wheel. It was as if the boat were waiting to be born. To be given a reason to exist. Many people would have been spooked by the aura radiating from the boat. Not Jed, though. The moment his hands touched the wheel, he felt a connection. He and the boat became one soul. He felt he'd returned to his origin. As the feeling consumed him, he couldn't hear his mother's voice calling him. Not until the lights came on did he wake from this spiritual connection.

"Jed, honey. Are you up there?" he heard her ask.

For a single tick of the clock, he considered not answering. "Yeah, Mom, I'm here."

"It's getting late, come in and eat so we can get going."

Unbeknownst to Jed, his mother knew this boat. Her life had changed forever the last time she'd seen it. What had started out as a fun day had turned into a life of never-ending interruptions, of sleepless nights. She had not thought about the boat itself for years. Somehow, she had assumed it was long gone. But here it was, bigger than life. How wrong she'd been about all of this. The boat was here and Jed's father wasn't.

Now she was in a battle for her right to be Jed's mother. The problem, at least in her mind, was that she hadn't been given many chances to show the softer, kinder side of herself.

That was, until she'd come back here and seen Jed again. True, she'd come for the money, but now she wanted more. She wanted her son. She wanted to be a mother.

Had Jed gone to Deb's this morning, he would have found the door locked. Ashley Walters knew he had an uphill battle with this case and had asked everyone involved to be in his Redman Village office by seven A.M. to prepare. He also wanted to know who was going to show up and who wasn't. As a man dealing with facts and details, surprises were not part of his plan. Ashley knew the standard rule the judge would be working from. It would be up to him to prove that Jed's mother was not the best person to be his guardian.

The absence of Jed's birth certificate was still a concern to him, in part because the lawyer he was up against, Thomas Tompkins, was known as a bottom feeder. City lawyers called his kind an ambulance chaser. Whenever Ashley saw Thomas, he was reminded of a character in a new sitcom called *WKRP in Cincinnati*. The character's name was Herb Tarlek. Tom was always looking for the quick buck, that one case with a big payoff. The idea of making an honest living by working for his clients rather than the payday was not a conscious thought for him. It would be just like him to have the birth certificate and hold onto it until the exact moment he needed it, or keep it hidden should it work against him. That was the one thing that bothered Ashley most about Tom. He was smart but lazy, and Ashley just didn't abide lazy people.

The fact that Ashley was not the lazy type was what had endeared him to the working class of New Ireland. Ashley had learned early in his career that this was where the real money was. The people around here were happy to pay for his services if they knew they'd get their money's worth. In fact, at the moment he'd realized this, he'd also understood the true meaning of a book he'd read recently: *Think and Grow Rich* by Napoleon Hill. Ashley had money and all it offered, but he also had family, friends, and respect from the ones who mattered to him. His life had indeed become rich in every way. Perhaps this was why he found himself taking on more and more of these types of cases for hard-working people like Deb.

But this case was the toughest he'd had to date. Everything was stacked against him. Winning would take everything he had, all of his knowledge, all of his skills. Including one skill which did not come naturally to him—that of being ruthless. Ashley had prepared for this case more diligently than for any case he'd ever had, and he was ready. Even so, he knew they would need something hard work and preparation could not influence; they would need a little luck for things to go their way.

Ashley waited until seven-thirty to call everyone into his office. All were there but one, the one he needed most. Having expected this, Ashley dispatched a man he had standing by to find and, if possible, bring that person to the courthouse. This type of case almost never went into a second day. Tomorrow would simply be too late.

So that everyone was on the same page, Ashley spent the next hour going over the plan while reminding them that things could change depending on the judge and any surprises that might come up. As soon as he was comfortable that everyone knew their roles, he dismissed them with the reminder that court started at nine o'clock sharp.

Meanwhile, Jed and his mother met with their lawyer. Seeing him walk in with Bradley did little to make Jed feel good about their chances. Jed had known from the beginning that he himself would have little to do with the actual case. As his mother, Bradley, and Mr. Tompkins talked, Jed's thoughts returned to his father's boat. *Why hadn't he gone aboard before*, was the question running through his mind. Since he'd left the wheelhouse, he'd felt the boat calling him. The outcome of the case didn't seem as important as it had. Standing on the deck of his father's boat, to return to the place he was earlier this morning, was the only thing Jed could think about.

At times like this, Jed had fallen into the practice of doing something all good writers do. He pulled out his journal and began writing. He didn't notice the funny look that came to Tompkins' face. He was busy writing before he lost the words being offered up by his mind.

Connie assured Tom this behavior was normal for Jed. Bradley shook his head and chuckled.

"What are you laughing at?" asked Connie.

"There's no doubt whose boy that is. He's every bit his father," answered Bradley.

This, Jed heard. He stopped long enough to say, "Thanks, Bradley, that's the nicest thing you've ever said to me," then returned to his writing.

There was also a third party working on the case who was still unknown to any of the others. Polly had come up with an idea, and had asked Winnie and Richard to meet her at the school early this morning. She'd also called in and asked the school to bring in a replacement for the day so that she could help with Jed's case. The three of them met in the parking lot, and Polly quickly asked her question.

"I had a thought. Do either of you know anything about how or where Jed was born? I'm thinking that the word *origin* is a reference to his birthplace."

Winnie had heard the story of where Jed had been conceived, but she'd never spoken of it. She wasn't sure she could speak of it even now. As it turned out, she didn't have to.

"Jed wasn't born here," said Richard, before a pig-grunt laugh escaped his throat.

Winnie looked at him with a sense of both fear and relief in her eyes and heart. Of course Richard knew the story. Richard seemed to know everything about everyone.

"What's funny about that?" asked Polly impatiently.

"He wasn't born here, but he was conceived here," continued Richard with a smirk on his face.

"Where Richard? Where was Jed conceived?"

Richard was delighted to tell the story. Most of the time people didn't want to listen to him, so when someone asked for it, they got it. Richard went on and on as Polly patiently listened, until he mentioned the boat, then she interrupted.

"That's it!" she said. "The boat is the place of origin! That's what Jed's grandfather was referring to. Do either of you know where this boat is now?"

"No offense, Miss Wright, but you're crazy," said Richard. "Remember, this took place years ago. That boat's long gone by now. Who would keep a boat knowing what had happened on it? No one, that's who. That boat's got bad karma."

Polly hadn't considered the time lapse, or the superstitions lobstermen place on their boats. But what else could it be?

"No, it's not gone," Winnie said. "I know where it is."

"You're kidding!" Richard's voice was stronger than Winnie and Polly had ever heard it.

Looking up at both of them, Winnie stated, "I've seen it."

Both Richard and Polly were elated by this news. They had somewhere to look, a way to help Jed. Finally, they felt as if they could contribute.

"I'll go in and get you both excused from school. Then you can show us where the boat is and we'll start looking," said Polly. As she turned toward the school, Winnie spoke again.

"I...I can't go."

"What do you mean, you can't?" said Richard.

"He's still mad at me for taking the journal," said Winnie. "I can't go break into his barn and make him madder."

Winnie's head dropped into her hands as she began to weep. She wanted to go, she really did. She just couldn't. Miss

Wright took Winnie's hands into her own and said, "Winnie, I understand, I really do. As a teacher I have to make decisions on whether or not to get involved with my students all the time. But hear me out. If Jed's mother wins, she could take Jed away from us and you'd lose him forever. So I'm going to tell you what I've learned. If you care for someone, really care for them, and they care for you, they'll forgive you if what you do is for the right reasons. Now, I know and you know that Jed cares for you. This is your chance to prove your love, by putting it at risk. Whether or not he knows it, Jed needs you to be there for him now. So what do you say, will you take us to the boat?"

Miss Wright's words were just what Winnie needed to hear. She smiled and got herself back together.

"Come on, Richard," she said.

Polly watched as the two of them took off for Crockett's house. Then she went in and explained to Mrs. Welsh what was going on. Approval was given and Polly headed for Crockett's house as quickly as she could without appearing undignified. Time seemed to be moving slower and slower as she crossed the patch of ground between the school and Crockett's place. But knowing that time was against them, she decided to give up on appearances and took off in a jog.

She could see a small door left open in one of the barns. As she reached the driveway, a rosebush reached out and scratched her on the leg. Thankfully, she'd worn jeans on this day. A mark was left on the cloth, but the thorn didn't penetrate the skin. Inside the barn, she was amazed at how much bigger a lobster boat looked inside of a building than it did out on the water. Polly thought about how a boat resembled a life, as board by board it grew to completion, with both large and small parts. It was a small part of Jed's life they would be looking for inside this fully grown boat. She couldn't help wondering how they would ever find such a small piece of life on such a large boat. If in fact, it was there at all.

CHAPTER 32

It's Not the Days, but the Events that Matter in Life

If there was any question as to the position of the judge, it was cleared up with his opening statement.

"Having looked over your preliminary statements, there are two things I want to make perfectly clear. First, despite the presence of a state-issued guardianship, it's my position that a child should remain with a parent. The burden here is on you, Mr. Walters. It's up to you to prove that Constance Baxter is not a fit mother."

"Secondly, it's my opinion that, regardless of the outcome, Miss Baxter made a difficult but proper choice in leaving Jed as she did. Her only mistake was in not confirming that Jed's father was still around, a mistake which I have chosen to overlook."

"Therefore, knowing this, Mr. Walters, are you prepared to move forward with the case?"

Most lawyers might well have been put off by such a bold statement from a judge, but not Ashley. No, he liked knowing where things stood, what he needed to do in order to win a case. The judge's position also meant that if Tom Tompkins had the birth certificate proving Jed was a minor, it wouldn't matter. This case was about the character of the people involved, and not the facts. If anything, Ashley's case had just gotten better.

"Yes, your honor, we are," he replied.

"Very well, then, bring your first witness forward," commanded the judge.

Ashley looked around. The missing witness was still not present.

Ashley called Deb to the stand. He spent the next twenty minutes asking her questions about Jed's upbringing, thereby revealing salient aspects of both Deb's and Jed's character. About all those special times in a boy's life when his mother had not been there—how Deb had filled those shoes admirably. The fact that Jed had been, not just content, but happy all those years. How his life had not been lacking. If anything, he had benefited from Deb's presence, not to mention the positive impact of his grandfather's influence. How Jed was more a man than a boy now, a result that had nothing to do with his mother.

Ashley knew that the testimony Deb was giving provided as much benefit to Connie's case as it did to his. But he also felt it was important to show Deb as the one who had been Jed's guardian for all those years, and that the state had made the proper decision by righting a wrong which had gone on far too long. Yes, it was a risk to present this type of testimony, but it was a necessary one.

Once Ashley had finished, it was time for Tom's cross-examination. Tom had few rules when it came to how he did things. One of these rules, which he never broke, was that when things were going his way, he didn't get in the way. "I have no questions at this time for the witness, your honor," he said.

Next Ashley called up Irene Black. Irene had shared her story with him, and him alone. Ashley knew there was no way he could substantiate the statement she was about to make without his star witness, but it would buy him time. As she was taking the stand, the three investigators were combing that boat, port to starboard, bow to stern.

* * * *

Despite having grown up in a lobstering town and her recent experience working with Jed, Winnie knew very little about boats. Polly knew even less. Thank goodness for Richard. It was he who knew the layout of a working boat. How every nook and cranny was used for storage, each tucked-away space accessed by a trap door. Door after door was opened, only to find the space empty. An hour passed with no results. Polly came back to her method of asking questions in the hope of finding answers.

"Okay you two, what are we forgetting? Let's think for a moment. Where would you put something on a boat in order for it to be safe? Even if the boat sank?"

After a few minutes Richard jumped up with an "I've got it!" and headed up on deck. He made his way to the bow, where a dinghy just big enough for one person and a few supplies were kept in case of emergencies. Richard untied the dinghy, flipped it over, and reached into the belly of its bow. There it was—a package wrapped in foul-weather gear for protection. Richard set the package on the seat of the dinghy and unwrapped it as Polly and Winnie looked on excitedly. Inside was a collection of items, including what they were looking for nestled in a brown folder. One quick look told them what they needed to know.

"Let's go, guys," said Polly, "we need to get this to the courthouse as quickly as possible."

The three of them sprinted to the school parking lot and took off for Redman Village. Polly looked at her watch. It was after nine, and Redman Village was a good hour away. All Polly could do now was drive and hope they'd make it in time.

* * * *

Back at the courthouse, Ashley began by saying, "Miss Black, in your own words, please tell us what you know of Constance Baxter."

"Well, my knowledge of Constance comes from my mother."

Tom spoke up. "Objection, your honor. The witness is presenting secondhand information. Does she have any proof of what she's about to state under oath?"

"Sustained, Mr. Tompkins," ruled the judge. "Miss Black, do you have any proof of what you're about to state?"

"I have my mother's diary," she answered.

The judge motioned for the diary to be brought forward. Irene opened it to the place she'd bookmarked. As everyone else sat waiting, the judge took time to read the entry. This was exactly what Ashley had hoped for: even if the judge ruled against allowing Irene's testimony, he'd taken the time to read the diary, which substantiated it.

Before the judge had finished reading the entry, the doors to the courtroom opened and in walked the person Ashley had been waiting for. Now it didn't matter whether or not the judge let Irene Black speak. A few more minutes passed before the judge set the diary down.

"Miss Black, I'm going to enter this journal into evidence, rather than have you give us a verbal account of it. You may step down."

"Mr. Walters, do you have any other evidence to substantiate what I've just read in this diary?" asked the judge.

"Yes, your honor," answered Ashley. "I have a witness who found the person mentioned in the diary entry you've just read."

"I see," said the judge. "I'm going to take a recess so that the prosecution can read the entry. Court will reconvene at ten-thirty." He dropped the gavel and left the bench.

Tom, Bradley, and Connie walked up to the bench so that they could read the journal entry. Jed sat still. His mind was not on the case. In fact, he'd now lost interest in the whole thing. His thoughts kept returning to the feeling he'd had on his father's boat. He just couldn't shake it, until he heard a familiar voice.

"Sorry I was late getting here, Mr. Walters," said Gus. "My truck gave out on me. It's a good thing you sent a man to fetch me."

"That's alright, Gus," said Ashley. "The important thing is you're here now. As soon as the judge gets back, I'm going to put you on the stand. If you have any questions, now is the time to ask them."

"Nope, I'm geared up and ready to haul back," answered Gus.

Seeing Gus there gave Jed his first bit of doubt about the outcome of the case. Though it did take him a second to be sure it was Gus. He was washed up, clean-shaven, and even his hair was combed. Jed knew that for everything Gus was not, he *was* an honest man. If Gus was there to testify on behalf of Deb, there was something Jed didn't know. Jed's interest in the case was renewed. He looked up at his mother. The look on her face was one of worry. Bradley, on the other hand, looked scared, while Tom seemed to be upset. Jed thought he heard Tom say something like "Why wasn't I told about this?" but he couldn't be sure. As Jed thought about joining his mother, the judge reentered the courtroom. With a slam of the gavel, court reconvened.

"Mr. Walters, do you have any more witnesses?" asked the judge.

"I do, your honor," answered Ashley.

"Proceed then," said the judge.

"I call Gus Blood to the stand."

Gus stood up and slowly made his way to the stand. Once he was sworn in, Ashley asked Gus to tell them about the day he had found Jed's dad, Zachary Crockett, out on the harbor all those years ago.

Gus heaved a deep breath and said, "I was just finishing up pulling my traps on the east side of the harbor's mouth when I seen Zach's new boat sitting just off Rockledge Island covered with puffins. I noticed his dinghy was missing off the bow, so I looked toward the shore, but it weren't there neither. Earlier that morning, I seen Zach leave the harbor with them two sitting over there," he said, pointing toward Connie and Bradley.

"Anyways, I made my way next to Zach's boat and hollered, but no one called back. So I pulled away, and dropped my anchor, then rowed over in my dinghy to check things out. When I got aboard, I saw that things were a mess all over the place. It looked to me like people had been partying. Word was out that Connie was a girl who liked a good time, so I headed for the cabin, thinking I might get me an eyeful. What I found was Zach sitting there in his skivvies with his head in his hands. Looked to me like he didn't really have his bearings."

Gus then looked at Jed. "Sorry you have to hear this, Jed. But it's the God's honest truth."

Jed smiled and nodded slightly, giving Gus some comfort.

Seeing that Gus was going off track, Ashley brought him back. "Gus, please continue."

Gus looked back at Ashley. "Sure, sorry. Anyways, I give Zach his clothes, then I went back to my boat for some coffee and grub. When I got back, Zach was coming around. We looked the boat over to be sure it was all right."

Tom Tompkins spoke up. "Objection, your honor. This is all very interesting, but how long—"

"I ain't through, you piece of shit," said Gus. He was standing now and everyone was taking him seriously.

"Mr. Walters, I suggest you get control of your witness," said the judge.

Before Ashley could answer, Gus did. "Sorry, your honor."

"Do you think you can go forward while behaving yourself?" asked the judge.

"Yes, sir."

"Very well, overruled. Please continue, Mr. Blood," said the judge.

"We couldn't find any real damage to the boat, but I could tell Zach weren't ready to head back. He drank some of the coffee, then he told me what had happened."

Gus looked back to Jed. They both knew that hearing what Gus was about to say would be as difficult as saying it.

"Zach told me that Connie had talked him into taking her and Bradley out on the boat. Once they were out on the water, Connie offered him a drink as she rubbed herself all over him. He never took much to the drink, so he refused. Anyways, Zach said he managed to keep her off him till he got the boat anchored. It wasn't till then that he noticed Bradley there was out cold. Connie there talked Zach into making a trip to the island, or so he thought. As he got the dinghy into the water and ready, she went below for some food. When Zach went down to get her, she was naked as a jaybird and jumped on him, knocking him down. He hit his head and fell to the floor in a daze. Before he knew it, she had his pants undone and had him straddled like a bolt through an engine block. Zach knew it was wrong, but his mind gave in to his body's desire."

Before Gus could go on, the courtroom doors opened again and Polly, Winnie, and Richard came running in. Richard couldn't contain himself. "We found it your honor!"

A guard stepped in front of Polly, stopping the three of them just inside the door. Polly looked a bit embarrassed, but rather than try to explain herself, she handed the folder to the guard and sat down. Winnie and Richard followed her lead.

"Bring that here," said the judge.

Just as he'd been all morning, the judge was deliberate in his actions. After taking time to read the document, he looked at Gus and said, "You may step down, Mr. Blood, your testimony is no longer needed."

As Gus moved back to the public seating, the judge addressed Jed.

"Jed, please stand. I have here your original birth certificate. You, young man, are over the age of eighteen." He turned to Ashley Walters and continued. "Therefore, I hereby remove the right of guardianship from your client, Mr. Walters. Jed has the legal right to do as he pleases with his life and his inheritance, so long as these actions are within the limits of the law."

Cheers from the small group ensued until the judge slammed his gavel.

"Court has not been dismissed. Take your seats and be quiet." The judge turned his attention back to Jed. "Young man. The woman beside you is your mother, regardless of how or why you were conceived. Nothing will ever change that, but if you ask me Deb, Irene, and these other three are your family. You keep that in mind as you decide what to do with your life from this point on."

Jed looked squarely into the judge's eyes and answered, "Yes, sir."

"Good," said the judge. "Hearing no objection, I hereby declare—"

Once again the doors to the courtroom opened. "Your honor," said a well-dressed man who was clearly a lawyer. "I have an objection."

The judge looked at the guard and said in frustration, "How many rabbits are going to scratch their way out of this briar patch and into my courtroom today? Secure that door this instant."

"May I approach the bench your honor?" said the stranger.

The judge motioned him forward while asking, "What is your purpose here, Mr....?"

"Randell, your honor. I represent someone who is challenging for their rights to the estate of Jedediah Rumford Crockett."

"Do you, now? Let's have a look." Once again the judge found himself reading an unexpected document. Again he turned to Ashley. "Well, Mr. Walters, it seems your work has just begun. Mine, however, is done, Mr. Randell. This case was to determine the guardianship of Jed here, not the ownership of the estate. Case dismissed."

The gavel went down for the last time.

CHAPTER 33
Outside the Door

No one had noticed that Irene Black hadn't returned to the courtroom after the recess. For months now, she'd planned for this day and looked forward to all that it offered. For on this day, all of her mother's, as well as her own efforts to make the day a reality were about to bear fruit. How many letters had she written and sent? How many news clippings had she cut and mailed? All so they could be sure, and not a moment too soon either, or so she thought. Irene missed seeing Polly, Winnie, and Richard show up with the birth certificate. Her mind was focused and on task, consumed with its own personal joy. For it was because of her that Mr. Randell had entered the courtroom. For she now stood on the granite steps of the eighteenth-century courthouse awaiting the arrival of her pen pal. She couldn't help but wonder if this was, in a way, how an expectant mother felt while waiting for the arrival of her baby.

Granted, she wasn't giving birth in a physical sense, but emotionally, spiritually, she most certainly was. For the first time since taking over for her mother in this role, Irene gave in to the feeling of personal joy.

A car was entering the parking lot. Could this be the one? Irene took out the photo she'd received in one of the letters and held it up. Her eyes moved back and forth from the picture to the figure walking toward her, while the heart in her chest told her how much this moment meant to her, to so many of them.

* * * *

Connie was outraged by the claims Mr. Randell had brought forth. She had gotten right into the face of Mr. Walters demanding to know the details. However, try as she might, she was stonewalled by the fact that Jed was of legal age, therefore she had no right to know anything. She had been well aware of this fact, and had done her best to keep it hidden. The smug looks that Walters and Randell proudly displayed on their faces, though for different reasons, only enraged her. After trying for several minutes, she turned to her own lawyer demanding he do something. But there was no sympathy to be found there. Mr. Tompkins had taken the case with the understanding that he would only be paid if they won. Since they had not, his interest in the whole mess was over. He just shook his head and walked out of the courtroom.

Bradley's role in the proceedings was reinforced when he said, "Does this mean I don't get the car?"

Through all of the revelations, all of the commotion, Jed had not moved. The judge's words had commingled with the emotions he'd been reliving from his father's boat. Despite everything going on around him he wasn't the least bit upset, actually, just the opposite. It was as if all of this was meant to bring him to a place of resolve, a place of comfort with his life and who he was.

Ignoring Bradley, Jed stood up and walked over to Winnie. She was talking to Deb while Polly and Richard looked on. Only Winnie saw him coming, and it was Winnie he made eye contact with as he approached. This contact took them to a place only those in true love can go. A place where they could be themselves wherever they were, no matter who else was around.

As Jed spoke, the room filled with the majestic aura they

created.

"So you found it," he said.

"Well, Richard was the one who actually found it," Winnie replied.

"Where was it?"

"It was on your father's boat, in the dinghy."

There it was again—his father's boat, which had sat idle and quiet all those years until now. Now its secrets were coming out, while the boat itself was becoming more and more important to Jed. His emotions were running wild, like a bottle being tossed around by the waves.

"What made you think to look there?" he asked.

Winnie hesitated before answering. She glanced at Polly and Richard. "We got the idea from one of the entries in—"

"The journal!" shouted Richard. "It said your mother sent a package to your grandmother, and that your grandfather put it in the place of origin."

Place of origin. Jed thought about these words for a second. Origin meant the beginning, the start of something. He'd just heard the story of how life began for him on his dad's boat. Is that why his visit to the boat was giving him all of these feelings? Of course it was. That was the connection. The judge was right. Connie might be his mother, but New Ireland was his home, and Deb, Winnie, and Gramps were his family. This revelation brought Jed a new feeling, one of contentment, of being grounded, as if he belonged to something greater than himself.

The next voice to fill the air was Connie's. "I'm his mother and I demand to know who is trying to take what's rightfully mine—uh, I mean Jed's."

"You had it right the first time, Connie," said a new voice from the back of the room.

Everyone turned to see who it was, but only a few of them knew. Jed heard a sound from Deb that could only be described as pain, but not the physical kind, while his mother said, "No, it can't be."

The rest of the room was silent, without expression. Except for Gus. Gus, with a crooked smile and squinted eyes, had that look a lobsterman gets when he knows something the other fishermen don't.

It was Mr. Walters who spoke next. "Mr. Zachary Crockett, I presume?"

Had he heard right? Was this true? Jed looked at the man. All he had to go on was the fuzzy person he'd seen in those old movies at Gramps'. Jed looked at his mother, then at Deb. Their expressions were different, but they had the same meaning. Bradley was still steamed over losing the Corvette. It was the only payment he'd asked for in return for all he'd done.

Apparently forgetting where he was, Bradley walked toward Zach speaking with anger.

"Zach, you ass! I should have finished what I started on that boat years ago."

As Bradley reached Zach, his right hand was back, ready to strike. But before he could swing, his left cheek collapsed under the pressure of a fist that sent him tumbling over the row of benches. He landed upside down, and that's where he stayed.

Zach looked at Jed and spoke to his son for the first time. "Nice punch. Thanks, son."

Hearing this from his father for the first time seemed as natural as if it had been the thousandth time. "You're welcome, Dad," Jed heard himself say. As if he'd been saying it his whole life.

Once again, it was Mr. Walters who moved things along. "Well, I think we've had enough revelations for one morning. I'd say some of you need time together, to get acquainted, or reacquainted, as the case may be. If that's all right with you, Mr. Randell?"

Randell smiled and said, "That's fine with me, Mr. Walters. I'm sure the details of our case can wait a bit."

Connie, however, was not satisfied. "Well, it's not okay with me!" she sputtered.

"But Mom, you said you left me in New Ireland because you thought my dad was here to take care of me, and now he is," said Jed. "What else could you want, but the best for me?"

With that, Jed turned to his father and said, "I'm going home. Mom and I have been living at Gramps' for a while, but I guess we'll have to move out now. Maybe Deb will let me move back in."

Zach felt the same kind of comfort Jed did, and he also chose not to question it. He simply accepted it as Jed had. "How about I give you a ride back and we'll figure it out on the way there?" he said to his son.

Connie was flabbergasted. She could think of no rebuttal. She had lost her bid to gain control of Crockett's estate, and any influence she'd had over Jed. And thanks to him, her man was out cold on the courtroom floor. What was she to do now?

Deb watched as Jed and his father headed for the door. She'd long ago given up believing Zach would ever enter her life again. Jed had filled that need through the years since that first day at the bakery, eating a bear claw. Watching the two of them now, she could be no prouder. The two men who meant the most to her were united for the first time, walking arm and arm.

As they reached the doorway, they stopped and turned.

"You coming, Deb?" said Zach.

"How about you, Winnie?" said Jed.

The two women looked at each other, then together they walked toward the men. For once, there was no itch to scratch and no patches that needed mending.